3/7/07

W9-CEI-279

To Nancy,
May all your weeds
be Wildflowers
R. Paul

CABBAGE REQUIEM

R. L. Paul

Cabbage Requiem

All Rights Reserved © 2004, R.L. Paul

No part of this book may be reproduced, or transmitted in any from or by any means, graphic, electronic, or mechanical, including photocopying, recording, taping, or by any information storage retrieval system, without the permission in writing from the publisher or author.

Helm Publishing

For information or to order this book contact:
Helm Publishing
3923 Seward Ave.
Rockford, IL 61108

815-398-4660
www.publishersdrive.com

ISBN 0-9723011-9-4

Dedication

**To Jo Marie, editor, critic and lover, for her
inspiration and encouragement**

Acknowledgment

Christine DeSmet, the members of the Troubadours Writing Group, Judy Emerson, Dain Trafton, PhD., and Drs. Jeffrey Behr, and L.P. Johnson who helped me at various times during the writing of this novel. I am indebted to all of them. I am also grateful that Dianne Helm, and Helm Publishing, had enough faith in my work to publish it.

CHAPTER ONE

CABBAGE REQUIEM

George Konert wanted to kick at the pile of pale-green early cabbage sitting on the concrete floor. He caught himself. Old men with brittle knees must manage frustration. If only he were young enough to propel the soccer-ball sized heads across the basement floor, he'd rid himself of some bitterness. Why, he wondered, didn't he croak last spring before he put all those plants in the ground? Now, he had to deal with all this unwanted produce. He glared at the offenders. Some crops, like tomatoes and leaf lettuce, deserved to be treated with dignity. Tomatoes reminded him of rosy-cheeked youngsters, leaf lettuce the delicate fan of an Asian beauty. But cabbage? Where's the elegance in cole slaw, sauerkraut and flatulence?

The coolness of the basement relieved some of the weight from the oppressive heat of a typical Ohio July morning. To survive the muggy mid-nineties prediction,

1

George had finished harvesting twenty-nine cabbages by nine in the morning. One by one he'd carried them up the path from the garden, through the basement door and into the exposed basement. Compelled by some unwanted urge, he'd washed each head, placed it on the cabbage pile to dry and collapsed into the tarnished chrome and black plastic chair Grace had banished to the basement years before.

He sighed. When had gardening become such an effort? Once, he could work all day, drink a beer, shower and be fresh for whatever was next on the agenda. Now he needed to rest to make it up the stairs and avoid the chest pains he carefully hid from the doctor during his annual physical exam. George reasoned that medical geniuses earning outrageous sums should be able to find any symptoms without his help. Moreover, at seventy-eight, George had little desire to extend his present incarnation.

He rubbed his hand over the familiar plastic arm of the chair. When Grace was alive he'd promised to take it to the dump. Now he didn't throw it out because it just didn't seem to matter anymore.

Lately, he sensed her presence and often talked with her. "Why am I plagued with all this cabbage, Grace?"

"As always, you planted too much," she answered. "Give it to the neighbors."

"I'd throw it in the trash before I'd give anything to these neighbors. They don't know if I'm alive or dead. Hell, they're all so new to the neighborhood they wouldn't know I once had a wife and kids. Now if the Martins still lived next door instead of that shyster lawyer O'Hara and his prissy wife, or the Gills and the Johnstons hadn't moved, and the girls hadn't left home and you hadn't died of cancer, I might feel differently. But, these people don't deserve my cabbage!"

Instead of feeling rewarded for all of his backbreaking, knee-grinding effort, the cabbage harvest really upset him. He detested cabbage. Grace hated it, too.

Now he was up to his ass in the stuff because his friend, Tom Wembley, gave him some plants, and he felt obligated to stick them in the ground. Usually surplus crops brought him some joy. Being awash in green beans and tomatoes, cucumbers or zucchini validated his efforts and made up for the times one of his crops was ravaged by varmints or victimized by some blight or parasite. He could accept the unpredictability. It was a gardener's reality.

George reached down and rubbed his knee even though he knew far more than a little friction was needed to make his arthritis disappear. Though his stomach hadn't sent a message, his watch told him it was time for lunch. He'd force something down--a beer at least. He pulled himself up from the old chair and stood for a moment to make sure of his balance. As he limped toward the stairs, he turned for a final look at the problem heads.

Upstairs, George rummaged through the fridge looking for baloney and cheese. He found only Swiss cheese. When he removed it from the Baggie, it stunk and was covered with a crust of green mold. It wasn't that he couldn't cope without Grace. He just didn't care. Like the cheese. She wouldn't have let the cheese get moldy, and they wouldn't be out of cold cuts. Plus, Grace had a bread fetish. When she didn't make bread, she always had a loaf of fresh whole-wheat for his sandwiches and toast. Now his bread came in three forms--stale, hard and none, the latter being the present situation.

It wasn't his dotage George couldn't stomach. It was the lack of doting. There hadn't been any since Grace died. Not only did the neighbors ignore him, but the few friends and acquaintances who were still alive hardly ever checked on him. He understood some had problems of their own but as far as he knew none had an affliction that prevented them from dialing a phone. At least his own daughters called once in awhile.

One time when he was visiting Jill in Chicago he

happened to see his name written on her calendar. *Call Dad!* It was written in the same square with *Send Dawn a B-Day Card.* Why would his oldest daughter need to remind herself to call, and who the hell was Dawn? Did Anne have him on her to-do list as well? When he passed on, he wondered, would they each write reminders to themselves? *Attend George Konert's funeral.*

On those occasions when he'd flown to Chicago to visit Jill and her husband, Stewart, Jill was gracious and attentive. In Columbus when he stayed with Anne and Bret in their Taj Mahal, his treatment was more royal but just as warm. These occasions were uplifting. He enjoyed being with his family, and their activities and interactions provided impetus for him to reconnect with others. Unfortunately, the return to his empty house and all-consuming garden erased his fleeting intentions.

When the girls and their husbands visited him, he wasn't as pleased with the results. Trying to reciprocate in kind to children with more lavish lifestyles was impossible. So to make up for his more limited resources, he tried to prepare special meals and wait on them. These efforts seldom satisfied him. He only seemed to make his guests uncomfortable and embarrass himself. He'd see them cringe and roll their eyes at his attempts.

Then he'd become resentful. Maybe he was a little slow or clumsy. So what? He was trying, dammit. He knew he had flaws. Why couldn't they ignore them so he could enjoy their company? He was their father after all. Soon he'd be out of their lives altogether, dead, planted and gone. Then they could laugh about him all they wanted. It hurt that they were all he had left to show for his life. Not one grandchild. Just a history that died with Grace twelve years before.

Frustrated with his lunch preparation, George decided to improvise. He'd use crackers instead of bread. There weren't any. He placed the cheese on the cutting board and sliced off the mold. Then he cut four chunks, smeared them with mayonnaise and topped each with two sweet pickle slices. He surveyed his concoction with pride. However, his first bite announced rancid cheese. He spit the unchewed mouthful into the sink. The remainder went into the garbage.

To kill the taste he moved to the garage refrigerator for a brew. At least that would be well stocked. Wrong. After much searching, he failed to find even one lonely bottle tucked behind the large unopened can of tomato juice and a long forgotten package of rolls dated March. He poked at the rolls. Rock-hard. They followed the cheese into the garbage.

The time had come to face another ordeal. Shopping. Grocery stores always threw him into a bad mood because he was sure he'd be cheated and overcharged. In his mind the store was an adversary, and shopping, a war.

In some families the husband purchased the groceries. Not theirs. Grace was the shopper. For a year or so after she died, he accepted the duty like a good soldier. After that the challenge grew old, and he resented the effort it required.

When Grace was alive, George groused about the food she selected. Since her death, she evened the score by harassing him on his trips to the supermarket. Though he sensed her presence on other occasions, he could always count on her to *help* with the shopping. Pushing the cart down the aisle, he could feel her urging him toward some wholesome item and away from the high fat content foods he liked. At times he resented her interference, but most of the time, like today, he was pleased to have her company.

In the bakery, he reached for a package of French donuts. Before he could get them into the basket, she grabbed them out of his hand and dropped them on the floor. As he stooped to pick them up, he said, "Come on,

Grace. Don't keep me from joining you."

While returning the donuts to the shelf, two bemused matrons who were eavesdropping smiled at him. He averted their stares and wheeled on to canned goods for some baked beans.

"Please don't embarrass me again, Grace, or I won't let you shop with me."

From beans he moved to produce to buy grapefruit. He picked one up and squeezed it. "This lousy fruit isn't worth fifty-nine cents," he said in disgust. He flipped it back onto the pile and jumped back from the ensuing grapefruit avalanche. By the time the last of the errant spheres cascaded to the floor, he was already bending to pick them up. Fortunately, the produce manager nudged him aside, and not needing any additional encouragement, he made a fast getaway. He pointed his cart to the dairy section.

A half-gallon of skim milk went into the cart, and then some Swiss cheese. Before moving on he debated over a pint of half and half for his cereal. When he was a child, he poured the cream off the top of the bottled milk. That was ancient history. Grace never allowed anything but skim. He looked around and saw her shaking her head.

"Leave me alone, Grace," he growled. "I don't want to live forever."

Shopping was turning out as bad as he expected.

At the deli, he wanted ham if it wasn't too expensive. It was. He settled for summer sausage. At the meat counter, his heart was set on steak. Five dollars and ninety-five cents a pound was a bundle, but he picked out a nice T-bone anyway. He waited for Grace's reaction. There wasn't any. Maybe she was tired of protecting him from himself. In his head he could hear her say, "Go ahead. Dig your own grave."

Then he saw the chips.

"No chips," he heard.

So she was going to take a stand on the chips. Well, so would he. "I'm getting 'em, Grace. The biggest bag they sell." He looked around. Silence. Grace was gone. He felt guilty as hell.

His final pick-up before moving to the checkout was a case of beer. As he placed his purchases on the counter, the packer asked, "Paper or plastic?"

"You decide, but be careful of the chips. I don't want them smashed."

"Yes, SIR!"

"And don't be a smartass."

The packer shrugged.

The checker looked up from her scanning and grinned. George sensed a conspiracy and decided to fight back. When she handed him the register receipt, he studied it carefully and handed it back to her. "It can't be that much," he said. "Do it again!"

"Again?"

"Yes. Again!"

Turning to the boy packing the groceries, he yelled, "I thought I told you not to smash the chips!" He grabbed the bag from the top of his sack and rattled them under the nose of the startled kid. "Look what you've done. You've broken them." Smashing a few chips for emphasis, he said, "I want a new bag."

The boy stood immobilized.

"Get going! Get 'em!" he said putting on his most satisfied smile. "It's going to take awhile for the little lady to refigure the bill."

The shoppers behind him who were enjoying the byplay moments before began filtering to faster-moving checkouts. If they were disgruntled, George didn't care. He felt no remorse. He'd won the war and to hell with the casualties.

Driving the old Chevy home from the store, he was proud of the way he pissed everyone off and never lost his composure.

When he was younger, he had a terrible temper. One of his worst exhibitions was the time he lost it with his oldest daughter, Jill, and her friend, Amy Martin, from next door. The two girls had been putting on a play in the basement using the old outfits Grace had kept for playing dress-up.

It was late summer. He'd sorted and stored his excess from the garden on the big metal table by his workbench and gone upstairs for a shower. The girls understood that his part of the basement was off limits. However, before the performance they needed props and broke the rules. Not only did they use some of his tomatoes and peppers, but they chose his prize burpless cucumber. As he, Grace and Anne watched the show, he observed his produce being violated and threw a tantrum. He blurted a blast of invectives that sent the girls up the stairs crying.

That brought Grace to her feet, shouting.

"Who the heck do you think you are, yelling at Jill and Amy when they're playing so nicely."

"They were playing with my vegetables."

"You and your darn vegetables. I wish you didn't have that garden. You're a fanatic!" she yelled at him. "I'd rather buy vegetables at the store than deal with your childish behavior. And while we're at it, we always have way more than we can eat. Why don't you plant less or give them away?"

It was at that moment, when George was feeling most contrite, that he hatched the idea of having the girls sell the surplus. He smiled.

"What are you smirking about?"

"I'm sorry." He reached for her.

She backed away. "Don't tell me you're sorry. Tell the girls."

"I need to put the vegetables back," he said.

"If you don't go up there right now and apologize, you won't have any to put back. I'll personally smash each one and then go outside and pull up all your plants."

And so he'd climbed the stairs and apologized to the girls.

He missed those days when the children were young, and he worked like a fool at Kerr. Perhaps he missed sparring with Grace as much as their tender moments together. Mostly he was sorry he didn't have more important things to do than bitch about the cabbage he'd grown.

As he pulled into the driveway, tears formed. He wiped them away with the sleeve of his blue work shirt. Another thing that bothered him about getting old were the tears. He seemed to feel things more profoundly, and his emotions were closer to the surface. One minute he felt fine. Then, suddenly, he'd find himself bawling.

When Grace was alive, he wasn't like that. If anything, he'd been too taciturn. More than once she'd chastised him for his lack of sentimentality. Now he'd turned into the blubbering fool she'd always wanted, and she wasn't around to appreciate it.

George raised the garage door and entered the kitchen. Carrying the groceries from the car to the counter by the sink required two trips. When he was finished, he sat down on a chair to rest. Throughout most of his life George thought of himself as ageless. As the rest of the population decayed, he was the standard measure of their decline.

Recently, however, he'd begun to feel like some character in a horror flick who goes to bed youthful and then during the night his skin crinkles and his hair falls out and when he wakes up in the morning, he's too stiff to get out of bed. One minute he was young and the kids were selling produce from an old wooden wagon with yellow wheels, and the next they were leaving for college and then leaving for good. By the time he finally accepted their absence, he had to deal with being a widower.

After unloading the bags and placing the food in the refrigerator and cupboard, George broke open the case of beer and placed each can on the shelf in the garage refrigerator. He could still taste the rancid cheese, so he popped a can hoping to wash it away. He also opened the chips.

A half-bag later with the beer drained, he needed a nap. He dragged himself to the chaise on the screen porch. When he was stretched out on his back, his eyes closed. A gentle breeze cooled him, but it didn't bring on sleep. The cabbage pile on the basement floor kept entering his thoughts. What in hell was he going to do with them?

CHAPTER TWO

TURNING OVER THE SOIL

Each Saturday during the summer when Jill was ten and Anne was seven, George would fill the yellow-wheeled, wooden wagon with surplus vegetables for them to sell to the neighbors. In the beginning, George would trail behind to make sure they were safe. Jill, who was a full head taller than Anne, was the leader. She would pull the wagon with one hand and clutch Anne's in the other until they reached the driveway of a customer's house. Only then would Jill release Anne so she could race ahead and ring the doorbell. Together, they were a formidable sales team. Dressed in their matching homemade dresses, they were irresistible. The neighbors usually bought everything they had.

Once after another successful sales trip, George gloated about their exploits to Grace.

She shook her head and voiced her reservations. "They're taking advantage of the neighbors, George."

"That's ridiculous," he said. "Everyone profits. The neighbors get fresh produce for next to nothing, the girls fill their piggy banks, and I unload my vegetables. Has anyone ever complained?"

"No."

"So, if selling vegetables is so bad, Grace, why don't they turn the girls away instead of luring them into their homes with lemonade and home-baked cookies? Who gets hurt?"

"No one, I guess. It just seems more friendly to give them away."

"Give away the results of my hard work? Don't be crazy!"

The next Saturday he loaded up the wagon again.

By late summer his daughters were making their forays without George traipsing behind. Just as they were beginning another expedition on an August afternoon, a big storm was gathering. If Grace were home, she'd postpone the trip, but unlike his wife, he usually had trouble saying 'no' when they begged and pleaded with him. Pointing to the sky, he said, "The weather looks threatening. Maybe you should wait awhile."

"We'll be fine. Please Daddy, let us go," Jill said.

"I shouldn't." He watched Anne's mouth form a pout. "Well...I'll let you go if you promise to go into a neighbor's house and call me the minute it begins raining. I'll come get you with the car."

"We'll call, Daddy. Don't worry."

Even though they were responsible kids, he did worry. He worried about their safety and worried about the earful he'd receive from Grace when she returned from shopping. His apprehension grew as the sky darkened. He watched them round the curve by the Johnston's and head toward the far end of the street. The storm kept building in typical Ohio fashion–windy, noisy and full of lightning flashes.

Sitting on the stoop, his mood matched the blackness moving in around him. With the first drops of rain, he moved from the uncovered stoop to a drier spot by the door. He thought about tracking down the girls but hesitated. They'd call when they needed him. The rain increased. Another flash, a simultaneous crash, and the sky opened up. George raced for the car keys.

Easing the car out of the driveway into a sheet of rain, he squinted through the wiper-streaked windshield for a glimpse of them. When he didn't see the girls or the wagon, he began to panic. He was sure they were safe, but in which house? Reaching the end of the street, he reversed his direction and slowly drove back toward home. The gale bent smaller trees into arches.

The shadowy houses crept by. He searched for the wagon, but it was nowhere in sight. What if they'd gone off the street? Would they go near a strange car? Grace had taught them the 'Don't ride with strangers stuff,' hadn't she?

The windows fogged, and he used his hand to clear a view. As he approached the Gill's, he let out a deep sigh. Through the downpour he could make out the bright yellow wheels of the wagon parked under the eaves of the garage. He pulled into the driveway, took a couple of deep breaths and ran for the front door. His finger shook as he pushed the button. He waited. A clap of thunder answered. The rain quickly drenched his clothes and soaked his tennis shoes. He rang again.

Finally Sarah Gill opened the door. "I'm glad to see you," she said. "Jill told me to call you, but no one answered."

"I was out looking for them." His eyes darted past her.

"They're in the kitchen."

"Thank God!" The knot that had been strangling his stomach loosened. "I was sure they were okay," he said. "I wasn't worried."

Their eyes met. "Of course, you weren't," she said.

Jill and Anne were playing Monopoly with Timmy Gill.

"Hi Daddy," Jill hollered. "Mrs. Gill bought all the vegetables we had left for $1.50. Altogether, we made $4.35."

George blushed. "That's great," he said.

Looking down at the puddle surrounding his drenched shoes, he said, "I'm making a big mess in your hall."

"It's just water. Would you like a lemonade?"

He glanced out the window and saw the tempest abating. "No, now that I know they're safe, I'll go home and put on some dry clothes."

"I'll bring them home when they finish their game. Don't expect them soon. You know how endless Monopoly is."

He grabbed her hand. "Thanks for being home and taking them in."

"It was nothing," she said.

A woodpecker rattled George from his dream. As he scrunched to an upright position, he squinted at his watch. His nap on the porch chaise had lasted much longer than he planned. The smell of cabbage locked in his nostrils returned him to the problem languishing in the basement. Once before when he'd had a cabbage glut he'd looked into selling it at the Saturday Farmer's Market. When he learned the vendors were charged five dollars to sell produce, he decided it was a dumb idea. He probably didn't have ten dollars worth to sell. Now, with only twenty-nine heads to sell, the farmer's market made even less economic sense. Though he considered it heresy, maybe he should succumb and give the stuff away. Grace would like the idea.

He decided to phone the supermarket and see if they would buy his cabbage. When someone answered, he said pleasantly, "Produce manager, please."

George heard the page. A voice picked up. "Produce."

"Hello, this is George Konert. I have a large garden. Would you like to buy my surplus cabbage?"

"How many cases do you have?"

"Cases. I've got twenty-nine heads. How many cases is that?"

The voice shouted to someone in the background. "A guy's got twenty-nine cabbages to sell. Do you want 'em?" He was laughing when he returned to George. "Sorry. We can't use them."

George growled, "What's the matter! My cabbage not good enough for you? It's better than that garbage you sell!"

"Sir," he said patiently, "if you had twenty-nine cases, we'd consider it!"

Insolent bastard, he thought as he slammed down the receiver.

To calm down, he went to the garage, grabbed another beer and returned to the chaise. The hated O'Haras were mulching flowerbeds in their back yard. He'd noticed them before and grudgingly credited them with maintaining a more presentable yard than the Martins ever did. Even their kid, Sean, was pitching in. He was dragging the mulch from one bed to the next so his parents could place it around the perennials. A fourteen-year-old helping his parents was a rarity, George thought. Usually the punks were playing video games at the mall.

While he watched them toil, he tried to recall why he disliked them so much. Being honest with himself, he probably wouldn't have liked anyone who lived in that house. That was where the Martins had lived. No one could replace the Martins. They'd shared in the childhood and adolescence of his children, and Liz Martin was Grace's closest friend. They learned bridge together, took care of each others kids and practically ran the PTA by themselves while the children were in elementary school. Bill Martin grieved with him when Grace died. As newcomers, the O'Haras knew nothing about this history. They were just bodies inhabiting a real neighbor's home.

The rift with O'Hara began a few months after they moved in. When George awakened in the morning after a stormy night, he noticed the trunk of the magnolia that grew by the back door had split. Half the tree was flat on the ground. The wound looked fatal. He was shaken. The magnolia was Grace's tree. One spring years before, he had planted it as a surprise for her birthday. She loved the tree and cared for it in its infancy like it was a newborn child. Later, when it matured, they delighted in its fragrant blooms. The year after Grace died it failed to bud, and he feared he was going to lose it, too. Then the next spring it had more blossoms than ever, and he credited Grace with reviving it. After that it continued to flourish until that fateful windstorm.

As he stewed about the magnolia, he noticed a shingle lying near the hydrangeas. His eyes traveled to the roof, and he noticed several more missing. Missing shingles meant hiring workers who would overcharge him to fix the roof before it began leaking.

O'Hara was in his front yard picking up debris. The lawyer pointed to a pile of six or eight shingles. "These must be yours?"

"Yeah, they're mine. Did you have any damage?"

"Just a few sticks to clean up . . . and your shingles." The lawyer laughed. George didn't like being laughed at, particularly by some damn attorney just after he'd lost Grace's magnolia.

"You're lucky. I lost my favorite tree."

"You can always plant another one."

"You insensitive SOB. You don't understand!" He turned his back on him and stomped away. Since then, whenever George pictured O'Hara's surprised expression, he felt a twinge of regret. That storm must have been at least four or five years ago, he thought. They'd barely spoken since.

George glanced at his watch. Three-fifteen. The cabbage problem still wasn't solved. He weighed his options. The store wouldn't buy them, nor would he pay the fee to sell them at the Farmer's Market. He couldn't eat all of them, nor could he preserve them in any palatable form. He wouldn't throw them away or give them away. There was only one solution. Wait for Grace to tell him what to do.

He didn't wait long for her answer. "You planted too much like you always do," she said. "Don't be an old fool. Give the darn stuff away."

Leaving the chaise and porch behind, he moved to the bathroom to relieve himself of the beer that had collected while he rested. As he washed his hands, he peered into the mirror and saw the visage of a wise but tormented soul. Then an idea flashed. Most of the time his best insights came while he was in the bathroom. The den or the living room seldom yielded such brilliant thoughts, only the bathroom.

He walked to the attached garage and began searching through the junk that had accumulated where Grace's car had been parked. Under the porch cushions he'd vowed to throw out, he found what he was looking for. The wagon was covered with dust. In order to pull it into the driveway, he had to move some boxes and the old mower that hadn't worked in years. He tilted his head and studied the wagon. Although it squeaked when it rolled, and the yellow wheels were pitted with rust, he declared his idea workable.

When the wagon was filled with cabbages, he

leaned against the car to catch his breath. All those trips to the basement had exhausted him. After a good night's sleep, he'd retrace his children's old route. At fifty-cents a head, he wouldn't get rich, but with some luck, he'd be cabbage-free by noon.

The following morning, he pulled the old wagon to the far end of the street and started his venture by ringing the doorbell where the Olson's used to live. No one answered. He began to zigzag back and forth across the street and stop at every house. No one was home at any of the next three houses. He griped at Grace. "What's the matter with these modern women? They should be home." Then he added, "They're just like our daughters. Always gone. No wonder I don't have grandchildren."

A woman in a sweat suit bought his first cabbage. With dismay, he could sense she bought it just to get rid of him. Two more no-answers galled him before a harried young mother with an urchin clutching her leg welcomed him as if she'd been waiting all day for him to arrive. After the initial shock, he began his pitch.

"I've got some excess cabbage from my garden. Would you like some?"

"Would I? We love cole slaw, don't we, Rachel?" She reached down and ran her hand over the girl's straight white hair. She hesitated and asked, "Are you from the neighborhood?"

"Down at the end of the street. The gray house. I'm George Konert."

"What a nice treat, Mr. Konert." Then she added, "I'm Mary Alexander, and this is Rachel. My sons, Jimmy and Kevin, are playing badminton in the backyard, because their best friends are away at camp." She gestured for him to follow her. "You look a little flushed. Won't you come in for a drink?"

George followed her to the kitchen. She filled a large glass with water and sat with him at the table as he drank it. Rachel ran off.

He tested his sales skills. "I have more cabbage in the wagon. Would you like another head or two?"

"Sure, if you can spare them."

He remembered how Grace told him he'd never be good at sales. Maybe she was right. He knew he didn't have the guts to charge this neighbor for his cabbage. George brought two more into the foyer. Rachel reappeared. "You have a lot of cabbage!" she said.

He creaked to a squat to speak to her at eye level. Mary stood over them. "I grew twenty-nine in my garden this summer, and I'm growing another thirty."

"We don't have a garden. My daddy plays golf."

George looked up at Mary, then said, "No one can do everything, Rachel."

"I wish I had a garden."

He handed the cabbages to Mary. "Don't I owe you something for these?" she asked. "They're beautiful."

He paused. Then he winked at Rachel and patted her on the top of her white hair. "No. I'm an old man without much to do. I thought I'd be neighborly today."

"Thank you very much," Mary said. She studied him. "Mr. Konert?" she asked. "Do you like children?"

George sensed Rachel watching him. "I'm kind of out of touch, but I've always enjoyed them. Why?"

"Oh, I was just thinking..." she paused. He could tell she was struggling with her words,"...maybe you'd like to have lunch."

"Today?" He stared at her and chuckled. "No one's asked me to lunch for years. Sure, why not?"

When Mary called, her sons joined the group for toasted cheese sandwiches. Jimmy, the twelve-year-old was at the tripping-over-everything stage. His squeaky voice amused George. "I play soccer," he said. "Did you play soccer when you were young, Mr. Konert?"

"Soccer was a European game. We hadn't imported

it yet."

Subconsciously, George patted his bad knee, "I played football, but America's game was baseball."

"I don't like baseball. I strike out all the time."

"We have something in common. So did I."

He glanced at Kevin. He saw a face full of freckles and bright red hair. "I'm a good hitter," Kevin said.

"I'll bet you are." Kevin was shorter but more athletic looking than Jimmy.

"I hit a home run every time I bat."

"That's bull, Kevin. You're not better than me at anything except farting."

George glanced at Mary.

"That's enough you two. We have company."

When Kevin finished his sandwich, he began telling George about all the games he could play on the computer. George showed some interest until Kevin attempted to explain in detail how each game was played, at which point Kevin's monologue became too much for George and his eyes glazed over.

His glance took in all three children. Nowadays, he wondered, were all children like this or were the Alexander kids especially outspoken and precocious? If they were the norm, perhaps God was telling him he wasn't equipped to handle grandchildren. Not that he was in any danger of having any. Anger seeped into his gut. His damn daughters. At least they should give him a chance to find out.

When they finished eating, George said, "Maybe you kids would help me in my garden someday."

Rachel jumped from the chair and grabbed Mary's hand. "Can we, Mommy?"

"Maybe sometime, dear, or maybe Mr. Konert will visit us again."

"I'd like that, but right now I have to go. I still have cabbage to...give away."

"Way to go, George!" Grace whispered in his ear.

After thanking Mary for lunch, George continued on to the Johnston's old house. How long had they been gone, he mused. Ten years, maybe? He rang the bell. A woman in curlers and a bathrobe cracked the door and told him to come back another time. He tried to explain his cabbage was free, but she closed the door in his face.

Suddenly, he was becoming pooped, and his knee was hurting. Two more 'no' answers didn't help his attitude. Neither did finding himself in front of the Coleman's. They were the parents of the neighborhood delinquent, Brad. The thought of giving them anything left him cold. He limped on.

His next stop was old Mrs. McConnell's house across the circle from him. It had been several years since he'd talked with her. The thought upset him. She'd been a good friend to Grace and neighborly to him. Sure she used to yell at the kids when they cut through her yard to the next subdivision, and his own children were afraid of her, but that was nothing. He still should have been checking up on her.

He pulled the wagon up the driveway, climbed the stoop and rang the bell.

When she answered, he was shocked to see a shriveled up skeleton of a woman standing before him, her back arched with osteoporosis.

"What do you want?" she said.

"I brought you a gift." He held out the cabbage.

"Put it down. I'll deal with it later. You stay here." She turned and disappeared into the darkness.

George squinted into the hallway.

After a long wait, she returned carrying a paper bag. He smelled cookies. "I just baked them. Take them to your wife."

"She's been dead for twelve years."

She shook her head. "I didn't know."

21

Reaching down, she picked up the cabbage and backed away from the door leaving him standing wide-eyed on the stoop. He was about to turn and leave when he heard her call from far down the hallway, "Thank you for the lettuce, Mister."

Returning to the wagon, he reached into the bag, removed a cookie and took a bite. The senile old gal still baked a delicious chocolate chip, he thought. And she'd given him a whole bag full. For what? A smelly cabbage? Guilt seized him.

Since Grace died, he'd avoided his neighbors, even the ones he liked best. Suddenly, he was tired of being mad at everyone and everything.

A glimmer of what he had done to himself surfaced. Grace was there to hear him. "You knew, didn't you, Grace? Pretending I could live without you and slaving in my garden instead of facing my grief. What a fool. All the effort. All the hiding."

He gazed at the gray wood-sided house at the end of the street. He could see the corn stalks rising from his garden in back. He grinned. "But, Grace, you'll have to admit, *my* idea to give all the cabbage away was brilliant."

He waited for her response, but only heard a car honk on Riverside. "I'm glad we settled that. Now if you will remind me, I'll return the fifty-cents to that lady who bought my first cabbage."

The O'Hara's red brick home loomed ahead. This was the stop he most dreaded but most needed to make. He trudged up the short walk from the driveway to the porch. He rang the bell. No one responded. He relaxed. Maybe they were gone. He rang again. The door opened and Cheryl O'Hara was staring at him.

"Hello," he said.

"Mr. Konert! Is something wrong?"

"No. I've brought you some cabbage from my garden." She seemed confused, so he repeated his words more slowly. "I have some cabbage for you." George thought she understood and handed her two of the remaining heads.

She took them but continued staring. "But why?"

The transaction had become a little more uncomfortable than George had expected. He shrugged and said, "Because I thought you might like them."

"Oh! Well, thank you. Won't you come in for a moment?" He followed her into the foyer. "This is very nice of you. I was just . . . surprised." She called into the family room where George heard a TV. "Guess who's here!"

"Who?"

"Mr. Konert from next door."

"Really? What's up?"

"He brought us some cabbage. Turn off the game and come here."

Mike O'Hara unfolded from the chair and joined them. "When you were picking this morning, I wondered what you were going to do with all that cabbage. Why did you plant so much?"

"I made a big mistake."

"Really?"

George grinned. "I mean I always planned on giving the cabbage away to the neighbors."

"I'm glad we were on the list. Thanks for including us. Want a beer?"

"A beer would be fine," George said.

"The Reds are just starting. Do you want to watch with me?"

George mumbled something for Grace to hear. To the O'Haras it sounded like, "That's a great idea."

CHAPTER THREE

CULTIVATING

George rose with the sun and worked for an hour or more in the relative coolness, hoeing around his cucumber, tomato and green pepper plants. He checked the tassels on the ten rows of sweet corn, attempting to gauge when the ears would be ready to pick. This year the weather delayed his corn planting so he guessed he wouldn't be ready to harvest until the second week of August. Then it would undoubtedly come on so fast he'd have far too much for his own use and have to give some away. He chuckled at the total silliness of vegetable gardening. Take the little green cabbageworms he found gnawing away at the winter cabbage. Had they been munching on the summer cabbage several weeks before, he would have had a solution for his overabundance. Let the creatures ruin the crop. But, the tiny late cabbage plants brought out his nurturing instincts. They needed his protection, so he went to the basement, filled the sprayer with his own non-toxic concoction and eradicated the invaders.

It was nearly eight-thirty when he stopped for breakfast. While he was eating his cereal on the porch, the phone made one of its infrequent intrusions. Lifting himself from his chair at the second ring, he hobbled toward the sound. Four rings. Five. He grabbed the receiver on the sixth, cleared his throat and said, "Konert's." His voice came out gravelly. He coughed.

"This is George. Who? Oh, hi, Mary." There was a long pause. "I don't know." Then, a shorter pause. "I'm not sure." Pause again. "If you think I can do it...I'll try...Friday morning then. I'll be there." He hung up and eased himself back into the chair. This could be interesting, he thought.

He returned to the porch. As he was looking out over his garden, something in the kitchen startled him. He swung around to see his deceased wife watching him from the doorway. Her timing was impeccable. She always appeared when he wanted her opinion.

"Why am I baby-sitting for these kids, Grace? So I can play grandpa?"

No answer.

"Do you think I'm nuts?"

Still no answer.

"I shouldn't ask. You always think I'm nuts."

She faded away.

"Okay, I'll find out for myself."

He returned his gaze to his garden and the familiar wooded tapestry beyond. High in the maples, the crows mocked him. Moving from the chair to the chaise, he lay back on the pillow and closed his eyes. The monitor of his mind played out images of chunky, little white-haired Rachel and the Alexander boys. He grinned. When the crows ceased their racket and just as he was drifting off to sleep, he shrugged and said, "So what's wrong with playing grandpa?"

On Friday morning, George dragged his wiry frame to the Alexander's. The door opened, and he thrust a bag of vegetables at a surprised Mary.

"What's all this?"

"Just some tomatoes and cucumbers I picked for you this morning."

As she carried them to the kitchen, she glanced back at George and said, "If you picked all these this morning, you must get up with the birds."

He pointed to his temple. "At five-thirty every morning the alarm in here goes off."

"I'd be dead if I got up at that hour."

"If I don't wake up at that hour, I *am* dead," he chortled. "Rising early is God's tariff for allowing me to live through the night."

"My Uncle Jack said he never slept when he got old."

"I'm glad I'm not that old yet. How old is he?"

"When he passed away, he was seventy or seventy-one."

"I'm seventy-eight. Your uncle never made it to old."

He surveyed Mary. She was tall and lean with a classic high-cheeked face and long straight sandy hair pulled back from her forehead. Her voice was perfectly pitched, the mellow type of woman's voice George liked. He could clearly hear what she was saying despite his dubious hearing without having to suffer the shrillness that spewed from some female mouths. Though he was no good at judging ages anymore, he guessed she was probably in her late thirties.

He looked past her to the living room. "Where are the children?"

"Jimmy and Kevin are fighting over the computer in the den. Before long they'll wake Rachel." She pointed to the hallway. "I imagine by now Jimmy has given up on Space Invaders and Kevin is playing Yatzee."

George raised an eyebrow. "I don't know a thing about computers, but I know a lot about Yatzee." He rubbed his palms together. "I used to play the original Yatzee with my daughters."

"It's the same on the computer. Come on, let's find the boys."

They entered the den. As she predicted, her older son was hanging over Kevin attempting to irritate him. George stuck out his hand to Jimmy. He high-fived it.

Then Mary said, "Kevin, Mr. Konert's here."

His eyes stayed glued to the monitor.

She waited a moment before raising her voice. "Kevin, stop that game and say hello to Mr. Konert."

"Hello, Mr. Konert," he said without looking up.

George saw Mary's anger rising and waved her off.

"Is that Yatzee?"

"Yeah," Kevin answered.

"Well, I'm a Yatzee champion. Will you play me when you finish your game?"

Without a trace of a smile on his freckled face, Kevin declared, "I'm the best nine-year-old Yatzee player in the world. No one can beat me."

"Kevin!" his mother cautioned.

"They can't, Mom. Dad can't and neither can Jimmy."

Jimmy slugged his arm. "I can beat you anytime I want."

"Ha! I'm the best."

George was fascinated with the byplay. He didn't remember his daughters competing when they were young. He remembered their yelling, whining and snippiness, the running to their room when they had their feelings hurt and the hugs when they were pleased, but never overt combativeness. George eyed the two boys and smiled.

This was a lot more fun.

He turned to Kevin. "I'm impressed, but I wonder how you'll do against the oldest living World Champion. I'm the Yatzee King. No one has beaten George Konert in thirty years."

Kevin eyed him.

As Mary retreated to the hallway, he whispered, "Of course, I haven't played in thirty years."

George pulled up a chair as Kevin cleared the screen. After showing George how to work the computer, Kevin challenged him to a head-to-head battle. Jimmy watched the action and fell to the floor laughing when George won. After the second win, Kevin jumped on Jimmy, and they began wrestling. When George meekly suggested they quit fighting, Kevin skulked off to an old leather easy chair, threw his feet over the arm and put on the earphones to listen to some CD contraption.

"Now you have to play me, Mr. Konert," Jimmy said. "I'm just as good as Kevin."

"Or just as bad," George said. A few minutes later he whipped Jimmy, too.

"You're good, Mr. Konert. Can we play again?"

"Sure, if you can handle losing again." Part way through the game Rachel joined them. She was wearing a pink shorts outfit and tennis shoes, which called attention to her sturdy legs. The top didn't quite cover her protruding tummy. Clinging shyly to the doorframe, she wouldn't budge despite George's coaxing. Finally he said, "Jimmy, get Kevin to play with you for awhile. Rachel and I need to talk."

She ran to the bookcase, picked out a video and handed it to George. "Will you watch Winnie the Pooh with me, Mr. Konert?"

He stared at it, and said, "I don't know what to do with this thing."

"You can't work a VCR?" Kevin giggled. "Even

Rachel can work a VCR."

"Can you roto-till between the cabbage plants?"

"Probably. What's a roto-till?"

Rachel grabbed the video from George and placed it in the player. Running to the couch she patted the seat next to her and said, "Come watch Pooh."

George dropped onto the soft cushions. As her brothers started a new game, Rachel snuggled next to him. He put his arm around her tiny shoulders. She responded by patting his hand. Suddenly, an alarm went off in his head. What would Mary think if she saw him with his arm around her four-year-old? Every day on TV or in the newspaper he read stories about pedophiles or old men being charged with molesting children. The world was so sick nowadays. He glanced over at the boys. They were so engrossed in their game they were unaware of his presence. Still, he was uncomfortable. He lifted his arm from around Rachel's shoulders and struggled to his feet. She studied him for a moment, and then returned to watching Pooh.

He moved behind Kevin and Jimmy and followed their moves on the monitor. Thus distracted, his self-consciousness waned. "Who's winning, Kevin?" he asked.

"My brother's so lucky he makes me puke."

When "Pooh" was over, Rachel ran to George and stood next to him and watched the end of the Yatzee game. Her tiny hot hand grasped his gnarled index finger. George worked his finger free and enveloped her hand in his. A sausage in a bun he used to say to his kids when they were small.

When Kevin lost again, he began badgering George to give him another chance to win. He was about to play when Mary entered wearing a red, plaid apron and a huge smile. "I've already done a lot. How are you all doing?"

Jimmy laughed. "Kevin lost every game."

"I did not."

"I thought nobody could beat you, Kevin."

29

"They just got lucky, Mom."

She winked at George. "Maybe you ought to play Rachel."

"She doesn't know how to play."

"I think that was your mother's point," George said. "Maybe you'd have a chance against her."

Kevin made a face and looked away.

George felt bad. He didn't like rubbing it in, but Kevin was an easy target. "I'll tell you what. Rachel and I will take you on. Okay, Rachel?"

"I have a bit more I'd like to do, Mr. Konert. If you can stand another hour of this, we'll have lunch."

George motioned for her to go.

When Mary left, Rachel asked, "Will you fix my pigtail, Mr. Konert?"

George looked helplessly at the open door. "Why didn't you ask your mother, Rachel?"

"Because I wanted you to do it."

Kevin said, "Your hair's okay, Rachel. Let's play Yatzee."

George said, "Don't you know a woman can't do anything until her hair is just right? OK Rachel, I'll fix it for you." He undid the bands, tightened the braid and rebanded it as the boys watched wide-eyed.

"How did you learn to do that?" Jimmy asked.

"I invented braids."

"Were you an Indian or are you just old?" Kevin asked.

"Just old."

He moved a chair next to Kevin for Rachel to sit on and started a new game. They proceeded to clean his clock. When the game was finished, Rachel said sweetly, "Kevin's not very good is he, Mr. Konert."

George looked at Kevin and saw his face redden. Not wanting to add to his humiliation, he said, "Kevin's an excellent player, but he needs to learn that luck plays a big part in winning games. If he finds some luck, he'll be hard to beat next time."

"Yeah! Wait 'til next time."

Mary entered the room to say she was finished and had lunch on the table. She invited George to eat with them. While he walked next to Kevin toward the kitchen, George patted him on the back and told him how impressed he was with his play.

Kevin looked up at him and smiled.

Once they were seated, Mary served cheddar cheese on crackers with split-pea soup. After a few sips, George exclaimed, "This is the best soup I've ever eaten."

Kevin stared at him like he'd lost his marbles. "It tastes awful."

George glanced at Mary for her reaction before saying, "Do you know how difficult it is to make pea soup, Kevin? You should eat the whole bowl out of respect for your mother's hard work."

Kevin's eyes narrowed as he listened. Then he asked, "Can I have a peanut butter sandwich, Mom?"

"Me too, Mom," Jimmy said.

"Why don't you kids try some more soup? You may like it."

George nodded his agreement.

When Kevin and Jimmy gagged and grimaced, Mary gave in and told them they could make sandwiches.

George shook his head. "I can't believe you boys would rather have peanut butter than this wonderful soup." He winked at Mary. "When I was young, we were so poor my mother used to make stone soup so I'd have one hot meal each day."

"What's stone soup?" Kevin asked.

She'd place a clean white rock in a kettle with water and boiled it. When the rock was just right she'd throw in some bones with a little meat on them, a potato or two, some vegetables and simmer the pot for a long time. Then

31

she'd taste it, and if we had some cream and butter she'd stir that in."

Kevin's eyes narrowed. "Was it good?"

"It was the best soup I'd ever tasted until today." He glanced at Mary. "It was sure better than eating grass and leaves and the stale bread the neighbor lady threw on the ground for the birds."

"Yuk!" Jimmy said. "You're kidding us."

"Just be glad you're not poor."

The whole time George was spinning his yarn and downing his soup, Rachel was matching him spoonful for spoonful. When Jimmy noticed her bowl was empty, he said, "Rachel, you ate all your soup!"

"It's better than an icky old peanut butter sandwich, isn't it, Mr. Konert?"

When they finished lunch, George excused himself and stood up to leave. He looked at the kids and said, "Your parents should be proud of you. You're wonderful children and so bright. I learned about computers and VCRs. Thank you for spending the morning with me."

Kevin turned to his mother and asked, "Can he come play again, Mom?"

"Of course. Mr. Konert can come anytime he wants."

The boys raced for the den. Rachel started after them, reversed, and skipped back to George. She wrapped her pudgy arms around his leg, and said, "I love you, Mr. Konert."

"I love you too, Rachel." While he pulled a handkerchief from his pocket and dabbed at his eyes she ran off. "She's really something," he told Mary. "I wish she was my granddaughter."

Mary chuckled. "And, Kevin?"

"He's a winner, too." George laughed. "Well, maybe not today."

At the door, Mary told him about the closets she'd

finally cleaned out and the two dresses she'd cut out for Rachel. Shaking his hand, she said, "I can't thank you enough. If you hadn't been here, the kids would have interrupted me so often I wouldn't have accomplished anything." She fidgeted and lowered her eyes. "This is awkward. But I should pay you for your time."

"No. I should pay you for reintroducing me to young children. I wouldn't think of taking a cent."

"Don't be silly. I won't feel comfortable asking you to help out next Friday."

"Next Friday, huh? That might be all right, but before I commit, I have to confer with my appointment secretary."

"You do that, and let me know."

"I'm kidding, of course. What time do you want me?"

"Eleven?"

"Eleven it will be." He tossed her a mischievous grin. "I'm now thinking I should be compensated. Even though the marketplace doesn't place much value on an old man's time, what if I were to take some of your delicious soup as payment?"

"By all means," she said and returned to the kitchen to fill a container. She laughed. "I'm sure the boys won't mind."

That evening, George confided in his wife. "These kids like me, Grace." Tears filled his eyes and a few drops peppered his blue work shirt. "Do you realize how long it's been since a child has liked me?"

At eleven sharp on Friday, George returned with a bag of squash. Mary looked inside. "What kind of squash is this?"

"Spaghetti squash. When my children were young, they loved it. I thought yours might too."

"I've never cooked it."

"I'll show you. It's so simple the kids could do it."

"Hmm," Mary said. "If it's that simple, you and the kids can prepare lunch while I finish pressing the washed curtains in Jimmy's room."

Mary yelled, "Hey, you guys, come here. You're going to help Mr. Konert cook lunch."

"We don't know how to cook," Jimmy hollered back.

"Mr. Konert will teach you. He's cooking spaghetti." They stampeded to the kitchen and joined George.

"Where's the spaghetti?" asked Kevin.

"It's not exactly spaghetti," George said. "But it tastes like spaghetti." He turned to Mary and said, "I need spaghetti sauce. Can the kids go to the store with me to get some?"

Mary crinkled her brow. "Well...I don't know."

George read her concern.

She added, "Wait. I think I have some in the pantry."

"That's even better."

Before letting the children cook, George insisted they wash their hands, even though hand washing wasn't a ritual he followed with any consistency at his house. George reached into the bag and pulled out three medium sized squash.

"I don't see the noodles," Rachel said.

"They're inside."

Kevin picked one up and examined it. "No, they're not. Noodles come in a box."

"Believe me, they're in there. The trick is getting them out, and I know the magic."

Later, while the sauce simmered on the stove, George cooked each individual squash in the microwave. The children were mesmerized as he held each scalding vegetable with a hot-pad and sliced it lengthwise. The escaping steam was a perfect prelude to the magic of forking long strands of golden "spaghetti" from the squash.

Rachel clapped her hands and ran to find her mother.

Jimmy said, "That's cool."

"That's not spaghetti," stated Kevin. "You're fooling us."

"It's better than spaghetti," answered George.

"I want real spaghetti!"

"Be quiet, Kevin," Jimmy said. "Mr. Konert says his is better."

"Okay, but it's still not spaghetti."

After they devoured the meal, and the children scampered off to play, Mary said, "You're a great cook."

"I was showing off today. At home, I don't do too well. I learned to cook after Grace died. I had to. Otherwise I would have starved."

She studied his craggy face. "The children are learning so much from you. I wish my husband had some of your traits."

"They're not traits. They're things I've learned over time—a great deal of time." He smiled. "It took Grace years to train me."

"You're too good to be true."

He burst out laughing. "Wait until Grace hears that."

Mary walked him to the door as Winnie the Pooh wafted down the hall.

George said, "Can the children come to my house sometime and learn about gardens?"

"I'll have to do a lot of selling. Dan thinks you're too old to be in charge of his children."

He felt a knot in the pit of his stomach. "I am old," he said. "But, too old?" Then he flashed a hopeful grin. "Tell him I'm much younger when I'm with his children."

On the walk home, George's imagination worked overtime. The scene unfolded with Dan reading the newspaper at the dinner table while Mary cleared the dishes. The children were off playing. She said, "George was here all morning entertaining the kids."

Dan placed the paper on the table and said, "You know I don't like that old goat hanging around."

"Who cares what you like. The children love him, and he likes it here. He seems so lonely."

"I suppose he'll be coming to dinner soon?"

"No, but he had lunch with us. He wants the kids to come to his house and pick vegetables."

"What? You can't entrust our kids to a geriatric specimen just because he keeps you in fresh produce."

Mary's face reddened. "When they're with him, I get projects completed."

He shook his head. "No way. I don't want some old fart fooling with my kids." Then he warned, "You never know about old men."

By the time George arrived home he was fuming. He summoned Grace. "How can he think I'm an old fart," he whined. "He's never met me."

"You're seventy-eight. You are an old fart, George. Also, you may find the little scene you dreamt up was way off the mark."

The next day Mary called. "If you want the kids to come work in your garden, Wednesday would be a good day."

"So you won?"

"What?"

"You convinced your husband I was competent enough to entertain the children."

"Oh, that. I never asked him."

***

When he awoke on Wednesday morning, George was apprehensive. He wanted the visit to go off without a hitch so Mary and Dan wouldn't find fault with his efforts. To make sure there were enough vegetables to pick, he made an inspection tour around the two-foot-high fence that surrounded the garden. Starting at the east end, he paced the forty feet to the back corner where the corn was head-high, and turned to traverse the sixty-foot length of the south barrier. He chuckled at the thought of his little fence being a barrier. Maybe it kept out the rabbits and ground hogs but it did nothing to stop the deer that occasionally grazed in the flood plain behind his property. Until he found the ultimate repellant, they used to wreak havoc on his beets and beans. Then his farmer friend Tom Wembly told him about using male urine as a deterrent. Ever since, he'd filled plastic milk bottles with his fluids. Walking the two-hundred foot circumference sprinkling his tinkle, as his girls used to call urine, must have given the O'Haras a few laughs, but it sure kept the deer away. When he finished his inspection, he was pleased. Carlisle's hot muggy nights had loaded the plants.

While he waited for his pickers' nine-thirty arrival, George distracted himself by reading the paper. Between columns he dozed. When the door chimes awakened him, he brushed away the open newspaper spread across his chest, creaked to his feet and limped to the foyer.

"Good morning," he said as he opened the door and ushered them into the living room. "Any last minute instructions for me, Mary?"

"Not for you, but I have some for the children." She turned to her children standing in a row pawing at the rug like quarter horses in the starting gate. "Don't wipe off your sun screen and behave, and do exactly what Mr. Konert tells you."

"We will, Mom," Jimmy and Rachel replied at once.

"Kevin?"

"Okay!"

Mary kissed each child, and left saying, "I'll see you about one."

George called his platoon to order. With Jimmy leading and George bringing up the rear barking orders, they marched down the stairs to the exposed basement, past the sink in his garden room and out the door to the garden. He sat down on the bench by the faucet and hose and gathered them around him.

"Listen up troops," he hollered like a sergeant from some old 'B' war movie. "We have a lot to do today, and we'll start by picking beans." He explained how they should hold each tender branch with one hand while they pulled the beans with the other. "That way you won't hurt the plants."

They moved to the fence, and he lifted Rachel and placed her on the other side. The boys and he stepped over the hurdle. Ahead loomed five rows of beans. George pointed to two of the rows. "These are played out. No need picking them. We'll concentrate on the other rows. Jimmy, show us how to pick beans."

Jimmy squatted next to a plant, held the branch and picked off three pods exactly as George had instructed.

"That's simple," Kevin said.

"Okay, show us."

Kevin reached town and tore off two beans and a branch.

George looked heavenward for inspiration. Before he could chastise him, Rachel pushed Kevin out of the way and said, "You're dumb, Kevin. Let me do it."

Kevin nudged her away, but she found a plant and carefully picked the beans without hurting the plant. "See how, Kevin?"

George grinned and released them. They began stripping the rows like an army of migrant workers. As they picked, he monitored the results.

Fifteen minutes into the job, Rachel said, "I have to

go potty."

George hadn't planned on that. He took off his straw hat and mopped his face with his blue handkerchief. "How bad?"

"Bad."

"Okay, we have to go up to the house. Do you guys have to go?"

"No," Jimmy said.

"Kevin?"

"We'll keep picking."

"Just continue like you are. You're doing a great job. We'll be right back."

When they arrived at the basement door, he pointed to the downstairs bathroom and Rachel ran ahead holding her crotch. He sat down on the old chair and waited for the flush. When he heard the water in the sink, he stood up. "You washed your hands, Rachel?"

"I'm a big girl."

"You certainly are."

"Mr. Konert, I don't like picking. I'm tired."

Now what, he thought. He couldn't leave her in the house alone, couldn't leave the boys unsupervised in the garden, and he couldn't be two places at once.

"We're not anywhere near done, Rachel."

She smiled up at him and pulled him outside by the hand. "We're smart. We'll think of something."

Once outside, he heard yelling coming from the garden. He and Rachel rounded the lilac bushes and saw the boys wrestling in the dirt. During the melee four or five bean plants were destroyed. He was furious.

"Everybody on their feet," he yelled. The boys jumped to attention. Dirt and debris covered their white tee shirts and tan wash pants and stuck to the suntan lotion on their face and arms. "I want to know why you guys were wrecking my beans?"

"We were racing to see who could pick the most

39

and Kevin started breaking the plants."

"I did not. You cheated, Jimmy. You had the best row."

"Honest, Mr. Konert, I was just trying to get Kevin to quit, and he started fighting."

"So your tussling smashed those plants."

"Maybe," Jimmy said.

George stepped over the fence and peered into each of their baskets. Jimmy's was all beans. Kevin's was full of plant parts. "Kevin, we need to talk. Step out of the garden."

"Don't make me quit, Mr. Konert. I'm sorry. I'll do better." He began crying and Jimmy laughed.

George pointed at Jimmy. "You're out of the garden, too."

"What did I do?"

"You laughed at your brother. I don't like that." George stepped back over the fence and took a deep breath. He looked toward the sky and summoned Grace for help.

Rachel came up from behind and tugged on his hand. "Mr. Konert, who's Grace?"

He stared at the child. Had he actually spoken Grace's name or was Rachel telepathic? He recovered by saying, "Somebody I know, and wish was here."

He turned and faced the boys. Kevin had found a clean spot on the bottom of his shirt to wipe his eyes. Jimmy had his arm around Kevin's shoulder and whispered, "I'm sorry."

"Whew," George said.

Now that his workers were under control, George called a quick meeting. "Crew, we have some decisions to make." He made eye contact with each boy. "I can't give you back to your mother as filthy as you are so you're going to have to take showers when we're done."

"Then we'll just have to put on our dirty clothes again," Jimmy said.

George retorted. "Well, you can't go like this. You'll have to go naked."

Kevin glanced at Jimmy and then George. "Mom won't like that."

George began laughing, "You have a point. No shower."

"Yea!"

Now for the second decision. "I already know Rachel's feelings on the matter. Do you boys want to quit? Let's have a show of hands. Everyone who wants to quit, raise his hand."

They stood like statues.

"That's settled except now we have another problem. Rachel is tired but wants to be with us. Any suggestions?" All blank faces. "All right, you boys pick. Rachel and I will supervise."

Jimmy and Kevin moved back into the rows of beans. A few minutes later, Rachel asked George to help her over the hurdle so she could join them.

"How did I do that, Grace?" he whispered.

After the children finished the bush beans, they moved on to the pole beans. When many of the pods were too high to reach, he joined them. Rachel pulled at George's shirt. "I'm tired."

"When we finish the beans, we'll take a drink break, okay?"

She nodded.

With the sun beating down on them, George led them to the hose and showed them how to drink from the stream and wipe handfuls of water over their faces and neck. While the children sprawled on the grass around him, George sat on the bench mopping his face with his damp handkerchief. He closed his eyes. They flew open at the sound of Jimmy's startled yelp. Surveying the situation, he saw Kevin had turned the hose on him. "Kevin," George yelled, "Bring me the hose."

Whether it was accidental or premeditated, George was greeted with a blast of cold water. By the time he reached the nozzle, Kevin was half way up the lawn toward the house, laughing. George started laughing, too. Just for fun, he sprayed Jimmy and sent him scurrying after his brother. When Rachel waved her arms and hollered, "Me, me," he sent a fine spray her way. Only then did he shut off the faucet.

The boys returned and George asked, "We've got work left. Are you up to it?"

"What's left to pick?" Jimmy asked.

"Tomatoes, cucumbers and green peppers."

"How do we do them?" asked Kevin.

"That's what I'm going to show you."

While George explained his cucumber picking technique, Rachel said again, "I'm tired."

He groaned. Spying a plastic basket, he took Rachel by the hand and with the boys following moved to the shade of the corn stalks. He turned the basket upside down. Motioning to it, he said, "Come on Rachel, sit on your throne."

She gave him a quizzical look. "Don't you understand? You are the Queen. We are your subjects and will do anything you ask because you are Rachel, the Queen of the Garden."

She giggled. "Does that mean I can have something I want, right now?"

"Of course. You're the Queen."

"I want some lemonade."

"Later."

"I thought I was the Queen?"

"You are, but I'm the King."

She smiled up at him. "Okay, Mr. Konert."

The boys moved through the cucumber hills and green peppers. Soon, filled baskets surrounded Rachel's throne.

When they were about to start on the tomatoes, Jimmy said, "I have to pee."

George took off his hat and scratched his head. "Bad?"

"Bad."

Contemplating another trip to the house on his aching knee, he asked, "Ever gone in the woods?"

Jimmy shook his head.

"Then this will be your first." He pointed to the far side of the property. "Go."

Kevin ran after him. "I'm going, too."

George grinned at Rachel. "You stay on your throne, Queeny."

When the boys returned Kevin asked, "What's that tall stuff with the yellow flowers, Mr. Konert?"

George pretended he didn't hear, because he knew if they picked the okra the smell of the pods would get all over their hands and already filthy clothes.

"What's it called?" Kevin persisted.

"Okra."

"Can I pick it?"

"No. You can't reach the pods. You're too short."

"No, I'm not."

"You'll smell bad when you're done, and I don't want to have to tell your mother why you stink."

Jimmy laughed. "Everyone knows Kevin stinks, anyway."

"Yeah," said Kevin. "I don't care if I stink."

Rachel heard the commotion and joined them. Soon all three were pulling pods from the stalks. When the row was picked, their hands and clothes reeked just as he'd predicted. Rachel returned to her throne while the boys completed their last job, picking tomatoes.

When they were finished, George motioned to the house. "Your mother will be here in an hour, and I need to clean you up and feed you by then.

43

"Can we make spaghetti again, Mr. Konert?" asked Kevin.

"No, we're having sandwiches and chips."

"I want spaghetti."

"Me too," said Rachel.

"Next time," said George.

Just as they were sitting down to eat, Mary phoned to ask if it was all right if she was late. Dan had taken the afternoon off, and they wanted to run some errands. After a moment's hesitation, George said, "No problem," though he wasn't sure he meant it.

After lunch, George took the three of them down to the basement and showed the boys how to wash vegetables in the sink. "Remember guys," he said, "Some of those vegetables are going to your house. I don't want a speck of dirt on them. And absolutely no water fights."

Rachel yawned. He took her by the hand, limped up the stairs to the living room and sat with her on the couch. She slipped off to dreamland resting her head against his shoulder. Placing a protective arm around her, he fell asleep, too.

From far off, he heard voices. A man said, "Look at this, Mary. Doesn't this give a new meaning to the word childcare? We walk in off the street, and he doesn't even know we're here."

"I do hope the boys are here somewhere," Mary said.

"Don't bother asking the old man."

George opened his eyes and saw Mary and Dan standing over him. "I guess I dozed off," he said feebly. He extricated himself from Rachel without waking her and creaked to his feet. "I feel terribly irresponsible."

"We should have returned sooner. Taking care of kids can take a lot out of you, particularly when you're not used to it."

"You're telling me. I'm exhausted. I guess I am

showing my age." He took a few steps toward the open basement door. "I better check on the boys."

Dan followed him down the steps. They found the boys covered with mud and soaking wet, working at the sink.

"Hi Mr. Konert. Hi Dad. Kevin and I are washing vegetables."

Dan said, "What are you going to do with them? You don't eat them."

"We like the ones Mr. Konert grows."

Dan stepped to the sink and picked up a handful of wet beans. "You're actually cleaning each bean separately?"

"We have to. Mr. Konert said we can't take them home unless we get all the dirt off."

"He did? Well, he's absolutely right. Nobody wants dirty vegetables."

Later after George and Dan returned to the living room, Kevin burst into the room carrying a bag of cucumbers and peppers. "You should see all the vegetables we picked, Mom. There must be a ton of them. We picked beans, tomatoes, cucumbers and some smelly things . . . what were those smelly things called, Mr. Konert?"

"Okra."

"And okra and peppers, and I had a cheese sandwich for lunch with a tomato. We had lots of fun."

Kevin set the bag by the chair and flew from the room.

"He, of course, was not taxing at all."

"Well . . . ."

"You needn't say more. How did Rachel do?" Mary asked.

"She was the Queen, and very regal."

Rachel rubbed her eyes and stretched. Dan bent to pick her up. "I was taking a nap," she said.

"You weren't the only one," Dan said. "I saw Mr.

Konert sleeping, too."

George grinned sheepishly.

"I was Queen of the Garden," Rachel said. "I made everyone work hard, and I had my own throne."

"It was just an upside-down basket," George said.

Rachel squirmed from Dan's grasp and ran after Kevin and Jimmy who were bringing up bags of vegetables and placing them by the front door.

Rachel ran back to her father and reached her hands high above her head. "Smell," she said.

He bent over and took a whiff. "Whew! Stinky! They need a good scrubbing."

"I said they'd stink if they picked the okra, but, no, they had to do it anyway."

"The Queen, that's me, made us do it."

Rachel ran over and hugged George's leg.

Dan watched with an amused expression and said, "I can't take all this excitement. We better get going." He placed an arm around Mary.

George walked ahead to the door and opened it. Jimmy grabbed a bag and carried it to the van. Kevin and Rachel rushed after him. "Thanks, Mr. Konert," they yelled in unison.

Mary followed the children. "Thanks, Mr. Konert, for everything."

George could tell Dan was hanging back. "I'm sorry I fell asleep. Something awful could have happened."

"Forget about it. It turned out all right." He reached down and picked up the remaining bag. "In fact, seeing you with my kids today, I realize you could probably teach me a few things."

"Thank you, Dan, but I doubt you need my help."

After closing the door, George plopped into his easy chair. With his head crunched against the cushion, he sighed and let his lids fall shut. "You know what, Grace? I really may be too old for this."

CHAPTER FOUR

TILLING

George climbed the three concrete steps of the stoop and rang the bell. His knee throbbed. He waited, and then rang again. The door finally opened and a woman half his age and twice his size looked down at him. She was squeezed into a gray sweat suit.

"What do you want?" she said.

"I'm George Konert from up the street." Her blank expression made him squirm. "A month or so ago back in early July I sold you a cabbage for fifty cents."

A spark of recognition shone on her face. "I remember. Nice cabbage, but I don't need another one."

"Good thing. I won't have any more until fall, but I've brought you some tomatoes and green peppers." He shoved a bag at her which she handled like it contained a bomb. "That's not really why I came back. After I charged you for the cabbage, I gave the rest away." He fished two

47

quarters from his pocket. "Here's your fifty cents."

She tilted her head and started laughing, a big rumbling, full-gutted boomer. "Now I've seen it all. A salesman with a conscience." She opened the screen door and motioned for George to follow. He protested, but was overruled.

"You look like a guy who needs a cup of coffee." She thrust out her hand as he entered the foyer. "By the way, George, I'm Gert."

He followed her into the kitchen and sat down at the maple breakfast table. While she busied herself preparing coffee, he amused himself with the action of her ample buttocks in the too tight sweat pants.

"I'm out of filters," she said, and left. George used her absence to allow his eyes to travel the room. Everything was organized. No newspaper stacks, no dirty dishes. He was mildly surprised. It was an unexpected contrast from the disheveled appearance of his hostess. She returned with a roll of paper towels.

"Maybe this will work as a filter." She tore off a few sheets and fiddled with the coffee maker. A dark liquid began pooling on the counter. She dammed it with the towel roll.

George watched her struggle. "I don't need any coffee. A glass of water will do."

"Nonsense. It's almost ready. Talk to me about cabbage, young man."

"Cabbage? Let's see . . . I grow cabbage the same way you brew coffee. I put in plants, struggle with worms and end up with something no one wants in the first place."

"I beg your pardon. There are no worms in my coffee."

"I assumed that. I was trying for an analogy."

"I got it."

"It was kind of a stretch, wasn't it?"

"No worse than my coffee making."

48

A few minutes later, Gert served him in a mug with 'Chowning's Tavern' written on it.

George pointed to the mug. "You've been to Williamsburg?"

"Yeah. Mom and I . . . Cripes! I keep forgetting she's here." Moving to the door, she yelled, "Mom, get your butt in here. We've got company."

"You talk to your mother like that?"

"I have to. She's deaf as a post."

"I'm not deaf as a post."

George turned and saw a trim, attractive gray-haired woman in her late sixties or early seventies slip through the doorway into the kitchen.

"Gert, I may be auditorally challenged, but you don't need a bullhorn to get my attention. Also, you could show me some respect." She smiled at George. "I'm Catherine, the mother of this circus barker."

"My name is George Konert. I live up the street."

"Well, George, as a member of my generation, weren't you taught to respect your parents?"

He nodded.

"This . . . person treats me like I'm one of her floor scrubbers."

"That's not true," Gert said. "I treat them better."

"When the hospital mixed up the babies in the nursery, I treated Gert like my very own even though I knew the cute dark haired one was really mine. Still, she's ungrateful."

"Because you called me the foster child."

"I was just kidding."

Gert was laughing so hard she was tearing. "And were you kidding when you moved without telling me, and I came home from school and the house was empty?"

"You know that's a lie," Catherine snickered. "You caught the wrong bus. You forgot we moved." They both broke up.

49

George's eyes darted from one to the other.

When it was over, Catherine turned to George and repeated her earlier question, "Shouldn't I receive some respect?"

"I think a daughter should honor her parents," George answered.

"See Gert!"

"I see very clearly. As usual, Mother, you've managed to turn my friends against me. That's the gratitude I get for bringing a man into your life."

Catherine blushed.

Gert beamed. "Since you and my guest are in cahoots, I'm leaving. You'll have to find someone else to trample. I'm a sensitive flower that wilts when I'm crushed." With an exaggerated turn, she stomped from the room.

Catherine grinned and poured herself some coffee. She sat across from George. He surveyed her. Petite and mouthy. Grace was like that, and he loved her for her feistiness, though he usually barked back when she ragged at him. They had some delightful confrontations. It was when she was subdued that he knew something was bothering her. Then instead of letting her talk it out, he'd withdraw. God, he was stupid then.

He gestured toward the door where Gert had disappeared. "Are you two always like this?"

"Only when we're showing off." Catherine placed a finger to her lips and winked at him. "Shh, she's listening." Then in a normal voice, she said, "She's really quite disturbed, you know. She abuses me."

"I heard that, Mother." When Catherine laughed, George heard a refined edition of Gert's laugh.

"Mom, tell George the truth." Catherine rose to bring the coffee pot to the table and refill their cups. "Tell him I won't have booze in my house, and it upsets you because you can't have your cocktail."

Catherine nodded her confirmation.

"I'll admit it if you'll stop eavesdropping."

Gert returned to the kitchen. "I'm going to the grocery."

"You're not going to the store looking like that, are you?"

"Bye, Mom!" She grabbed a Coors Beer baseball cap and crushed it down over her hair.

Catherine threw up her hands.

At the door, Gert turned and said, "You're a great audience, George. Come back soon." She slammed the door after her.

He heard the garage door grind open. Then the vehicle roared out of the garage and through the window George saw the red four by four barrel down the street. "She really moves out in that truck."

Catherine was slumped over her coffee.

"I should say. It's the love of her life. It's the only vehicle we have and normally it's loaded with mops and pails, equipment for her business. Do you know how embarrassing it is being transported in a truck with 'Gert's Maintenance' written on the side?"

"Not exactly Cinderella's coach!"

"It's not so bad at night. But when we drive in broad daylight, I'm mortified."

George shifted his position. "Mind if I ask a question?"

"Why do I put up with it?" Catherine shook her head. "I don't like talking about my mistakes."

"I wanted to know why you're living with Gert."

"I know, but I don't want to share that. Tell me about your life."

"Okay. I've lived seventy-eight uneventful years."

"I don't believe it."

"It's true."

He began his story, and long after he should have

51

stopped he was still filling her with details. He couldn't believe he was sharing his past with a person he'd known for under an hour. But it felt good to chat with a woman around his age who wasn't dead. He was amazed his monologue interested her at all. She kept saying "go on" and "fascinating" so he rambled on telling her about his bad knee, how lonely he was without Grace and his disappointments with his daughters.

"I don't understand their lifestyles," he growled. "Jill is a businesswoman and works all of the time. Anne does nothing but entertain herself. Their emphasis is on money and things." He shook his head. "They moan about different aspects of their lives not being fulfilling. I told them, if you'd have children, you'd get fulfilled in a hurry. But they don't listen. If I had my own grandchildren, at least *I'd* be fulfilled. They could visit me when they got older, and we'd garden together like I do now with the Alexander kids." He paused. A smile found his lips.

"Despite my griping, I've liked my life." He gazed into her gray-blue eyes. He was startled. He saw tears. "I've said something to upset you?"

"No. Listening to you, I realize what I've done to myself. Everyone has heartbreaks, but each time you've suffered a loss you've kept moving ahead."

"Maybe. So what have you done to yourself?"

"Quit. That's what I do." Catherine's eyes took on a faraway look. George sipped from his now cold coffee and waited for her to continue. Instead of answering, she pointed to the window. "I haven't been outside all day. Is it warm?"

"Seventy-three at noon."

"How about a walk, George. I feel all cooped up here."

George rubbed his knee, hesitated and said, "I'll try. Can you tell your life story in three blocks?"

"If we walk slowly."

"Perfect. I can handle slowly."

Brightness clawed at his eyes as he hobbled after her to the sidewalk. She noticed his limp. "Maybe we should go back."

"My doctor says to walk on it, but I think he wants me to make it worse so he can put in one of those artificial knees." He took her arm and turned her in the direction of his house. Walking at a leisurely pace George waited for her to begin her autobiography. Instead she remained silent.

On the other side of the street, he spotted a young girl riding her trike in the driveway. He nudged Catherine. "That's Rachel Alexander, the little girl I sit for." He yelled at her. Rachel jumped off her tricycle, ran to the edge of the street and waved.

"Can you play, Mr. Konert?"

"Not today, Rachel. Maybe tomorrow." She trotted back to her trike.

Catherine said, "She's a beautiful child. Her white hair reminds me of my granddaughter, Nicole."

"You have a granddaughter?"

"And a grandson, Peter. They live in Seattle with my younger daughter, Marianne, and her husband."

"That's a long way."

"Further than you think. I haven't seen them in two years."

"But at least you have grandchildren."

"Yes, but no relationship with them. Unless they read my letters, they hardly know I exist."

"Why don't you go visit?"

There was no answer.

"If they don't have room for you, stay at a hotel. At least you'd see them."

"Oh, their house is big enough. It's my daughter that doesn't have room for me. Along with being a mom and a wife, she's a trial lawyer. She can't possibly handle being a daughter, too."

"Marianne sounds just like my Jill. Always busy, and into herself. Yet, if I had grandchildren, anytime I wanted to visit them I'd buy a ticket and show up on their doorstep with or without an invitation."

Catherine stopped walking and clutched his arm. "George, why do you think I moved in with Gert?"

He confessed he didn't know.

"I moved in with her because I don't have any money!" Her grip on his arm tightened. "Do you know how bad it is to be old and not have any money?"

"No." But it had to rank up there with being old and not having grandchildren.

She said, "Perhaps you've heard enough of my life?"

"The walk was your idea. So I decide when I've heard enough." He flashed her a quizzical look. "Why don't you have any money?"

"Because I'm stupid. I trusted my husband with our finances even though I knew he wasn't a financial whiz. He was forever getting into get-rich-quick schemes. After he died and the bill collectors began hounding me, I faced the truth. Until then, I was oblivious because he always gave me enough money to spend. After he died, I found out he cashed in his life insurance. It took a second mortgage on my home to bury him. Then I lost that, too."

"What did you do?"

"I begged Marianne to help me, but she refused. Actually she didn't refuse, she just had a million excuses for why she couldn't help, and I stopped asking."

"So Gert came to the rescue?"

"On the day of the auction in Cincinnati, she showed up, loaded my clothes and a few remaining personal items into her truck and brought me to Carlisle. I don't know where I'd be without her. I was out of options. She never did ask me if I wanted to live with her. Probably afraid I'd say no. In the five months I've been here, she still hasn't asked."

"You probably should have gone to her in the first place."

"I couldn't. She was always Floyd's girl. Big and blustery. Not refined like Marianne. We weren't close when she was growing up. It was always Floyd and Gert. Catherine and Marianne. Marianne received all my attention because we had so much in common. I was a terrible mother to Gert."

"That's why she brought you here! Because you were a terrible mother."

Beads of perspiration formed on Catherine's forehead and she wiped them away with the back of her hand. "Seems I'm always misjudging people."

"No more than the rest of us."

At the end of the street, George pointed to a gray, wood-sided home. "That's where I live. Maybe you'll come back some day and see my garden. I'd fix you a drink."

"I'd like that. You're a nice man, George."

She held his arm as they headed back. At Gert's house, the red truck was parked halfway into the garage. They squeezed past it and pounded on the locked kitchen door.

Gert was still wearing the cap when she greeted them. "Here the lovebirds are. I was about to send the senile police out looking for you."

Catherine said, "Do you always have to be so crude?"

"What your mother is trying to say," George said, "is when you say things like that she gets embarrassed and can't show you how much she appreciates all you've done for her."

"George, you shouldn't say that."

"Maybe not, but somebody should."

Gert's stunned expression startled him. She left the room.

Catherine took two glasses from the cupboard and filled them with ice and water from the fridge. When she returned, she placed one at her spot and the other in front of George who now had his left leg propped over a chair.

"It hurts a lot?"

He shrugged.

"I'm sorry I made you walk so far."

She sat quietly, drawing a line with her index finger in the condensation on her glass. Raising her head, she glanced toward the living room. "If you're listening, Gert, I do appreciate all you've done. You're a wonderful daughter."

CHAPTER FIVE

PLANTING

The next morning while George was picking corn and checking his tomatoes for hornworms, he could hear the roaring motors and screeching brakes of the going-to-work crowd down on Riverside. He chuckled. Why be stressed? So what if they docked you a few bucks for punching the time clock late? How would that pittance make a better life? Still he knew what they were feeling. He was like that once, always rushing, heart palpitating, stomach churning. When he was the breadwinner, he knew the gnawing fear of upsetting his superiors, the risk of getting fired. He'd felt that way right up to the day he retired. What foolishness, he thought. But then, was that worse than now when he was without responsibilities and had more time on his hands than he could handle.

Since his stomach hadn't sent a breakfast alarm, he lingered in the coolness of the basement cleaning his tools.

Before spending the last hour on his green folding campstool pulling weeds, he'd planned a breakfast of scrambled eggs and bacon. Now with his body aching and sweat beading his forehead, cooking, and particularly cleaning up afterwards, seemed like too much effort.

Lately everything seemed like too much effort. Even the garden was becoming such a burden he'd thought of giving it up and moving to a condo. Perhaps he'd be less bushed living in one. Except living in a condo didn't solve anything. He'd still have all the picking up and cleaning, cooking and dishwasher loading and unloading he detested. If he wanted to stop gardening, he should just quit planting. He didn't need to move to do that.

Then there were the new apartments connected with the retirement complex. If he lived there, he'd have lots of people to talk with every moment of every day and still have his privacy when he wanted it. Retirement centers had dining rooms, housekeeping and maintenance services, and when he became too feeble or demented to live independently, they'd tie him in a wheelchair and whisk him away to the nursing section. All he had to do for a lifetime of leisurely living was write a big check each month. He ran a veined hand through his thinning hair. Forget it George, he thought. That's not the way you want your life to play out.

What he really needed was some live-in companion to keep him company and help with the chores. Maybe even a wife. "I said maybe even a wife, Grace. That's it–a strong young wife to do all the work. Or better yet, Grace, how about a strong, young, rich wife who'll roto-till, plant and weed my garden while I drink beer and direct her from a chaise." He searched the barren concrete walls for a sign from Grace. "Pretty good idea don't you think? Of course, I'll still do the harvesting because that's the fun part."

Suddenly, the basement room filled with Grace's laughter.

It was nearly eight-thirty when he creaked to his feet and grunted up the stairs. Instead of entering the kitchen, he backtracked to the front door and brought the newspaper in from the stoop. Walking into the kitchen, he slipped the rubber band from the rolled paper and placed it on the closet doorknob with a bunch of its predecessors. Wednesday, August twenty-first it said at the top. Damn, he thought. Wasn't yesterday Wednesday? The paper man was always leaving him a day old paper. He checked the calendar on the refrigerator. In Tuesday's square, he'd written, "Clean out bird feeder." Yesterday, he'd cleaned out the bird feeder, so it must be Wednesday after all. "Sorry, paper man," he said as he tossed the paper onto the counter.

George opened the fridge and poured a tumbler of orange juice that he sipped while he filled a bowl with All-Bran and poured on two percent milk. When he was seated at the table, he began separating the newspaper, placing each section one on top of the other in its order of importance. The sport section went on top, then the front page. The local news, which contained the obituaries lay at the bottom. The remainder was set aside for the recycle bin.

For George, the most coveted piece of information in the entire paper was the previous night's score of the Red's game. Like fanatics of a different ilk who'd never dare begin a day without consulting their horoscopes, George's feelings were so closely intertwined with the fate of his Reds that the box score was the key to how his day would unfold. Nothing sent him flying as high as a win or spiral him into a day-long gloom like a Reds defeat. As a die-hard fan, he actually relished having his emotions inflamed by his Reds.

Grace once chastised him for getting all excited over a dumb baseball game. He passively agreed with the silliness of it rather than show her some real emotion for criticizing his interests. Now if she were to meddle with his choice of emotional stimulus, he'd tell her crying over a Red's loss beat the hell out of boredom. So rather than remedy this roller coaster of Red's induced mania or depression, he was content to have the substance of his day manipulated by the outcome of their games.

He picked up the sports page and eyed yesterday's score. It would be a good day. They won 9-8.

After scanning the rest of the sports pages, he placed his bowl, spoon and glass in the dishwasher. Then he gathered the two unread newspaper sections and headed for the chaise lounge on the porch. On a nice day like today, finishing the paper on the porch after breakfast was the perfect prelude to a morning nap.

Beyond the wooden fence that a woodpecker was intent on rat-a-tat-tatting into Swiss cheese, Mike and Cheryl O'Hara were mowing and trimming their yard. Seeing them at work suggested to George it might be the weekend. To confirm his suspicions, he rechecked the date on the front page of the paper. It still said Wednesday, August twenty-first. That raised another question. What kind of lawyer could do yard work on a Wednesday morning?

George scowled. Years before when he was working at Kerr, he always knew what day it was. Monday the work-week began. In the fall, winter and spring, he bowled on Tuesday nights. Grace and he watched their favorite TV shows on Wednesday night, and Thursday night he stayed home with the kids while Grace played bridge. Friday was payday and the family usually went to The Dolphin for a fish fry.

Since Grace died and he wasn't working, he found it difficult to adjust to a week without reference points. Wednesdays, Fridays, Sundays; they were all the same. No day had much to distinguish it from another. How could he develop a rhythm in his life when he never knew what day it was? He looked out through the screen toward the woods and said, "Fix me, Grace. I'm out of sync."

Reaching the chaise lounge he sat down on the edge. At one time when he was younger, he'd swing his legs onto it. Now he had to slowly slide his right leg onto the plastic cover and use both hands to lift and guide his bad knee next to it.

Once settled, he began scanning the front pages for the latest murder or natural disaster. Unlike some people who were into politics, George found blood and gore far more interesting than political propaganda. As a teenager, he mimicked his parents' views and idolized FDR. But his opinion changed radically when FDR involved America in World War II. When the wave of patriotism spawned a steady stream of dead young men, George sensed a betrayal. He began to believe what others were saying, that Roosevelt entered the war to get the country out of the depression. With the booming factories turning out war materials and their owners becoming millionaires, he saw nothing but cynicism in his former hero's decisions. After that turning point, he believed all elected officials were contemptible. He held fast for sixty years. Not even the most charismatic politicians could ever capture his imagination enough to change his mind.

He folded the front page and began flipping through the pages of the local section to the obituaries. George never missed reading them. He was compelled to see if any of his contemporaries had succumbed. Before his cabbage give-away when he was at odds with his world, he wouldn't have cared if his own name had appeared. Now he hoped he'd hang around awhile. In that regard, the obituaries were comforting, because many of the deaths were men and women in their eighties and nineties thus reducing his concern about his own impending demise.

Other than his aching knee, George usually wasn't preoccupied with his own morbidity. Unlike some of his peers whose conversations mainly contained regurgitated medical reports, he didn't pay attention to the consistency and frequency of his bowel movements or how tired he'd been feeling lately. If he was tired, he napped. Whatever he eliminated was flushed away and forgotten. He was more worried about the health of his garden plants than his own vital signs.

Not that George was a fool. Despite his cynicism toward physicians, he saw his doctor periodically to have his ticker and blood pressure checked and receive a lecture on eating right to lower his cholesterol. Also, he was motivated to take his daily blood pressure pill and aspirin, because it assuaged his one major fear, having a crippling stroke. His only other precaution was avoiding foods that upset his stomach or irritated his hiatal hernia. He hated the pain and discomfort when his innards acted up.

No longer could he be as cavalier with his body as he was when he was young and macho. Heck, back then if he'd cut an appendage, he'd rub dirt into the wound to stop the bleeding. Not any more. Life was tenuous enough without borrowing trouble.

George treated obituaries as invitations to social functions. Funerals and visitations presented opportunities for him to break up his routine and get out of the house. Over the years, he'd developed detailed guidelines for determining which services he'd attend and which families received sympathy cards. After all, putting on a white shirt and tie and climbing into his blue serge suit was a major effort. Not everyone was worth it.

The response of the deceased's family to Grace's death was the prime determinant. If either spouse attended her visitation or funeral, he'd reciprocate. In some cases if George were later given a reasonable excuse for the absence, he'd still attend. Otherwise it didn't matter how close the relationship was before Grace's death. If they'd copped out, they went on George's black-list and were forever shunned.

When George did attend a service, he went out of his way to visit with other old-timers and renew long-ago friendships. Usually, he found these meetings enjoyable. However, sometimes these connections were bittersweet. It troubled him when old acquaintances needed walkers and canes or appeared demented. In those instances, he was sorry he'd come. He preferred his memories to the realities of today. The exception was the time he ran into a pathetic old man and realized it was one of Grace's former suitors: George felt ecstatic. When he compared his own relatively robust health to the decrepit old guy, he couldn't wait to chide Grace about him.

The next most important criteria for determining whether he'd attend a service was the potential for a decent meal. While his system wasn't foolproof, he knew certain denominations like the Methodists and Congregationalists were more likely to put out better grub than others. His experience also taught him that late morning funerals provided better grazing opportunities than afternoon events. The only sure bets were eleven AM funerals held at a Methodist church where the deceased had well-to-do children or grandchildren living in Carlisle to foot the bill for the spread. George never missed those.

As he studied the obituaries this morning, on the lower part of the third column, he spotted the name, Anthony Parrino. He checked the age. Seventy-five. While he hadn't seen or heard about him for more than sixty years, it appeared from the obituary that Tony had lived in Carlisle most of his adult life and worked for Atlantis until he retired. He was sorry he hadn't known that. Tony's older brother, Jake, was George's best friend and protector in high school and one of the more interesting characters he'd ever known. George often thought about Jake, and had he realized Tony lived in the area, he would have enjoyed connecting with him.

63

Before committing to Tony's services, George went over the facts. The article didn't mention a country club affiliation or give any other indication that the deceased was well off. It did mention he was survived by a wife Evelyn and three kids. Two lived locally. That was a good sign. There might be a bountiful spread. He didn't want to go hungry. Predeceased by parents and brother Jacob, it said. He checked the service information. Tuesday, 10:30 AM. That was a positive sign. But St. Paul's Cathedral? The food at a Catholic funeral could be sparse. He was certainly looking for more than wine and wafers at the altar. What to do? What to do?

George folded the paper and placed it in his lap. He looked out over the gardens to the silver maples swaying in the gentle breeze. Even with all their traveling, both he and Grace agreed few places in the world were as idyllic as their own porch on a clear summer day.

His eyes became heavy. A nap was imminent. He glanced at the O'Hara's progress and scanned the yard. The little gray squirrel that raided his birdfeeder was chattering in the horse chestnut by the path. The woodpecker was back rattling the fence. George stretched and filled his lungs with rose scented ambience. His head fell back against the cushion and his eyelids closed.

He'd go to the funeral, he thought.

CHAPTER SIX

BUDS

When George awakened, it was a clicking noise that caught his attention. It wasn't repetitive like a clock, but the intermittent sound of . . . . Very familiar. What was it? He squinted through the screen. Aha! Grass clippers. O'Hara was cutting the unwanted grass around his shrubs.

George stretched his back to remove the kinks that inevitably appeared after he slept. He was in no hurry to rise, so he lay back on the chaise and daydreamed. Tony's obituary had brought Jake back into his consciousness. After sixty-some years of occasional reflection, it felt good to recall their antics.

When George finally hoisted himself to his feet and looked over at his neighbor's yard, a large butt in scarlet shorts stared back at him. The clicking stopped. The butt moved on. The clicking started again.

"Is that you, Mike?" George hollered.

"Yep. A hell of a compromising position to be in,

don't you think?"

"Not for a lawyer," George said as he opened the screen door and walked down the steps to join him. "I've heard if the price is right, some lawyers will take virtually any position. Need some help?"

"Not from you after that comment. Actually, I'm about done."

"What exactly are you doing?"

"Cutting anything long and green growing in the mulch that doesn't have flowers on it."

"That's explicit enough. Cheryl's orders?"

He nodded. "It's not my idea of fun."

"Then I'll treat you to a beer."

George limped around the front of his house to the garage refrigerator and removed two cans. By the time he returned, O'Hara had finished and was mopping his face with his shirttail. George handed him a brew.

"So, you always do what Cheryl tells you to do?"

"In the yard."

"When Grace was alive and I was working at Kerr, the yard was my domain," George said. "It was the one place I was in control. She ruled everywhere else, except the office. The VP of manufacturing bossed me around there."

"Weren't you a supervisor."

"Actually, I was the superintendent."

"So you're exaggerating a little."

"A lot. But it gets me sympathy."

Mike laughed. "From whom?"

George shrugged.

"By the way, thanks for the brew. What's new in your life?"

"Nothing's ever new in my life," George said, "But while I was daydreaming on the porch, I thought about an old high school friend of mine. I'll bet you didn't know there was a time when I had a bodyguard."

"Why would you need a bodyguard? Was your family in the Mob?"

George laughed. "Hardly. But when I was young, I attracted bullies like Valentino attracted women. I was the perfect prey--a big, athletic kid who didn't fight back. In football where the game had rules, I was plenty tough. But off the field where fighting was uncontrolled, I was gutless.

"That's where Jake came in. He was exactly the kind of guy I wasn't, a totally fearless street fighter. With his well-deserved reputation for being crazy, most bullies avoided him, and when I was around, me."

"Built like a bouncer, I suppose."

"Not really. He was stocky, but smaller than me and most of the guys he took on, and mean as hell. Today they'd say he had an attitude.

"One day in our sophomore year he told me he'd been watching Terry Bates and Jerk Dawson pushing me around. He offered to beat the crap out of them if I'd help him with his schoolwork. I took him up on the deal, but wondered aloud why his sudden interest in grades. He told me his old man threatened to kill him if he didn't graduate from high school, and if I'd help him learn stuff, he'd see that no one messed with me."

O'Hara said, "Sounds like a good arrangement to me. But I'm having trouble envisioning you with a punk for a bodyguard."

"You know, O'Hara, I never considered Jake a punk or troublemaker. However, I admit he attracted trouble. His I-don't-give-a-shit attitude was so contagious I'd get involved in his shenanigans, like our bike attacks on Douglas Street hill. That darn hill was a full block long and steep as a mountain. If I was alone, I'd bike down it squeezing the life out of the handlebars and riding the brake. When I was with Jake, he'd charge over the crest with a full head of steam spreading his arms and legs like a human bi-plane. Like a fool, I'd occasionally mimic his

67

craziness."

Mike said, "Sounds like a high school chum of mine who took his bike down a toboggan slide in the winter and broke his collar bone and three ribs."

"That's Jake. He was always coming up with a new wrinkle. Fortunately, I didn't try to copy the stunt that almost killed him. Instead of his bi-plane routine, he flew down the hill lifting the front wheel of his bike over each crack in the concrete. Halfway down, he raised the front of the bike and the wheel dislodged and took its own course down the hill. Without a wheel the fork dug into the asphalt, and Jake flew over the handlebars. He landed face-first twenty feet down the hill and skidded to a slow grinding stop at the curb. When I got to him, I thought he was dead."

"What did happen?"

"He broke his wrist and jaw and bruised his larynx. His face looked like hamburger. Also, the doctors said he had a brain concussion, but as goofy as Jake was, who could tell?

"The first time I visited him after the accident he looked awful. His face was covered with bandages, his jaw wired-shut and his wrist was in a cast from his thumb to his elbow. I stayed for only a few minutes, and I'm sure he didn't care.

"The next time most of his bandages were gone, but he had to stay cooped up in the apartment until his throat and concussion healed. Being alone was driving him nuts."

"You were his savior."

"Exactly. All his wild schemes required an accomplice, someone gullible like George. For example, take the escape rope made from sheets caper. Why I ever let myself get mixed up in that gig, I'll never know.

"With his jaw wired shut and the injury to his voice box, Jake wasn't supposed to talk. So he communicated by gesturing and writing notes on a clipboard. *What if there was a fire, and I needed to get out in a hurry?*

"That note sucked me in. After a succession of messages I found myself dragging every sheet from every stripped bed and closet into his bedroom and tying them into a rope which I tied to the leg of his bed. He then put down his clipboard, slipped his arm from the sling and helped me push the bed to the open window. The rope went out. It was about four feet short of the ground. I hung my head out the window and saw the white line dissecting the red bricks. For the first time, it occurred to me that someone might actually climb down that sheet-rope, and I had a sinking feeling that Jake assumed it would be me.

"He picked up his board and wrote, *Try it.* I realized if his crazy plan didn't kill me, my parents would for trying it. 'Forget it,' I said, and tried to convince Jake that the fun was making a three-story long rope, not using it."

"I can tell you what happened next," Mike said. "He slid down the rope."

"Like a one-armed acrobat. Once he was safely on the ground, he waved at me to follow. When I refused, he gave me the finger and performed a version of a hopping chicken with one wing flopping. That's motivation for any male teenager. I moved onto the sill and reached gingerly for the rope. Once it was firmly in my grasp, I swiveled and wrapped my legs around it. Slowly, I began descending until I was even with the second floor windows. That's when I saw the flashing lights of the squad car. I dangled there as a patrolman rushed up to Jake and began yelling at him. Jake pointed to the wires in his mouth and shook his head.

"The policeman turned his attention to me and hollered, 'Hey, what are you doing up there?'

"Since I was wondering the same thing myself, I didn't answer and continued lowering myself hand-over-hand until I reached the ground. The patrolman stared at me and then at Jake as he waited for an explanation. Jake was getting annoyed because he couldn't tell the cop what we were up to because of his larynx, and it appeared I'd gone dumb. He tapped the policeman on the arm and pointed to the third floor window. The cop looked up and shrugged. He wasn't into charades. Jake gestured for a piece of paper to write on. The cop checked his pockets and shook his head.

"In exasperation, the cop said to me, 'I understand why your friend can't talk but what the hell's the matter with you?'

"Behind the cop's back, Jake was doubled over and slapping his knee. I found my voice. Pointing to the open window I explained that Jake lived there, and we were practicing an escape from a fire.

"The cop said, 'That's the most ridiculous story I've ever heard. What were you really doing, robbing the place?' Then he began pushing me toward the squad car. Jake got between the car and us. Then he produced a key. The policeman took off his hat and scratched his head. He couldn't understand why we'd climb out a window and down a rope made of sheets if we could go in and out of the apartment at will. I meekly restated my explanation, and he said we needed to go with him to the station where the Sergeant would sort it out.

"Jake shook his head and fell to the ground. Whereupon, the cop pulled him up by the armpits. So I dropped to the grass. When he pulled me up, Jake sat down. Two kids on a teeter-totter. It was an impasse."

O'Hara said, "I'll bet that pissed him off."

"Oh, yeah. Plus we were starting to have fun. The cop car and the confrontation had attracted a small crowd of neighbor women and children. Finally, one lady stepped forward. The policeman looked up and demanded to know who she was. Incensed by his tone, she said it was none of his business, but if he must know she lived in the gray house next door and the boy with his mouth wired shut was Jake Parino.

"The cop pointed at me. She said she'd never seen me before, but the other one lived in that building. She pointed to Jake's apartment. Suddenly, her eyes widened as she saw the sheets hanging out of the window. She wondered what in the world was going on which, of course, was exactly what the cop was wondering.

"She told him Jake was always doing dumb things, but she doubted he was stupid enough to rob his own apartment. After the two adults competed for the honor of lecturing us on the danger of shinnying down a three story rope made of sheets, the cop climbed into his patrol car and sped off, the lady marched home, and Jake and I walked upstairs where I untied the sheets, remade the beds and returned the wrinkled linens to the closet. As I was leaving, Jake handed me a note. It read, *Come over tomorrow. I have a better idea.*"

"I can only imagine what bizarre scheme he had up his sleeve," O'Hara said.

"Frankly, I don't remember. He had so many." George smiled at O'Hara and asked, "Want another beer?"

"Sure, but I'll buy this time." He got up and headed for the house.

While Mike was gone, George remembered the time at high school football practice when he'd run right over Butch Hogan and made him look bad. Since Butch was one of the biggest and toughest defensive tackles on the team, his pride was hurt, and he began badgering him away from the field. No big stuff he couldn't tolerate, just a few shoves and general tormenting.

One day, Jake saw Butch shove George into a corridor wall. Slipping up behind him, Jake blind-sided Butch with a right to the pit of his stomach. The air whooshed out of him as he crumpled to the floor. Butch was gasping for breath when Jake jumped on him, grabbed

71

his hair and banged his head on the terrazzo a few times.

As they ran to class, Jake said, "Butch won't pester you anymore, George."

"What if Butch squeals?" I said. "You could get into a lot of trouble."

Jake said with disdain, "Only wimps squeal. Butch isn't a wimp. He won't say nothin'."

After the Butch pounding spread around school, Jake became a folk hero. Like an old-west gunslinger, every tough now wanted a piece of him. They came, one at a time, a steady march of wannabes. Jake stopped them all and blunted their bravado with bloody noses and missing teeth.

George was staring off into the distance and grinning, when O'Hara returned. "What's so funny?" he asked handing George a beer.

"Oh, just reminiscing about Jake. As his reputation soared, and it became known he was my friend, no one ever bothered me. My enemies assumed correctly that if they messed with me they'd have to settle up with Jake."

They carried their drinks to a spot in the shade of O'Hara's huge maple. After taking a long swig, George placed the can on the ground and leaned his back against the trunk. "You know, O'Hara, my part of the bargain wasn't easy. I tried hard to help teach him, but Jake wasn't into schoolwork.

"One time in order to avoid an F in English, he had to write a theme. His solution was to have me write it for him. I explained that if I did the writing, and it didn't sound like him, he'd get an F for cheating. I told him to write it, and I'd correct it.

"A few days later when he didn't come up with a paper, I assumed he blew off the assignment so I didn't say anything. Later that month while we were bowling, I asked him why he never turned in his theme. He acted hurt that I'd think such a thing and told me he had turned it in and received a B on it.

"That was incomprehensible. There was no way he could get a B without my help. So I asked him what the title of his paper was."

"*'Raising African violets.'*

"Since I knew he couldn't tell an African violet from a tomato, he had to be lying. When I questioned him further, he gave me a plausible explanation. He'd copied a paper his older sister had written several years before.

"Another time he got into trouble with Mr. Young, the no-nonsense football coach and our American history teacher. One winter day Mr. Young was called from the room. In the unsupervised chaos that followed, one of the class loudmouths offered Jake a quarter to jump out of the second story window. Jake went to the window, looked down and shook his head. He wanted a dollar. When the ante was raised, Jake climbed onto the sill, pushed open the huge double-hung and jumped into a snowdrift. Brushing the snow from his sweater, he looked up at all the faces crowding the window and took an exaggerated bow.

"He would have gotten away with his caper if only he'd beaten the teacher back to the room. Instead, when Jake burst into the room he ran into Mr. Young who demanded, 'Where have you been?'

"'Outside.'

"Mr. Young pointed and said, 'I don't remember giving you permission to walk out that door.'

"Jake laughed. 'You didn't. That's why I jumped out the window.'

"Mr. Young's face turned crimson. We waited for the huge man to explode. He stepped menacingly towards Jake who didn't budge an inch. When they were nose to chest, Mr. Young raised his fist to clobber him. Jake never flinched. He stood there grinning. The fist hung suspended. When Mr. Young noticed our shocked expressions his hand slowly loosened and fell to his side.

Backing away from Jake, he bellowed, 'You'll do a hundred push-ups every day in front of this class for the rest of the year!' Jake smiled and said, 'Thank you, sir. Can I start right now?' He loved being the class distraction. Three weeks later, the smirk was still on his face when Mr. Young called off the punishment."

"Totally incorrigible."

"Yep."

O'Hara took his beer and rubbed the cool bottle over his cheeks and forehead. "He had quite an effect on you. I've never heard you talk this much."

"He did. At the time, he was the most important person in my life."

O'Hara took a final draw on his beer and asked, "So what ever happened to Jake?"

"As we progressed through high school, Jake and I saw less of each other. The importance of our pact diminished. Not only had I become a football star, but when necessary I could mimic Jake's chutzpah to get out of scrapes with my detractors, and much to my surprise, Jake didn't need my help to pass his courses because he began studying semi-seriously.

"For a few weeks following graduation, we hung out together. We told dirty jokes and swapped lies about girls. With the help of more than a few illicit beers he'd stolen from his folks, I came close to displaying my feelings for him, but I never quite made it.

"That fall we separated. I left to study engineering at Ohio State, where I destroyed my knee playing football. Then the war broke out and the army rejected me. I finished college and began working at Kerr.

"Because of the Depression, Jake bummed around for a few years trying to find a job he liked. When Japan attacked Pearl Harbor, he joined the Marines because they were always in the thick of the fighting. He was going to be a war hero. Ironically, he missed the really big fight of his life. In boot camp at Paris Island, he was putting up targets on the rifle range when a stray bullet killed him."

"I wish you hadn't told me that," O'Hara said.

CHAPTER SEVEN

SEED SELECTION

They were lying in bed. George was on his back, his fingers interlocked behind his neck. Grace was reading a magazine. "Come on, Grace. I'm in the mood."

"Really? How exciting for you." She kept reading.

He rolled to his side and began rubbing his hand slowly up and down her bare leg.

When his caress moved to the inside, she let out a slight murmur. She flipped the magazine to the floor and found his mouth with hers. After several passionate kisses, she said, "Tell me Georgie, have you been a good boy today?"

"Of course," he said with a slight catch in his throat.

She whispered, "Then I have a reward for you," and swung her legs to the floor.

Flicking off the light, she removed her nightgown. George meanwhile was frantically extricating himself from his pajama bottoms. He felt her weight on the mattress. Then her naked body found his and in moments he was ravaging her, and she was in perfect rhythm with his every thrust. When he was done, she wasn't; so they continued until she was satisfied.

As they lay entwined, he spoke into the darkness. "I love you, Grace."

She answered him by kissing him again. Then he slept.

When he awakened, gray light filtered into his bedroom. Rain beat on the roof. He reached over to touch her and, of course, she wasn't there. The clock said five AM. He rubbed the sleep from his eyes and stretched. What an unexpected pleasure, he thought.

Instead of getting up, he decided to linger. He gathered an extra pillow and propping himself against the headboard, closed his eyes. Perhaps Grace would reappear.

He'd met Grace after the war. At the time his office buddy, Sherm Peterson, was hot and heavy with Sally, a buxom brunette. Sherm had extra tickets for a Benny Goodman concert in Columbus and insisted he come along and take a girlfriend of Sally's who was reportedly lots of fun. Sally had said, "I just know you'll like Grace a whole lot."

George was reticent. Since the war he hadn't had much luck with blind dates, one of several reasons he was still single at twenty-eight. But he was nuts over Benny Goodman.

He asked Sherm, "Can't I tag along as a single?"

Sherm answered through clenched teeth, "If I'd wanted a chaperone, I'd have asked Sally's mother. Take this woman or stay home."

So he'd succumbed to the date.

George glanced out the window to see if it was still drizzling. Because it was, he pulled the sheet up to his chin, and whispered, "How the years fly by." Sherm was gone now, dying of cancer about a year after Grace. And Sally? After that evening she dumped Sherm, and George never saw her again.

Sherm and Sally had picked him up at Mrs. Abernathy's in Sherm's new Studebaker. They'd driven around the square once for show and once again because Sherm missed the turnoff to Carpenter Street where Grace lived in a ramshackle gray Victorian. When Carlisle was in its adolescence, the home probably belonged to a banker or other wealthy businessman. Not anymore. Sometime in the recent past it had been converted into apartments.

After Sherm braked, George cut across the lawn and followed the veranda to the main entrance. He hesitated before ringing the doorbell below the third mailbox from the left as he'd been told. A voice through the screen door beckoned him to come down the hall. He followed the sound until his eyes lit on a moon-faced young woman with a smile as big as the doorway she filled. George was curious why she wasn't dressed for a dance, but he didn't ask.

"If you're George, you can come right in," she said merrily.

"And if I'm not?"

"Then you're stuck with me for the evening."

"So you're not Grace?"

"You look disappointed. Would you like me to be?"

As George struggled to answer, she exploded with laughter. Finally she grabbed his hand and pulled him through the door and deposited him in an easy chair that had lost its ability to hold a human. He was practically sitting on the floor. His greeter hovered over him like a prison guard. "What's the matter, George? Cat got your tongue?"

Before he could think of something to say, she moved to the couch, sat on the edge and grinned at him.

"I'm a bit confused," he said.

"Sorry, I just couldn't control myself," she said. "I'm Betsy, Grace's roommate. She'll be out in a moment."

He tried to explain away his discomfort but bungled it. She began giggling. He completed the rest of his vigil in silence.

Out of the corner of his eye he saw a slim woman in a bright canary-yellow sweater and full black skirt come into the room. He struggled to rise from the broken chair and failed. By the time he was standing she had stuck out her hand and paralyzed him with her mischievous eyes and wry smile.

In the moments that followed, he learned that Betsy and Grace were secretaries at the home office of Fidelity Insurance. They'd been together since forty-four.

Betsy said, "Unless some men find out how winsome and attractive we are, we'll be stuck with each other forever."

Two years later in '50 when he broke up the duo, Betsy was the maid-of-honor at their wedding. Then three years after that when Betsy married Rob, Grace reciprocated even though she was seven months pregnant with Jill, and the wedding was in Chicago.

After that every few years until Betsy's folks moved from Carlisle to Florida, Grace and Betsy would get together when she visited them. The last time he saw Betsy was at Grace's funeral.

To his surprise, being crammed with Grace into the back seat of the sedan for the two-hour drive to Columbus was anything but the ordeal he expected. He actually enjoyed being drawn into a real conversation with her. Usually on dates he clammed up and daydreamed while pretending to listen to the inane yammering of his companion. But Grace wasn't like the others. Ten minutes into the trip he realized he didn't need to trot out the dissertation on Benny Goodman's music he'd planned on using to relieve his boredom. His tongue and mind were well coordinated.

Other than one group discussion over the whereabouts of the dance hall, Grace and he were as separated from Sherm and Sally as if they were riding behind the glass partition of a limousine. They had their own air spiced by Grace's faint perfume. He was mesmerized by her pert, curly brown hair and dark eyes that flirted with his as she talked about her job. Her wit dazzled him. Then later, when she punctuated a sentence by touching his hand, an electrical storm raged through his chest and gut. It scared him for a moment, but he liked it. He liked it a lot.

At the dance hall the two couples crowded around a small round table to listen to the band. It was just large enough to hold their drinks. George had beer, and the others sipped mixed drinks. Even though he felt slightly embarrassed drinking beer, he always felt in control. He never knew what reaction he'd get from hard liquor.

Between numbers they chatted, but the minute the band began playing the next tune George "shooshed" them. As much as he was enjoying Grace's company, he didn't want Benny Goodman's clarinet or the swing music marred by conversation. There was plenty of time for talking with Grace while Sherm and Betsy danced to the recorded music between sets.

Toward the end of the evening Grace asked, "Aren't you going to ask me to dance?"

He explained about his bad knee and how unstable it was. "If we dance, I might fall and embarrass us."

"I'll risk the embarrassment. If you need to quit, tell me."

On the dance floor, he held her close and felt the magic of her body as they moved and swayed to the music. They danced to each slow number. When the band returned for the last set, George was disappointed they couldn't dance anymore. Grace was his whole focus now, more than Benny Goodman's glorious sound and more than the sore knee that would undoubtedly swell up like a balloon on the long ride home.

In the quiet of the back seat on the ride to Carlisle, Grace placed her head against his shoulder. He held her hand and played with her fingers. He wanted to kiss her, and several times he made a move in her direction, and she tipped her head back to receive him, but he chickened out. What if he was moving too fast, he thought.

When they arrived at her apartment and Sally and Sherm said their goodbyes, he took Grace's arm and escorted her to the door. While shuffling along the porch, she said, "You're quite a gentleman, George."

By the way she said it, he was worried she was mocking him. "You don't like your men to be gentlemen?"

She hesitated. "Yes, I do. Your behavior is refreshing." At the door, she took the key from her purse and said, "Thank you for a wonderful time."

He smiled and words began pouring over his lips like a waterfall. "Thank you for going with me. I had fun, too, and if you want to go out with me again, I'd like to go out with you, maybe to a Carol Lombard movie, or dinner or anywhere really."

She said anytime was fine, and she was free the next Saturday night, and he said, "Great. Saturday night it is."

As she fiddled with the lock, George put his hands in his pockets to keep them from shaking. Grace cracked open the door, then turned and faced him. His heart raced. Still he didn't move toward her. Finally she said, "It's all right to kiss me."

George stepped toward her. They embraced, and he kissed her several times. Suddenly, George heard himself say, "I'm going to marry you some day."

She burst out laughing, broke away and slid through the open door. "Wow," she said, "I didn't know I was that good of a kisser!"

George pushed away from the headboard and slowly lowered his feet to the floor. Rain was beating a tattoo on the window, precluding any outside work for the morning. He hobbled over to Grace's dresser, searched through a drawer and found her old jewelry box. Like the hundreds of other times he found himself touching and caressing the remaining symbols of their life together, he began crying. Even placing her small quarter-carat diamond engagement ring in his palm and opening and closing his fingers over it until it was the temperature of his hand did little to console him. So he placed the ring in the box, put the box in the drawer and shuffled to the closet for his robe. He shook his head sadly, "I sure miss you, Grace."

CHAPTER EIGHT

SEEDLINGS

The late August day had been a scorcher. So hot in fact that he hadn't been outside since early morning. Following dinner he decided to brave the diminishing heat and walk out to observe his garden. What he saw ruined his digestion. Two rows of four-inch high turnip seedlings had been eaten to the ground by some critter. Judging by their quick disappearance–the sprouts were intact that morning–the perpetrator was most likely a ground hog.

While mourning his loss, a swarm of gnats followed by a squadron of mosquitoes conspired to drive him to the safety of the porch. After figuring where he could buy more turnip seed the next day to replant the rows for a late fall harvest, he grabbed a glass of ice-tea from the refrigerator and plopped down on the chaise. His brain, as it so often did these days, carried him back to the early years of marriage when the girls were young. The piggy bank incident with Jill came to mind. It was one of the few times he could remember disciplining one of the children, and it furnished him with one of his most poignant memories.

When Jill was nine, she developed an acquisitive streak that eventually got out of hand. For some time she'd been stuffing every coin she got her hands on into the large ceramic polka-dot piggy bank Grace's mother had given her. Tooth Fairy coins, birthday money, even the profits from her vegetable sales clinked into her "Piggy." At first, George and Grace were pleased their daughter was mimicking their frugality. However, when Grace observed Jill banking her meager allowance instead of wanting to spend her own money on typical things like candy, bubblegum and hair ribbons, she became mildly concerned. She discussed her uneasiness with George one night when they were alone after dinner. He suggested they take a wait-and-see attitude.

All that summer Jill played with Lisa Metcalf, the Methodist minister's daughter who lived at the end of their street. Lisa was a bright and polite little girl and an appropriate companion for Jill. Much of the time the two girls played dress-up in the basement rec room with the collection of old clothes Grace had gathered. At other times they entertained themselves at the Metcalf's.

One Saturday the phone rang while George was home alone with the girls. It was Mrs. Metcalf. "I regret having to say this, but I saw Jill take some change from my kitchen counter and put it in her pocket. I didn't say anything to her, but I thought you'd want to know."

George was about to defend his daughter, when he realized the minister's wife had just solved a puzzle that had been plaguing him for weeks. Each day when he returned from work and emptied his pockets of keys and coins, he'd notice the next morning that some of the coins had disappeared. Until the phone call he wasn't concerned because he assumed Grace took them. Now he realized the truth.

"I'm sure it was difficult for you to call," he told Lisa's mother. "I appreciate your letting us know. It won't happen a second time."

Waiting for Grace to come home, he stewed. There were two teachings his father passed on to him that he never disclaimed. They were *hard work is a virtue* and *dishonesty in any form is a sin*. George was particularly enraged by stealing. During the war, he'd caught one of his better employees filling his lunch box with scarce pieces of lead. That afternoon he confronted the man as he was leaving and asked him to open his box. As George suspected, he was smuggling the lead out of the plant. Although the instance was the first conflict he'd ever had with him, he fired him on the spot. The man begged for another chance, but George was unrelenting. "I'm letting you off easy," he said. "I could call the police. They jail men who steal essential war materials."

When Grace entered the front door, George took the grocery bags she was carrying and set them on the kitchen counter. While she emptied the bags, he placed the milk bottles in the fridge and the ice cream in the freezer. Then he said gently, "Sit down. We need to talk about Jill."

A concerned look covered her face. "Is she all right?"

"When I get through with her she may not be." He spilled out the whole story and asked for her support with his plan to punish her.

"Isn't that too extreme?" she said. "What if we both talk to her?"

"This is too serious for talk. It calls for action."

"Okay, but please stay calm."

He nodded.

Tears formed in her eyes. "But, she loves it so."

"It's the only thing to do."

As planned, that afternoon Grace took Anne for a wagon ride. Jill wanted to go too, but George told her she had to stay home because they needed to talk about something important. When they were seated on the couch, he said, "I'm going to ask you a question, and I expect you to answer it truthfully." When she agreed, he said, "Did you take some coins from Mrs. Metcalf's kitchen counter?"

She squirmed.

He waited her out.

Suddenly her face clouded over, and she rained tears. He wanted to reach out to her, to hold her. Instead he asked again, "Did you take coins..."

"Yes!" she cried.

"And did you take my coins from the desk?"

"Yes."

"Why Jill? Why did you take them?"

Tears streamed down her face as she struggled for an answer. It hurt to watch her. He studied the floor before asking, "Did you need money to buy something?"

"No. I wanted them for Piggy," she whimpered.

"You stole coins to put in your bank?"

"Yes. Piggy likes coins."

"You mean you like coins."

She nodded.

George said, "Then you need to get Piggy and bring him to me." She stood up, wiped her eyes with her fist and shuffled to her bedroom.

When she returned, she handed him the bank. "What you did was stealing," he said. "You have to understand how serious stealing is and never do it again."

"I won't, Daddy."

"I'm sure you won't." He glanced at the piggy-bank. "My job is to make sure you remember. Go downstairs to my workbench and bring me the hammer, please."

"No, Daddy. Please. I promise I'll never, ever steal anything again."

"I accept your promise, but this has to be done.

Either you get the hammer, or I'll get it myself."

Jill slunk off. When she returned she said, "Please don't hurt Piggy. It wasn't his fault."

"Sometimes our actions hurt those we love. Now Piggy has to pay for what you did." He carried the bank to the front stoop and wrapped it in a towel. "I want you to break your piggy bank." She took the hammer and smashed it with her second tap. They began separating the coins from the broken china and placing them in a small box.

"What are you going to do with the money?" she asked.

"You and I are going to walk to Mrs. Metcalf's. You need to apologize to her. Then you're going to give her the coins to put in the church collection."

"Okay."

As they were walking to the parsonage, they passed Grace pulling Anne in the wagon. Grace shot George a quizzical look.

"Jill and I are walking to Lisa's. We'll return soon."

"All right. We'll talk when you get back."

George took Jill's hand and continued to the parsonage.

Upon their return, as she was about to enter the house, Jill looked up at her father. Her squeaky little voice took on a serious tone. "I feel much better now, Daddy, even though Piggy is dead."

He snatched her from the ground and squeezed her against his chest. His voice cracked as he said, "So do I."

That night as they lay in bed, George gave Grace all the details. He said, "I felt so cruel. It was the right way to handle it, wasn't it Grace?"

She scrunched nearer to him and placed her arm over his bare chest. "I couldn't have done what you did, but I'm glad you did it. I think you're remarkable."

She kissed him and said, "Turn off the light George. You've had a tough day."

As the children grew older, they developed distinctly different personalities. Jill became a take-charge type while Anne was more reticent. As parents, it was simple to observe their dissimilarities, but it was Grace who harnessed their proclivities. Whenever a task like dusting or raking leaves required a joint effort, Grace held Jill accountable for the outcome and let her work out the details with Anne. With Jill leading and Anne happy to follow, routine jobs were completed without the tedium of parental harassment that was usually required.

From today's perspective, George wondered if he and Grace had done right by their daughters. Instead of exploiting their differences, perhaps they should have encouraged them to strengthen their natural shortcomings. Did the family dynamic Grace established, and he condoned have a downside for their daughters' futures?

George couldn't argue with Jill's success. At a remarkably young age, she had become the forceful, industrious vice-president of finance at KTR in Chicago. Eighty-hour workweeks and courageous decision-making propelled her to the top of the corporate ladder and allowed her to shatter KTR's glass ceiling. But what if they'd raised her differently, George wondered? Would she be less driven and more inclined to produce grandchildren? Perhaps she could have felt as fulfilled caring for her kids as she was discussing her stock options and productivity bonuses over dinner at some trendy bistro with her nondescript husband, Stewart.

Stewart bothered him. He never fully understood why Jill married him. She certainly could have chosen a stronger, more interesting man. In his wary moments, George believed Jill married Stewart because she could control him. He considered Stewart the ninety-pound weakling bullies kicked sand on at the beach. Pasty-faced, scrawny and unhealthy looking, he was the classic model for the 'before' version of a Charles Atlas ad. Besides his physical appearance, George was troubled by Stewart's lethargic demeanor and passive temperament. When he and George were alone, they barely communicated.

What impressed, and to some degree, perplexed George, was how solicitous Jill was of her husband. When she was with Stewart, her hard-nosed persona evaporated. Instead of the dynamic corporate woman, George saw overt tenderness and affection. Evidently, Wonder Woman had a beating heart and Stewart was the catalyst that started it pumping.

Although Jill's marriage was a puzzle, Anne's whole life baffled him. She seemed content to bask in the glow of her oral surgeon husband's success and enjoy the trappings his career provided. Unlike Stewart who left him cold, he admired Anne's husband, Bret. Tall and ruggedly good-looking, he was at the pinnacle of his career professionally and financially. Yet, unlike Stewart who avoided him, Bret went out of his way to spend time with George and make him feel welcome.

While George had few problems with the way his daughters treated him, he concerned himself with the demands on Jill's time and the choices Anne made. To begin with, Anne and Bret lived in an exclusive area of Columbus in a home large enough to raise ten kids, yet she didn't have any. Secondly, she paid a maid and yardman to do all her work while she did nothing. How could she be satisfied with a life that revolved around playing golf and bridge at the country club, traveling with Bret to Switzerland to ski in the winter and entertaining lavishly? Where were the values he and Grace had taught her?

Even though Grace often said Anne was the brighter of the two, George thought they were each smart as hell. Both graduated with honors at Ohio U. When it came to sheer brilliance, Grace might have been correct. Anne achieved her honors in English with a minimum of effort. She was absorbed by other interests, like being captain of the All-School Party Team and heaping attention and affection on the current man in her life. While Anne played and chased, Jill worked her butt off to become the top accounting student in her graduating class. Jill's efforts attracted a Big-Eight accounting firm who offered her a position following college. Anne used her education to attract Bret and eventually marry him.

Grace joined his reverie.

"As long as Jill's comfortable with Stewart and Anne's content to be an adornment hanging around Bret's neck, I'll never have any grandchildren."

Grace scowled. "Why is it you think you deserve grandchildren?"

"I'm their father, aren't I? They owe them to me."

"And I'm their mother. I don't recall having any grandchildren, either."

"What difference does it make to you? You're dead. I'm not, and I want some."

She shook her finger at him. "Whatever you do, keep your cockeyed opinions to yourself, and for God's sake don't butt into their lives."

George sighed and closed his eyes. Then he said with resignation, "I suppose you're right...as usual."

CHAPTER NINE

SOWING

When the Alexander boys returned to school in the fall and Rachel entered kindergarten, George found a variety of reasons to stop by and visit with Mary. He might bring an old recipe of Grace's for Mary's file, acorn squash or, lately, a huge fall cabbage. Any excuse would suffice. Unlike other young people who trivialized the ramblings of their elders, Mary always acted like she was interested in what he said.

"Smell's good," he said when he arrived. "Is that fresh-baked apple cake cooling on the counter for me?"

"Sorry, George. It's for the church bake sale."

He feigned a huge sigh. "My neighbor across the cul-de-sac always has chocolate chip cookies for me when I visit her. I was hoping a trend was developing."

She motioned him to the table as she poured him a cup of coffee. "I could make you some cinnamon toast."

"Don't bother, I'm not very hungry this morning." Hiding his disappointment, he returned to a conversation they'd begun on his previous visit.

91

"Until I met Grace," he said, "I never gave a thought to spending the rest of my life with a woman. My days were filled with male things. Beginning in high school and continuing into college, I began to take notice of the attention some girls showed me. I didn't return their interest because I was afraid they were only interested in being around a football player. I didn't yet realize I was endowed with a magnetic personality and rugged good looks."

Mary laughed. "I'm sure it was your good looks."

"Not my personality?"

"Of course, the personality, too, but not just the athletic stuff. Many women don't think that's so cool."

"That's interesting. Some of my jock friends capitalized on their sports persona to capture the affections of the ladies. I avoided girls because I was an athlete, just as an acquaintance of mine who had wealthy parents was paranoid his friends only tolerated him because he had money to spend on them."

"That's pathetic," Mary said. "Didn't you date at all?"

"Of course. I even had a steady girlfriend once in high school. Her name was...I'm so bad with names. Why can't I remember a detail like that? I do remember she was a cute redhead, and we dated for several months one spring. Sheila...Shirley. Anyway, the thing I remember about her most was how comfortable I felt when I was with her. We were inseparable. We sipped malts at the Soda Shack, studied together on weekends, went to movies and walked to and from school every day.

"Even though Jake teased me about her–'Sandra, Sandra, face like a Panda'–that was her name, Sandra. I was happier being with her than being with Jake or any of my other friends. I'd call. She'd say when and where, and we'd do something together. Unfortunately, we were together so much we became bored with each other and

92

broke up."

"I had several steady boyfriends in high school," Mary said. "It was wonderful not needing to worry about having a date for Saturday night or some special function. Trouble was, in my era, the longer two people dated, the greater the expectations. If I wasn't careful, the relationship would escalate, and I wasn't ready for that. More than once I broke up with a guy I liked because of the pressure."

"When I was young, I'd never consider doing anything but kissing and messing around a little. Not that the urges weren't there. I just never considered acting on them. Though I don't believe my parents ever directly discussed it, I learned early on to respect girls. Anything but necking was off limits until one was married." George tipped his head back and poured down the dregs of the now cool coffee. Some spilled on his blue work shirt. "Even the football coaches got into the act. Coach Young lectured us that serious female contact the night before a football game would sap our strength and have a negative effect on our performance, and I believed him."

"That wouldn't work today, I'm afraid," Mary said. "Jimmy's only twelve, and I doubt he'd buy it. Today's kids are far too aware."

"I agree. When I compare the things young people do today with how we acted, I laugh at how backward we were. Yet, I think we were happier kids because we didn't have to deal with all those emotions until we were old enough to handle them."

Mary heard the bell on the dryer and excused herself. George let his thoughts return to the one time he could remember succumbing to his sexual fantasies.

It was his senior year in high school. The girl was Patsy Steinbach. Like all of the guys, he was aware of her shapely breasts augmented by one of the new brassieres that brought everything to a point. While they were

93

fascinating to study, he wasn't motivated to go beyond gawking until some of the guys on the team started pressing him to date her. She had hot pants, they said. He wasn't impressed. However, when they suggested he was something less than a man unless he took her out, he gave in and asked her to a movie.

They sat in the back row. Somewhere in the middle of the show he'd slipped his arm around her neck and she scootched over next to him and lay her head on his shoulder. That was the signal to stretch his arm down and grab her breast. He assumed this met with her approval, because she let out a little purring sound. Instead of being turned on, he became disgusted with himself. He couldn't wait for the film to end, because her noises distracted him from the movie plot.

Afterwards he walked her home, performed the obligatory kiss and concluded the whole breast touching thing was overrated. However, at practice the next day to the wide-eyed astonishment of his drooling teammates, he gave an X-rated fantasy play-by-play of his evening with Patsy.

"Sorry. Where were we?" Mary said when she returned.

"Maybe I ought to head home and get out of your way," George said.

"Please stay. My Uncle Jack used to tell me stories about his youth. I loved listening to them, and I love listening to you. Besides, if you don't mind, I can fold laundry as we talk."

"You're certainly a good audience. Grace used to tell me not to bore people with my endless stories."

"That's a standard line they teach in wife school."

"I didn't know that."

"You never went to wife school."

"But I did go to college. Let me tell you about going from a small high school to a huge university. To survive at Ohio State was quite an adjustment for an eighteen-year-old. Living in a dorm with hundreds of students was distracting. But playing football, trying to learn from pontificating professors preaching in front of enormous lecture halls and dealing with mountains of homework about did me in.

Then there were the Saturday afternoons in autumn when huge crowds of alumni milled around the campus and filled the stadium to watch our games. In my sophomore year when I became the starting halfback, total strangers sought me out, and it seemed everyone on campus knew me by name. I'd never been the subject of such mass attention. At first I was embarrassed because I thought I was supposed to know these people. After a while, I learned to accept their adulation. I called it halfback homage. I didn't know them, and they didn't know me. I was a football player, and that was all they cared about."

"Celebrity can be a burden," Mary said.

George winked at her. "There *are* worse things."

"I have to say, Mr. Konert, I'm certainly impressed. You were a certified *Big Man On Campus*."

"That BMOC stuff didn't impress my professors. Unlike some of my teammates who never studied, I wanted to learn. I wanted to be a great player and a good student so I traded my social life for good grades. Sometimes I wish I could have had their focus. There were so many chicks hanging around, I could have had my pick. As it was, I'll bet I didn't go out five times in my first two years."

"Cancel the BMOC," Mary said.

"I just didn't want to risk having some coed ruin my ambitions."

"You were smart. Dating can be a distraction," Mary said, folding a king-sized sheet in record time.

"In retrospect, I should have had more fun. My game got ruined anyway. In the fall of my junior year, I

95

tore up my left knee." He patted it. "I was having my most productive day ever. Then in the midst of a seven-yard run, a would-be tackler knocked me off balance. The cleats on my left foot dug in and another player threw a shoulder into my knee as I was falling to the ground. My leg ended up bent backwards under me, crushed by my own weight and the weight of the two guys that hit me.

"I was so scared, and the pain so intense I didn't remember being carted off the field. A few weeks later a team of doctors operated using the newest techniques available at the time. They claimed the operation was a success, but I was in agony. I dropped out of school for the year. I couldn't do much, because I was in a hip-to-toe cast for five months. Eventually the pain subsided, the knee healed and as long as I restricted my activity to walking and light workouts, I felt fine. But I was through as a top-flight athlete. Later, when I was much older and arthritis set in, I started hobbling around like I do now."

Mary shook her head. "Football is so violent. All that effort to become a great athlete, and it's wiped out in an instant. What a waste."

"That's how life is," he said. "One moment you're up. The next you're down. You're on top of your game, then a screech of tires, a heart attack, a cancerous tumor and your whole world changes. I always believed that a run of bad luck was followed by a good run. Then Grace got cancer, and I learned something I wasn't prepared for. Bad things continue to happen, and they only end when you're six-feet under. Sometimes I feel like if it wasn't for bad luck, I wouldn't have any luck at all."

"That's a terribly gloomy attitude, George."

"I know it is, and I'll add one thing more. Aging only drives the point in deeper."

Suddenly George clutched his chest. His eyes bugged out and sweat beaded on his forehead. Mary clambered from her chair and raced for the phone. With one eye on George she dialed 911 when he hollered, "Hang up. I'm okay."

"Are you sure?"

"I get chest pains all the time," he said. "They're from my hiatal hernia. The coffee probably kicked them off."

She hung up the phone and walked toward him. "You're sure it's not your heart?"

"Nah, I've never had any heart problems, but I have been having more of these attacks lately. When I see the doctor in March, I'll ask him about them."

When he stood up, the room spun. He caught himself by grabbing the edge of the table. Eventually his eyes focused, and he stood erect.

"Are you sure I shouldn't take you to the doctor right now?"

He forced a smile. "No, but I'm not so sure about the walk home. If you could drive me, I'd be grateful." Then he added, "Don't worry. I'll be fine after a little nap and an antacid. Sorry to scare you."

When George awakened from his nap, his pains were milder and easier to ignore. As he reviewed the conversation with Mary, he was surprised at the macabre philosophy his words conveyed. Admittedly, his life was spiraling downward toward its natural conclusion, but he didn't feel that sad about it. He'd had a fine life and a great marriage. Maybe what he really meant was he had no illusions about recapturing what he had and no prospects for anything better ahead.

Another element of the conversation shocked him. He'd never before examined how his knee injury had affected him. Until that morning's conversation, he'd never admitted to himself that he'd lost more than the opportunity to participate in a sport he enjoyed. He also gave up the adulation that came with being Saturday's hero. When he was playing, he took for granted all of the attention alumni and classmates bestowed on him. He expected pats on the back and certain girls to go all googley when he smiled at them, because he'd never known them not to. Then, at twenty, it suddenly ended. He was the lead goose in hunting season. One second he was leading the flock south, the next he was in a free-fall, tumbling and twisting until he was swallowed up by the earth.

During his football career, George was so focused on himself and what he was doing that he was oblivious to the world outside the campus. When he finally noticed, patriotic fever had become epidemic. America was at war. Boys like him were lining up to offer their youth to help defeat the Nazis and Japs. Proud parents encouraged their sons to enlist even though their pride was tempered by the awful fear of death. Already Carlisle had witnessed flag-draped caskets being carried from the train by uniformed soldiers and placed on tumbrels for the trip to the cemetery.

In the summer following his injury, George walked into the recruiting office and volunteered. In the weeks that followed, he rearranged his priorities, mentally cast off the student mantle and thought only in terms of his new role as an infantryman or parachuter.

When the doctors told him he'd flunked his physical, he was stunned. He was prepared to fight. He was not prepared for a 4-F classification that would brand him a shirker. While most of his ex-teammates would be or already were serving Uncle Sam, he'd be home with the women, children and old men too decrepit to fight for their country.

That night he considered other avenues for serving his country while drinking a few too many beers at the Varsity Lounge. He narrowed his choices to laboring in a munitions factory or being an assembler for a truck manufacturer. Eventually he decided he could better serve his country in the long run by slipping back into school and finishing his degree in Industrial Engineering.

Staggering home from the Varsity, he stopped to rest at the foot of the General Grant statue in the center of the square. About four AM, a patrolman beamed a flashlight at his face to wake him and send him on his way home.

The time he spent completing the requirements for his degree dragged. The difference from his first two halcyon years at OSU was dramatic. When he finally graduated, the lift he hoped for never materialized. Obtaining his degree wasn't a panacea. It didn't give him the self-respect he hoped for. He actually felt like a shirker.

He did find out his engineering degree was magical in the job market. Manufacturers of strategic materials for the war effort were booming and the need for educated employees rose with it. With the military cutting into the available manpower, the competition for new graduates was brutal. After sifting through his opportunities, George returned to Carlisle and accepted a supervisory-trainee position with Kerr Manufacturing Company. He may have had better offers, but George was comfortable in his hometown and knew and respected two of the key executives.

The next few years rushed by. Being single and unburdened by personal relationships, George worked twelve and fourteen hour days. Many were challenging. He quickly realized his textbook knowledge didn't always apply in a company that once made automobile hardware and now struggled with a huge defense contract making shell casings. A company ran differently in wartime, and he quickly adapted. Unlike what he had been taught, the business was measured by the number of casings passing inspection and shipped out. No one cared if the jobs were done inefficiently. Cost was never a consideration. If the plant reached its quota, the company flourished. The government made sure of that.

Most of the workers under George's supervision were women. They knew very little about industry. Until the war, they'd been "kitchen lifers." Despite their lack of experience, they learned quickly and eagerly responded to his suggestions. Even if their job was no more complex than soaking the shell casings in a solution to clean off the machine oil, he could sense their pride. They were helping win the war.

One of his favorites, Nan Jackson, usually sat next to him on the 6:25 bus each morning. Nan didn't work directly for George. She worked in shipping. Like most young people neither owned a car because, in addition to the cost, gas rationing only provided a dribble of fuel for their personal use. Instead, Nan and George rode the electric buses to work and rode their bikes most everywhere else.

Nan was a petite blonde who'd started at Kerr a few months after him when her husband was drafted. He got to know her quite well from their daily rides and periodic coffee breaks. They'd sit at the picnic table in the back of the factory and sip coffee as she shared her post-war plans. Her husband, John, sent her all of his paychecks to deposit along with Nan's own savings. They had their eye on a shoe store they wanted to buy after the war. Along with a home of their own, their plan included three children or even more if the first three were the same sex. At times, George might have shared his plans except by comparison his future seemed far more uncertain than hers.

When she wasn't on the bus one winter morning, he wasn't concerned because a flu epidemic had forced many workers to stay home. Two weeks went by, and still she didn't show. That's when George looked up Nan's friend in shipping to see how she was doing.

"When's Nan coming back?" he asked casually.

She stared at him. Tears glazed her eyes. "You haven't heard?"

"Heard what?"

"Her husband was killed parachuting into France."

"Oh, my God! Where is she? I'd like to see her."

"That might be hard. Her folks helped her pack up and drove her to their home in Springfield. I doubt she's coming back to Carlisle."

"I can't believe it!"

"Me either. Poor kid. I do have her parent's address, though, if you want to write her."

That night when he sat down to write he was so choked with emotion he couldn't get started. The next night was more of the same. Riding the bus, at work, or anytime he tried to come up with the right words to let Nan know how he felt, he failed. His mind whirred, but he couldn't get a thing on paper. What was he going to write? That he pitied her? Or, that lots of girls lost husbands in the war. Nor could he say, you're young. You'll eventually find someone else and own a shoe store. He wanted to write he missed seeing her everyday because he enjoyed talking with her, but that seemed lame. Or write the truth that at times he felt so lucky he wasn't fighting in the war, but no one would dare put that on paper.

In the end, he never did send the letter. Years later, whenever he thought about her and the un-sent letter he felt like a coward.

The next time he and Mary chatted he confessed about Nan. She said, "Everyone understands that most young people, particularly young men, find it tough to express heavy emotions." She passed him another muffin. "After fifty years, I think you should forgive yourself."

He sighed. "It's hard, but I suppose you're right."

She smiled. "I'm sure Nan has."

They sat quietly for a few moments as George pulled the paper from the muffin, broke off a piece and covered it with honey. After he took a bite, Mary asked, "Did you meet Grace during the war?"

101

"No. After." He shifted his weight on the wooden chair so he could straighten his legs. He said, "During the war Carlisle was a hard place for a 4-Fer like me to live. I was self-conscious in public for fear I might call attention to my draft deferment. During the war most people were super-critical of any man of draft age who wasn't in uniform. It wasn't unusual for me to be confronted with the dreaded question, "You played college football. Why aren't you in the service?"

"I had a stock answer. 'I wish I was serving but I ruined my knee and I'm 4-F.' Some people would scoff and call me a draft-dodger. Others would accept it. One man from my street said, 'Did you know my son, Walter, lost his leg on Iwo Jima?' A woman informed me 'my nephew was killed in Sicily.' Each time I'd say I was sorry and slink away."

Mary said, "I read that people pulled together during the War."

"In general, that was true. As long as you weren't a man with a deferment."

"There had to have been many young men with deferments. It sounds to me like you let your guilt get the best of you. Tell me you weren't always beating yourself up."

"I enjoyed my job. Work was a haven. Friends there didn't care about my draft status. However, my father did. He didn't want me living in his home. Looking back I think he was sensitive about his German heritage, and afraid if he didn't play the super-patriot role he'd be ostracized by his friends and neighbors. What was particularly painful was how easily he turned against me. When I was a college football player, my father used to brag about me. Once I was sitting out the war, I embarrassed him. Attitudes like his were mirrored in every neighborhood in every town all over America. Patriotism was a high stakes game. No one wanted to be the parent of a shirker.

"When I left my parent's home, I moved into Mrs. Abernathy's rooming house along the bus route. She was a sweet and lonely old soul. She'd arise early to pack my metal lunch-box with sandwiches and cook supper for me at whatever odd hour of the evening I'd drag home from the factory. Since her own son was stationed in California, I think she loved looking after me. I liked her a lot, too, and enjoyed chatting with her when the cold weather kept me inside. Other than that I spent my free time reading magazines and following the war on the radio in my room."

"Didn't you have any girlfriends?" Mary asked.

George grinned. "No, just Mrs. Abernathy. All of the female workers at Kerr were off limits because of a company non-fraternization policy. The few other eligible women I knew were uniform crazy. They'd hang out at the USO hoping to attract a good-looking young 'war hero' for a night of fun. Drinking, one-night-stands, kiss hello, kiss goodbye. Most were not willing to commit because more serious relationships ran the risk of ending tragically. A sniper's bullet or an enemy grenade, and it was over."

"So you never dated?"

"Not once in two years."

"Wow!"

"But each spring I planted a Victory Garden."

"A what?"

"A Victory Garden. With Mrs. Abernathy's blessing and a sharp spade, I ploughed up a large parcel of land on a vacant lot she owned behind the rooming house. Together we learned to raise vegetables. Since there was a shortage of fresh produce in the stores, gardening was one of the more patriotic activities a 4-Fer and an old lady could do.

"All summer long as we harvested our crops, we kept some for our use and gave the rest away. Our distribution plan was unique and gave us a lot of satisfaction. At the bus stop, I built a makeshift table from some old wood. Then we kept it loaded with beans, beets, and tomatoes, cucumbers, corn, squash or whatever else was freshly picked. Our big hand-printed sign said, *TAKE WHAT YOU CAN USE. LEAVE THE REST FOR OTHERS.* Everyone followed the rules. I'd get a thrill whenever I peeked out the front window and see people walk by and take a few vegetables. Even the bus drivers got into the spirit of the event. Sometimes they'd take a cigarette break by our table so their riders could jump off and grab some produce. All those smiling faces helped ease my conscience about not fighting with the troops at the front.

Mary was silent for a few moments, and then she chided him. "Gardens instead of girls, George. I don't know about you."

He laughed. "Look at me now. Not much has changed in sixty years, has it?"

CHAPTER TEN

ROOTS

When he answered the phone, Mary sounded frantic. "I need to talk to you."

"Are you all right?"

"I'm okay, but I need some fatherly advice. Maybe after lunch?"

"Come on over. Anytime."

He placed the handset on the cradle and lowered himself into his recliner. Grace appeared. She stood in front of him, hands on hips tapping her foot as she always did. He chuckled. She was always so impatient.

"What is it now?"

"Grace, how will I give decent advice to Mary? I have no practice. Jill and Anne aren't clamoring for my counsel. They never listen to me and probably never will. Why would I be any better with Mary?"

"You'll be fine, George. Just try." He felt her kiss on his cheek. "Maybe, you'll even learn something about yourself."

"I've always wanted to be a good father. I just haven't always known how."

"You've had your moments. Some remarkable moments considering you knew nothing about fathering before I got hold of you. Most men learn from their own fathers. Thank goodness you didn't. Forgive me for saying it, but yours was not a pleasant man."

George hadn't thought about his father for a long time. Grace was right about him. If there was a colder fish than his old man, he was encased in an iceberg. August Konert was a stern, humorless and demanding man who buried his emotions under a veneer of order and discipline. A second generation German-American, he was a skilled tool and die maker with an old country work ethic and dedication to accuracy not found in many of his fellow workers. Thus he was paid more than most and even in the slowest of times always had work.

During George's adolescent years, August Konert ruled their home. His assignments and demands kept his mother and George hopping. If all went well, and the assigned chores were completed in an orderly fashion his reward was benign silence. If, however, his demands were challenged or someone messed up a duty, his Teutonic temper would blow like a volcano and both he and his mother would feel fortunate to come away from the confrontation with only an earful.

The primary morning duty for a student in most homes was bathing and dressing for school. At the Konert home in the winter, George would hop out of bed, throw on his bathrobe and head for the basement to fill the stoker with coal. If there was new fallen snow, George was expected to shovel it and retrieve his father's newspaper so it was waiting at the breakfast table for him to read. Only then could he begin preparing for school.

While George followed his predetermined schedule, his mother prepared the breakfast August demanded--a menu of fried eggs, sausage patties, rye toast and strong black coffee. Her challenge was making sure his food was at his place on the table by exactly 7:10 so the breakfast was hot for the precise moment his father arrived to eat it and read his paper.

Grace was right, George thought. Thank goodness he didn't turn out like his old man.

Shutting off his memories for a moment, George lowered the footrest on the recliner and moved to the kitchen to search for something to nibble on. When he spotted an orange, he cut it into eight sections and using his front teeth cleaned the pulp from the skin of each section. Wiping runaway juice from his chin, he shook his head. How different those childhood meals were from the haphazard food-grabbings he and Grace called breakfast. Their morning meal attended by anywhere from one to four was a free-for-all of bowl-clanging, milk-splashing chaos. The noise level was as high as the tension as each participant fought over whatever obstacle blocked his escape. Unlike his parent's home, his home had few regulations, and only one was strictly enforced. No one left the house without kissing Grace. That was his rule. Or maybe hers. Looking back he wasn't sure who was responsible for it. But it was law.

George hoped it was his rule because he never remembered seeing his father show any affection toward his mother. Mornings were the worst. They ate in silence, his father tucked behind his newspaper. He could still see his mother standing over them in her drab, gray robe and slippers waiting for them to leave so she could clear the table.

George spoke to Grace. "I wonder if she ever ate breakfast. If she did, I never saw her do it. You know what else, Grace? I never remember him kissing my mother goodbye."

Grace said, "I once told you, if you ever acted like

your father, I'd run away just like your mother did. Only I wouldn't wait for you to die."

When George was born, his father was almost thirty-five. His mother, Kate, was ten years younger. What attention he received came from her. Surprisingly, considering his father's rigidity and need for order, his mother was the disciplinarian. It was her fussing that kept him on the straight and narrow. However, the specter of his father unleashing an assault was the ultimate deterrent to bad behavior. Whatever roles each played in his development, he learned early *that anything worth doing was worth doing right, that you are judged by the company you keep and to be a good boy.*

Grace used to kid, "Your parents taught you to be a good child. I tried to teach you to be a decent man."

"Perhaps you should have tried harder."

"It was like teaching a rock to sing."

For lunch, George cooked bratwurst. After polishing off two loaded with onions, a can of baked beans and a beer, he retired to the couch for a gut-rumbling snooze. As his nap was ending, and he was entering the half-light of wakefulness, his musings lighted on Catherine and Gert's unusual relationship. From there it was a short hop to thinking about Jill and Anne.

It was Floyd and Gert. Catherine and Marianne, she'd said. George reflected on Catherine's comment. Grace and I never had our favorites, he thought. *You do for one, you do for both,* was her motto and therefore his.

After all, when it came to the children, he mostly deferred to Grace. From the moment Jill was born, and he was handed her fragile body to hold in his uncertain arms, he felt insecure in his father's role. Perhaps if Grace had even a third as much confidence in his abilities as she did in her own, he would have learned more quickly. Admittedly, he was a slow learner. In actuality, she was short on patience. From his perspective, she had such supreme confidence in her mothering skills she didn't need him on the management team. In fact, she had little tolerance for his bumbling efforts. Thus, by the time Anne arrived, his accountability for the children consisted of the occasional task she delegated to him.

Fortunately, his growing duties at Kerr and his ever-growing income coincided with his reduced family role. The knowledge that he was a good breadwinner soothed his conscience.

When he and Grace were in their second year of marriage, his father was diagnosed with lung cancer. He died a year later at age sixty-five. Losing his father was a concept that startled him, but there wasn't any sadness. In fact, he was devoid of any feelings. At the time of his death, he felt like he'd gone "eeny, meeny, miney mo" over the open newspaper, and his finger had stopped at an obituary for an August Konert. He was that detached.

With his father's death came his mother's resurrection. Two months after he passed away she came to George and said, "I'm selling the house and moving in with my sister in California. Come on over and take anything you can use. I'll have an auction with what's left."

Grace and he picked through the household bones and came away with a single bed frame, mattress and a chrome and plastic dinette set for their home. Otherwise, they left everything else as it was. As they were packing up the rented trailer, Grace asked, "Isn't there some memento, some personal item you'd like to have?"

"Not a thing," he said.

When they were ready to drive away, his mother came running toward them. She was carrying a large rectangular box like one that might contain a newly purchased shirt. Handing it to George she said, "You might want this."

"What is it?"

"It's the scrapbook I kept of all your high school and college exploits."

He opened the box and rubbed his hand over the leather cover. "I never imagined you kept a scrapbook."

"Your father didn't know either. He liked your notoriety but was afraid you'd get a big head if we made a fuss over you. During the war, he . . . he wanted to deny you existed. I wanted you near me."

"I know. It's okay." George handed the box to Grace, placed his arms around her and said, "I love you, Mother." Then he kissed her goodbye.

In the weeks that passed before she left, he'd wanted to ask his mother why she was leaving Carlisle. After all, her only child and his wife and someday her grandchildren would most likely be here. But he never dared ask her the question. Then after dinner the night before she was to begin the long drive to Pasadena, he received his answer. She was wearing a new red dress with the high fashion shoulder pads, creme colored pumps and smiling through the brightest, most brilliant red lipstick he'd ever seen. He studied her and grinned. "Good luck, Mother," was all he said as he hugged her.

Then a year later at her wedding in LA, he walked her down the aisle and handed her off to Herb.

The doorbell rang. George rose slowly from the couch and stood for a moment to clear his head. Before opening the door, he peeked through the peephole and saw Mary wearing a windbreaker. She had a plaid scarf tied around her long hair, and her hands were thrust into the pockets of her Levis. She was being buffeted by a late October tempest.

Once she was in the hall, he quickly closed the door behind her, helped her with her jacket and threw her things on a chair. She declined coffee and they moved to the couch. George started the conversation, "So what's the problem that needs my brilliant advice?"

Mary lowered her eyes. "I think Dan's having an affair."

"Don't jump to conclusions," George said. "You need to convince me with facts before I'll give any advice."

"I thought you were my friend," Mary said.

"I'm doing what good friends do. Too often people make rash decisions based on circumstantial evidence, so give me the facts." He smiled, "Just the facts ma'am."

Her expression told him she didn't know "Dragnet" from a hairnet, so he suggested she tell him everything.

"For a month now, Dan hasn't come home until late on Tuesday and Thursday nights. He says he's working on a new project. When I ask him about the project, he says he's not far enough along to tell me about it."

"So?"

"When I called his secretary and questioned her about it, she said there was no new project that she knew about."

"Okay."

"When I confronted Dan he blushed and said I was certainly nosy, but he didn't want to tell me what was going on just yet. But, not to worry."

"So?"

"I'm worried. Dan is always sneaking around."

"With women?"

"Not that I know about. But he lies to me about playing golf. Says he's working when he isn't. I know he isn't playing golf in the dark, so what else could he be doing but chasing around?"

"Why do you suppose he doesn't tell you when he's playing golf?"

"Because he knows I want him home with the kids and me more often, and he's embarrassed to say he'd rather be golfing. When he's with the kids, he seems to love them, and they certainly adore him. So I don't get it. Maybe he feels inadequate because he's a lousy disciplinarian? I always tell him, 'You're not their pal, you're their father.' He bristles at the truth, and probably avoids them all the more, so I should keep my mouth shut."

"Let's see if I'm getting this. Dan doesn't always tell you when he's taking off from work to play golf. Sometimes he even lies about it. Now he's gone every Tuesday and Thursday night, won't tell you what he's doing, and you think he's having an affair."

"Right."

"Maybe, but he could be doing any one of a million things."

"Name one."

"He has a part time job to earn extra money to buy you a diamond pendant."

"We have plenty of money, and he knows I don't want a diamond pendant."

"He's buying new bikes for the kids."

"They have new bikes."

"Maybe he's taking a parenting course at the community college."

"Come on!"

"Maybe not. But I want to let you in on a well-kept secret about men. We're all a bit derelict in our fatherly duties. I used to drive Grace nuts with all the time I put into my garden when she thought I should be doing things with the children. My father always spent the cocktail hour at the neighborhood bar, but he never invited me. So it doesn't surprise me Dan plays a little more golf than his wife would like. I don't know why we do the things we do, but I'm afraid the selfishness of men is pretty universal." He stood up and took a creaky practice swing. "Maybe he's taking golf lessons."

"Sure, golf lessons in early November."

"To get ready for spring?"

"What am I going to do, George?"

"Confront him one more time. Tell him his secrecy

is driving you crazy. If he doesn't tell you what he's up to you're going to kill him in his sleep. Grace always threatened me with death, and I believed her. Men aren't too bright."

"What if he *is* having an affair?"

"What if he's taking golf lessons?"

"After I kill him for not telling me, I'll love him to death."

The next morning Mary called. Since George couldn't tell if she was laughing or crying, and since he was concerned enough and curious enough, he said, "Hang on I'll be right over."

Mary let him in and led him to the kitchen table. He tried to read her mood as she rummaged around in the bread drawer, came up with a cinnamon roll and set it in front of him along with a cup of coffee. He took a bite, looked around for a napkin before licking his fingers and drying them on his pants. Mary sat down across from him, her elbows on the table holding her face in her hands. Her long sandy hair partially covered her left eye. She said nothing.

"Are you going to tell me what happened, or do I have to strangle it out of you?"

She laughed. "The strangest thing happened last night. I confronted Dan. He begged me to wait until next week before he told me what he was doing. I did as you said and threatened to kill him in his sleep if he didn't tell me that very moment. So he did. Guess what?"

"He was taking golf lessons, and you kissed him."

"He was taking a vegetable gardening course at the University Extension. He told me his kids were going to have a vegetable garden next summer just like Mr. Konert's. Isn't that wonderful?"

"No affair?"

"No affair."

George's face clouded over. "Well I'm pleased for

you, but sad for me."

"Why?"

"When your kids have their own garden, they won't think I'm special anymore." He shook his head. "Who'll be my Garden Queen?"

Mary patted his hand. "Rachel will always be your Queen, and you'll always be special at our house. You'll be our consultant. God knows Dan will need one."

CHAPTER ELEVEN

CLEARING THE FIELD

For the Thanksgiving weekend, George flew to Chicago to spend the holiday with Jill and Stewart. When he arrived at O'Hare late Wednesday afternoon, Carlos, the company limo driver was there to pick him up. Carlos packed his bag into the trunk, closed the door and headed the vehicle out into traffic. While George sunk into the cushiony leather seats, the driver repeated Jill's instructions. "First I'm taking you to Mrs. Palmer's condo. After you've freshened up and changed into a suit for dinner, I'm driving you to her office."

"That will be fine, Carlos," George said, stretching out his legs. He yawned. In moments, he was asleep.

Through his fuzzy consciousness George heard tapping. He also sensed the limo had stopped. Reluctantly, he opened his eyes and glanced out the window. They were parked in the driveway of Jill's condo. The doorman tapped on the door again before opening it.

"Nice to see you again, Mr. Konert." He took George's arm and led him under the canopy to the massive glass front doors. "I'll let Mr. Palmer know you're here."

"Thank you . . . ." George was embarrassed. He couldn't remember the doorman's name. Carlos, who was following with the suitcase, came to his rescue. "Where do you want Mr. Konert's bag, Willie?"

"Anywhere, thank you, Carlos."

George waited in the lobby while Willie called Stewart on the house phone. When he hung up he picked up George's bag and led him into the elevator. Placing the bag on the floor, Willie pushed the button for the twenty-first floor.

"Mr. Palmer has left the door open for you." Pointing to the suitcase, he asked, "Can you handle it from here?"

"Of course, Willie. Thank you."

When the elevator stopped, George stepped off and followed the corridor to the open door.

"Hello," he hollered as he entered the apartment. When no one answered, he wasn't overly surprised. Stewart usually avoided him.

After helping himself to a glass of water, George wrestled his bag to the bedroom where he usually slept and set it up on a folding stand. He unpacked, placing his shirts and underwear in a dresser drawer and laying out his blue suit, shirt and tie on the bed. Stripping to his shorts and undershirt, he raised his arm and inhaled. The result sent him to the bathroom for a pre-dinner shower.

Later while changing into his dinner clothes, he heard a female voice coming from Jill and Stewart's bedroom. Was Jill home? Or? He was buttoning his shirt when his curiosity moved him into the hall to check out the voices. Standing outside their bedroom door, he strained to listen. Suddenly he sighed. The female voice was talking about a cold front moving into the area.

A few minutes later when he was leaving, he called to Stewart and said goodbye. Again there was no reply.

Carlos met him in the lobby. "That was a quick change. You look very distinguished in that handsome suit."

"It's my funeral suit. I hardly wear it anywhere else."

"Your daughter will be impressed."

"I would hope."

Driving south along Lakeshore Drive, George gazed at the empty beaches and windswept grey-green water of Lake Michigan. When they arrived at Jill's office, they parked on the street at the base of the fifty-story building. Carlos took out his cell phone and called Jill.

"She'll be down in a few minutes," he told George. "I'm going to have a smoke. You can stand outside with me, but it's pretty chilly. I think you'll be more comfortable staying in the car." George agreed and stayed put.

While Carlos stood outside his door smoking a cigarette, George watched the street action. On the sidewalk, business people and shoppers hustled in every direction. Men dressed in flapping trench coats tilted into the wind. Of more interest to George were the mini-skirted women with their delightful, long slender legs protruding from leather-covered torsos. His eyes followed their progress from the moment they came into view until he was forced to crane his neck to continue gawking. Like a typewriter reaching the end of a page, his gaze shifted back to the front of the limo to catch the next eyeful.

He rolled down the window and said, "Carlos, you have some gorgeous legs in this city. I wish Carlisle grew them like this."

"In Mexico, the women of my village have sturdy legs for working. That's why they wear those long brightly-colored skirts."

"I've been to Mexico, and I never thought of that."

"Me neither, until just now."

A few minutes later Carlos opened the door causing a wind gust to rearrange a few isolated strands of George's hair. Irritated, he interrupted his sightseeing long enough to spit on his hand and slick the errant tendrils back into place.

"Here comes Mrs. Palmer."

George cupped his hand over his ear. "Who?"

"Your daughter."

"Oh, good!"

George slid across the seat so Jill could get in. She moved next to him and threw her arms around his neck and kissed him. "I'm so glad you're here, Daddy. Sorry I made you wait. I had a few things to clean up so I could dedicate the whole weekend to my father."

After directing Carlos to the Chicago Chop House, she said, "I've got everything planned. Tonight at happy hour and dinner we'll get caught up. Tomorrow we're having turkey, dressing, the whole Thanksgiving thing at the condo."

"You're cooking a turkey?"

"Daddy, you've got to be kidding. You know I don't cook. I'm having it catered."

"I wondered."

"Unfortunately, Stewart's feeling lousy and will probably stay to himself."

"Good, then I get you all to myself."

"Daddy!"

He said, "I'm sorry." But he didn't mean it.

"If he's feeling better, the three of us will play pinochle. Otherwise, after dinner you and I can renew our cribbage rivalry, or you can watch the football games. Then on Friday, you can sleep in while I go to the office for a couple of hours."

George interrupted, "I thought you said you were done for the weekend."

Jill sighed. "I'm never done."

George looked past her at a man holding a small girl's hand. The child was pointing at the limousine. "You work too hard."

"I have to Daddy. It's my MO. That's how I've gotten ahead. Anyway, in the afternoon I'm taking you shopping for some new shirts and sweaters. Then we're going to Spiaggia for dinner. Just you and me. It's Stewart's idea."

George whistled. "That's quite a schedule. When do I take a nap?"

"Is it too much for you?"

"Nooo. I'm just 78 for gosh sakes. Only old people get tired." He took her hand. "But, here's the problem. No matter how hard I go, I can't sleep in. I'll be up at 5:30 on the dot. If I don't get a nap with all the activity you have planned, I'll probably fall asleep at dinner."

"What should we do then?"

"If I were making the schedule, here's what I'd like. I'd go to the office with you to see where you work. When you're finished, we'd shop for a bit, go for a late lunch and come home. Dinner could be Chinese carry-out."

"I can live with that." She started laughing. "Do you realize, Daddy, no one at work ever challenges my schedules?"

"That's what fathers are for. To come around once in a while and straighten their daughters out."

"I really think you're right."

She motioned to the brightly lit entrance as the limo came to a stop. "It looks like we're here. I hope you have an appetite."

"Who's buying?"

"I am."

"Then I'm starved."

119

Thanksgiving and the following day went according to plan. They ran from place to place, shared family stories and played cribbage. George felt exhausted and overwhelmed with the pace. At the times when Jill expounded on her career, he gained an insight into her personality that shocked him. In many ways, Jill was a carbon copy of Grace. Besides the obvious physical similarities, she also inherited Grace's directness, her ability to think clearly and her flair for organization. He was unconcerned that his own legacy was less apparent. After all, he wasn't competing with Grace to see who contributed the greater number of genes to Jill's construction. He was just proud the finished product was so impressive.

Seeing Jill in action, however, forced him to ponder a weightier question. Since Jill and Grace were so much alike, he wondered if he'd cheated Grace by insisting he earn the living, and she stay at home. The thought made him flinch. He'd rather think her destiny was predetermined by the mores of their generation, and since he'd never heard her complain about her lot in life, he assumed she was content with the role she played. God, he hoped she was.

Saturday's pace was equally hectic. First they visited the Shedd Aquarium--George's request--and later ate at Arnie's, which was Jill's. Then it was Sunday and time for George to fly home. As Jill was driving him to the airport, he said, "I had a wonderful time."

"It was fantastic. I wish you'd come more often."

"I would, but I'm afraid Stewart dislikes me. He hardly said three words the whole time."

"Sorry, Daddy. Stewart's not well. When he feels lousy, he wants to be alone."

"Well, I hope he feels better soon."

"Me too."

Returning from the trip, George was buoyed. On

the basis of his visit with Jill, he could hardly wait the three weeks until he'd be spending Christmas with Anne and Bret. With luck, the interim with Catherine would be exciting, too.

After Grace died and before he found Catherine he'd turned into a hermit. He'd resented the effort it took to get presentable enough to go out. Showering, shaving and dressing up were onerous tasks when he already knew he wasn't going to enjoy himself once he got to wherever he was going. Tonight while dressing for dinner, he made a remarkable discovery.

He and Catherine were dining at the Broadway Café, and he was planning on enjoying himself. After a relaxed dinner, she might even put her hand in his during the drive home and just possibly reward him with a thank you kiss at the door. He glanced at his image in the mirror. No wonder he was smiling.

Three days after their date he came down with the flu. For the next two weeks, he hardly moved from his bed. At the times he felt the worst, he was glad he was alone. Then he felt a little better and longed for Catherine's company. Still he didn't contact her. It was bad enough he was older than she was. He didn't need her seeing him indisposed, or, worse yet, feeling like she had to care for him like some invalid. When or if he ever felt better, he'd invite her over, and they'd have a fine time. But not now. He might suffer alone, but that was better than letting her see him in this moribund state.

George finally felt well the day before he planned on driving to Anne's for Christmas. He called Catherine.

"Merry Christmas," he said cheerily. "I'm going to see Anne early tomorrow morning."

"How nice for you. When I didn't hear from you, I thought you were upset with me."

"Why would I be upset? I think you're wonderful."

"Then why haven't you called?"

"I had the flu."

"If you'd let me know, I would have brought you some chicken soup."

"I don't like chicken soup. Anyway, I didn't want to expose a beautiful woman of your advanced age to a nasty virus."

"That's my George. Loathsome and thoughtful in the very same sentence. That's why I like you, I guess."

"You guess?"

She laughed. "Have a wonderful holiday with Anne and Bret."

"I miss you already."

"Ha! I'll believe that when I hear your voice when you return."

The drive through the Ohio countryside to Columbus was uneventful. Though it had snowed virtually every day while he was sick, perhaps twenty inches in total according to the paper, the roads were spotless all the way. When he drove into Anne's circular driveway that evening, he was greeted with an incomparable Christmas light display. Each tree and large bush was festooned with hundreds of small white lights, and the house was ablaze. Multi-colored brilliance snaked up the columns surrounding the spotlighted front entrance, and the windows facing the street were squared off with whole strings of red or green bulbs. Part of him was awed by the spectacle. Another part considered it gaudy and overdone. When he slipped out of the car, Christmas carols assailed him from speakers hidden in the shrubbery. He groaned. Only Anne would spend a fortune on such frivolity.

Standing by the car George stretched the shoulder and upper back muscles that had stiffened from the drive. Then he shuffled toward the porch and began his ascent. His knee cracked each time he mounted a step. Just as he reached for the bell, Anne threw open the door and wrapped her arms around him like a football tackle. When she finally released him, she said, "We're so glad you're here, Dad. We've been looking forward to seeing you for weeks, haven't we, Brett?"

"That's for sure." He extended his hand to his father-in-law. "Give me your keys, George. I'll park the car in the garage and take your things to your room. Is that okay with you?"

"Who wouldn't like that kind of service after a long drive. Thanks, Bret."

Anne put her arm through his and walked him through the foyer and down the hall toward the study. "Martha made some hot chocolate. We can chat by the fire while Brett gets you settled."

When they reached the study, Anne left to fetch the chocolate while he plopped down on the cordovan-colored leather couch and placed his legs on the hassock. He studied his surroundings. Bookshelves lined the museum-like room. Every inch of flat surface was covered with artifacts from around the world. Carved woodenheads from God knows where stood on the mantel, and a Persian rug lay on the floor in front of the huge stone fireplace. A fire blazed. The opulence made George uneasy.

When Anne returned, she chirped, "Well, how are you, Dad?"

He sighed. "Old, but kickin."

"That's a good thing."

Changing the subject, he said, "That's quite a light display outside."

"You like it? I gave our handyman, Francisco, carte blanche this year. Personally, I think he outdid himself." She poured his cocoa and placed the cup on the coffee table in front of him. Directing his attention to the Christmas cookies, she said, "Have one of Martha's cookies. They're scrumptious. Bret eats them by the truckload."

"Martha's the cook?"

"And the maid. She has her own suite over the

garage. Francisco goes home each night to his wife and children."

He wanted to ask, so what is it you do? Instead, he blurted, "I have a lady friend. Her name's Catherine."

"You do?" Anne ran her fingers through her long blonde hair. "I'm really surprised. I hope she's financially secure."

"Why would you say that?" he snapped.

She forced a laugh. "Oh, you know. I hear stories about designing women and stuff."

"Catherine's poor as a church mouse and lives with her daughter who owns a business that cleans offices. I wish she had designs on me."

"I wasn't insinuating...."

"And I'm sure she has more class than any of the women at that country club you belong to." Glaring at her, he struggled to his feet. "I'm pretty tired, which bedroom is mine?"

"Dad, it's only eight. Let's not fight. Whatever I said, I take back."

Bret entered the room. He glanced at Anne and then George. Ignoring their long faces, he told George, "Your bag is in your bedroom, and I'm ready to play pinochle." He began rummaging through drawers looking for cards. "The last time you were here you cleaned our clocks."

"Dad just commented on how tired he was," Anne said.

Bret straightened up. "That's too bad, maybe tomorrow then. Before you leave we want a chance to get even with you, don't we dear?"

Anne nodded.

As with most of George's tantrums, it ended instantly. He smiled at Bret, "I think beating you two at cards and a beer might keep me awake. I accept the challenge."

While Bret searched the refrigerator under the wet bar for a beer, George put his arm around Anne and whispered, "Sorry honey. I shouldn't have lost my temper like that."

"I apologize, too. My stupid comment was way out of line the way it came out."

The next two days passed at a leisurely pace. While Bret was seeing patients on Wednesday morning, George and Anne reminisced. Over lunch at the Country Club, George said, "I've been so miserable since your mother died and so happy since Catherine and I have become friends, it's like dying and going to heaven."

"I'm not sure I like the analogy, but I'm thrilled for you. Personally, I'm looking for a rebirth."

George gestured with a wave of his hand. "You're not happy with all this?"

"I love Bret and my lifestyle, but I need something more. Lately, I've been thinking about writing a novel."

Really?" George smiled.

"I've read darn near every book there is. Now I need to write one of my own."

"You were always creative when you were young. Remember the play in the basement using my vegetables?"

"That was Jill. But I remember the lightning storm when Jill and I were selling vegetables and you came searching for us. I also remember writing a book about our family for Sunday School. It was quite good for an eight year old."

"Was I in it?"

"Of course, silly. You and Mom were my heros. Jill was just a minor character."

"I'm surprised. I always thought your mom was the hero, and I was an outsider because all the time you were growing up, I was working long hours at Kerr."

"You were always there for me, Dad."

He reached across the table and grabbed her hands.

"Thank you for saying that, Anne."

On Christmas day they exchanged presents and feasted on Martha's Christmas goose stuffed with roasted chestnuts. It was his first experience with goose and even though he was filled to his eyeballs, he put in an order for leftovers the next day. After dinner, he returned to his room to rest and let his food settle.

While he dozed, he contemplated the day. On the one hand, he felt lucky. Many men his age couldn't enjoy a family Christmas. They were either dead or among the near dead in a nursing home. On the other, he felt deprived. Three adults and a maid sharing Christmas dinner wasn't a celebration. Christmas required children. He missed the yelping as the children rushed from package to package tearing at the wrappings to get at the contents. Those times in front of the tree were what Christmas was all about. Too bad he couldn't spy on Rachel, Kevin and Jimmy as they opened the little bank envelopes with twenty dollars in each he'd given Mary to place under the tree. There would be lots of mess, confusion and joy at the Alexander's today.

At breakfast the next day, Bret shook George's hand and thanked him for spending Christmas with them. He had to return to work.

George heard the Porche zip out of the garage and head out the drive to the street. He turned to Anne. "I hope he doesn't kill himself in that tin can."

"He's a good driver, Dad."

"He's a good man, too. I know I shouldn't say it, but I like him much better than Stewart."

Anne laughed. "I do too. What would you say if we were to take our coffee in the sunroom?"

"I'd say, good idea."

They walked arm in arm to the bright quarry-tiled room. Martha followed with a tray holding the cups and the silver thermos. When they reached the couch with the bright yellow floral print, George and Anne sat down next to each other. George sipped his coffee and let the sunlight dancing on the snow lift his spirits. He smiled at his younger daughter and found the courage to finally question her on the subject that continually gnawed at him. He set his cup on the end table and asked directly, "Why haven't you and Bret had any kids?"

Anne blanched. "We've been having such a nice time. Do we have to talk about that?" Tears welled up in her eyes. Without saying more, she stood up and walked to the bathroom for a tissue. When she returned, she sat on the floor with her legs crossed facing him. She gripped each knee with her hands to keep them from trembling.

He looked down at her and felt his own tears forming. "I'm sorry, Anne. This is more than I bargained for. It's none of my business."

"You had every right. I've always known how much you wanted grandchildren, and you deserve an explanation." She sighed. "As you know, Dad, I'm not a driver like Jill. I'm more comfortable in a supporting role. All I ever wanted for my life was a good husband and a couple of children to mother. When we were first married, we put off having children until Bret built his practice. During that time I could have taught or worked on my master's, but we thought I would be more valuable to him if I was out in the community doing charity work and socializing. So I became the good trooper and enthusiastically pitched in. I did my job well. Bret has often said I was as responsible for building his practice as he was."

She brushed the hair back from her face and waited for George to respond.

He shrugged. "I never knew any of that."

"I'm not surprised. Mom and I discussed things sometimes, but I'm sure she never shared my personal stuff with you."

"Why was that?"

"I don't know. Maybe she didn't want to bother you."

Anne uncrossed her legs, stood up and returned to the couch next to him.

"Anyway, once Bret felt established, we decided to start our family. After a year when we didn't have anything to show for our efforts, we both went for tests. The doctor concluded there wasn't a problem. 'Just relax and let it happen,' he said. Well, that's easier said than done. I became more and more tense trying to stay calm. I obsessed over having a child. I thought of nothing else. I'm sure that had everything to do with my not getting pregnant.

"Then mom got sick, and all the time she was dying I was falling apart. I couldn't talk with her about my problems, and you seemed so vulnerable I couldn't trouble you, so I did the only logical thing. I had a breakdown. Boy, was I a mess. I was hospitalized a short time. Later, during my time in therapy I was on some pretty powerful drugs. There was no way I could bear a child wondering if I'd be able to raise it. So we stopped trying. Now I could handle motherhood with ease, but I'm too old."

George was awash with emotion. Even though he'd been preoccupied with Grace's impending death and dealing with his own grief, he should have been sensitive to Anne's anguish. Any decent father would have sensed her plight and been supportive even if he couldn't fix her problem. "I should have known."

"No one knew but Bret and me . . . and my therapist, of course. I became adept at masking it around people."

"A decent father would have known."

"If you'd known, you'd have been frustrated because you couldn't have helped."

George put his arm around her and pulled her gently

toward him. She lay her head on his shoulder and sobbed. "God knows, I would have tried," he said.

She blew her nose on the Kleenex. A ray of sun streaked across her face. She raised her head from his shoulder and kissed him on the cheek. "That's the Dad I know best. The one who's always there to lean on."

George smiled. "And always will be."

That afternoon when he was returning to Carlisle, he began to have reservations about Anne's revelation. Now that he knew why Anne didn't have children, was he any better off? Was dredging up her pain worth it? What if his asking pushed her into another depression? Damn his bluntness!

Squinting through the windshield at the sun dancing on the snow covered fields caused his spirit to brighten. New thoughts crept into his old brain. If Anne regretted not having kids, his knowing the reason why wouldn't add any additional pain. The knowledge should bring them closer together. Fathers should know such things. He should know. If he'd never found out, he'd have gone to his grave with a tinge of resentment and be burdened with all those unanswered questions. Neither he nor Anne deserved that.

CHAPTER TWELVE

FIRST BLOOMS

George hated winter. Twelve years ago Grace died on a freezing, bone-chilling day. Winter was such a depressing time, full of foreboding. He mostly abhorred the frigid days because he was isolated. Though he was anything but a social butterfly, George still liked access to the people he chose to see at the times he desired to be with them. He resented the difficulties the cold and ice imposed on him. The possibility of slipping and breaking an arm or leg or having a heart attack shoveling a simple path to the mailbox gave him pause. In winter, spontaneity was packed away with the summer shirts. Even the simplest events required planning.

With February still a week away, he had at least two dreary months to endure until he could get back into his garden. The boredom drove him nuts. So did the short days. Awakening at 5:30 in the dark of winter with nothing to do and less to look forward to made him apprehensive. In summer, he embraced the early morning, because he could rush outside and complete his gardening before the day became stifling.

His winter wish was to sleep at least until daylight, but his built-in alarm wouldn't let him. One night, he vowed to change his sleep pattern by staying up until two o'clock. He awoke at his usual time. He tried a second night and was still awake before the sun. After a third attempt, he evaluated his progress. It seemed his late night experiment had left him in a state of complete exhaustion and a need for more daytime naps when he'd rather be awake. Another failed attempt was too demoralizing, so George settled for arising early and cursing the darkness.

Walking past the hall mirror, he peered into it and frowned. "George, you're pathetic. Instead of looking for a little fun, you waste the winter reading seed catalogs and crying in your Sprite and cranberry juice. So what if the weather is abysmal. You need some action, boy. Get off your rear and find some."

In the kitchen, he began rinsing the lunch dishes and arranging them in the dishwasher. After finishing, he took an inventory of his interests. The effort made him sleepy. He headed for the living-room couch. Placing his head on a throw pillow, he pulled his legs onto the corduroy and stretched out. He squirmed and twitched and couldn't get comfortable. When he finally found a position that suited him, his eyes wouldn't close.

He sat up and placed a pillow in back of his head. It was time for an honest self-appraisal. His first thought was reading more. But why start now? Except for the newspaper, nothing else in print ever interested him. TV? Boring except for pro football and his Reds. He enjoyed watching both except football season was over and baseball hadn't started yet. Was he supposed to watch soaps or wrestling for the next two months?

Some people liked movies. Not him. He'd gone to a movie one Saturday night a year or so ago. It was a fiasco. For seven bucks, he watched some unconvincing actors spout dumb dialogue as they chased tornadoes through Oklahoma or Kansas or some other desolate flat place. Watching the atrocity helped him understand why the critics called it a disaster movie. Halfway through when the smell of dead popcorn began to make his head ache he walked out and swore he'd never ever return unless perhaps "The Sound of Music," Grace's favorite, was playing.

George shuffled to the kitchen to fill a glass with half Sprite and half cranberry juice. When he returned to the couch, he resumed his assessment. An idea had been whirling around in his head for some time. He'd buy a DVD player like the Alexander's. As long as he was grasping for ideas, he decided to revisit it. If he had a player, he could watch movies at home in his work clothes with a beer and cheese sandwich or anything else he wanted without the stale popcorn smell. Moreover, because there were thousands to rent, he ought to be able to find one or two he liked. And if he did pick out a crapper, he'd only be out the four-buck rental and the time it took to flick off the machine.

Another advantage to a DVD player was it gave him a reason to ask Catherine over. She could have the cocktail her daughter, Gert, wouldn't allow at her house, and they could sit on the couch together and hold hands. He'd serve shrimp cocktail or a vegetable dip and chips, and when the movie was over they'd chat awhile before he'd kiss her and drive her home.

The grin that had emerged slowly diminished. Why was he thinking such foolishness? He didn't have the nerve to kiss Catherine or hold her hand. To date he'd only fantasized about such things. It was also possible she might dislike movies. Or chips. Or maybe she had a shellfish allergy, and he'd have to take her to the hospital emergency room.

So if Catherine wouldn't watch movies with him, he'd never go to the store, pick out a disc and watch one by himself. The damn DVD player would just gather dust until he died. In which case, he'd never recover the cost of the machine.

George shifted his position on the couch. Once he was upright with his bad left knee stretched out flat, he berated himself. "Shape up, George. You don't need some electronic gizmo to get through the cold weather. You need human contact. Just call Catherine and invite her to dinner or to play cards. She'll accept."

Every winter since Grace died, he'd crawl into a hole like a mole or some other hibernating animal and not emerge until spring. No more, he thought. Before long, he'd be underground permanently.

Returning to the couch, he began listing all of his experiences leading up to his current funk. The list was much more balanced than he thought. Two funerals for acquaintances from the past and an argument over a Mayoral candidate with his barber that turned into a shouting match, versus his holiday visits with the girls and several dates with Catherine. Maybe if he saw her more he could unbalance the ledger and time wouldn't drag on so. Suddenly he felt foolish. Feeling depressed is ridiculous, he thought. Throw out the old and let the new me emerge.

He dialed Catherine and invited her to dine with him at Pierre's on Saturday. When she accepted, he was ecstatic.

On Saturday morning, it was snowing lightly when George awakened. It finally stopped about one-thirty in the afternoon. He dragged himself to the garage and started up the snowblower. On one of his passes to the end of the driveway, he gathered up the mail from the box and stuffed it into his coat pocket. When he finished blowing and before removing his hat, coat and boots in the front hall, George sorted the mail and opened it. Among the usual junk was an invitation to the O'Hara's Valentine's Day party. He was elated. This was another opportunity to ask Catherine out. As long as he was still dressed for the cold, he opted to deliver his RSVP in person.

He trudged through the snow to the O'Hara's and rang the bell.

Mike opened the door and waved him in. "What's going on?"

"I just received your Valentine's Day invitation and wanted to accept."

"You could have just called."

"I know, but I wanted to ask you something face-to-face. Can I bring a friend?"

"Of course. Boy or girl?"

"A lady friend."

O'Hara raised his eyebrows. In a syrupy mocking tone, he said, "I see. And what's her name?"

"Cut that out. Maybe I won't come at all."

Mike hollered into the next room. "Cheryl, George Konert has a lady friend he wants to bring to our party. He promises she won't eat much. Is it okay?"

Cheryl yelled back, "Be nice, Michael." She padded into the hall. "Of course, you can bring her, George." Then she asked sweetly, "And what's her name?"

George grimaced. "It's Catherine. Catherine Newkirk."

"I can't wait to meet her."

O'Hara rubbed his hands together and said, "Oh boy! I can hardly wait, either."

On the day of the party, he picked Catherine up at two sharp, drove her back to his house and re-parked the car in the garage. After letting her out, he asked, "Do you want to come in for a minute?"

She shook her head. "But I have something I'd like to give you." She faced him and moved closer. He stood with his hand on the door handle. She tilted her face to his and kissed him gently on the mouth. "Happy Valentine's Day, George."

"That was nice. I hope I still don't have the flu."

"It's been two months. I think if you were going to give it to me I'd have it by now."

"I meant to say . . . . Oh, the hell with it." He pulled her to him, kissed her hard and felt like a teenager kissing a girl for the first time.

When they entered the O'Hara's foyer, George introduced Catherine to their hosts. Despite his fears, Mike didn't embarrass him in front of Catherine. As they moved into the living room, George sensed the other guests observing them. Then it hit him. They were oddities. He and Catherine were much older than the other guests. Though disconcerting, the age difference was understandable. If the O'Hara's were in their forties, wouldn't their friends be the same?

With a plate of canapés in one hand and a beer in the other, George recalled the stern lecture he gave himself about drinking and eating too much. Historically, he had trouble pacing himself at parties. One time in the wake of his overindulgence, Grace chastised him. "It's difficult being married to a man whose credo is, 'Anything worth doing is worth overdoing.'"

After some minor grazing, George found a space on the family-room couch for Catherine and him. From there, they chatted with each other and the occasional stranger who included them in a conversation. Then around five, Catherine asked to leave. She said she was tired, but George was sure she was bored with him. After thanking their hosts, they walked down the O'Hara's walk, around the snow-piled curb and up George's driveway to the garage. Catherine didn't speak the whole way. He had planned on suggesting they spend the rest of the evening playing cards or going to a movie, but decided not to risk a refusal. Instead, he pulled the opener from his coat pocket, raised the garage door and held the car door for her. They drove in silence.

When they reached her house, she placed her hand on his knee and said, "It's still early, George. Come in for a cup of coffee."

"I thought you were tired?"

"I don't like cocktail parties very much. Tired means I've had enough."

"When Grace said she was tired, it usually meant she'd had enough of me."

"I'm not Grace," she said.

"I know that."

He took off his gloves and turned on the vehicle's interior light. "If you want me to come in, I will."

She shrugged. "It's up to you."

Later that night after returning home, George changed into old clothes and began reading his new Sports Illustrated. Before long his thoughts drifted to Catherine. She was beautiful and smelled like lilacs, which was his favorite smell other than maybe burning pine needles and she was fun to be with. He liked those first few kisses in the garage, holding her hand, and feeling a little ripple in his stomach when she smiled at him. Unfortunately, like this evening, he also had a tendency to act like a fool in her presence. What was it about the woman that could turn him into an adolescent? Had she already gained so much power over him during their short relationship that she could addle his brain? Or had he always been a fool and only now capable of recognizing it?

While the freezing days continued, George knew that Catherine was the key to banishing his winter blahs. Each contact with her improved his disposition because she would spark some long forgotten pleasant emotion. He often caught himself smiling. At other times he'd feel angry for letting so much time slip by between visits earlier in their relationship. When you're almost eighty, anything can happen. One doesn't squander one's opportunities.

***

Several weeks later Catherine was all excited. Her daughter, Marianne, had invited her to Seattle for a ten-day visit in March.

"How am I going to get along without you?"

She laughed. "You'll be fine. There are plenty of fish in the sea."

"Not the Dead Sea."

After she left, George spent the first two days ordering all of his garden seeds. To celebrate his new relationship with Catherine, he decided upon some changes. Instead of planting the same old varieties, he switched part of his bean crop from Kentucky Wonder to Tendergreen, and after a hiatus of twenty years he bought some kohlrabi seeds. In the past they'd been a disaster, but this year he had a hunch they just might grow into something edible. At least, they deserved one more chance.

Once the seed orders were posted, George decided to tackle the downstairs bathroom. Though Catherine had never mentioned the twelve years of filth that had collected in corners, George was embarrassed enough to scour the room to meet the most stringent female standards. With the bathroom gleaming, he focused on the kitchen until it, too, passed muster. When he finished, he had nothing left to do except compare the cold and blustery forecast of The Weather Channel with what he observed through his own window. He felt trapped. Without Catherine, he'd be right back in the winter funk he vowed never to revisit again. Slipping his brain into overdrive, he came up with a potential solution to his crisis. He picked up the phone and dialed Gert.

"It's about time you called me, George Konert. I've been wanting to ask you about your intentions towards my mother."

"All you had to do was call, Gert. The phone lines run both ways."

"The Newkirk women are ladies. My mother says ladies don't call gentlemen."

George guffawed. "That may be, Gert. But what kept YOU from calling me?"

Pretending to be hurt, she said, "Underneath this rough facade beats the heart of a lady. It just doesn't show through the sweatshirts."

"You're so self-deprecating, I get sucked into your little game and say things that could hurt your feelings."

"I wish I knew what self-deprecating meant. I guess I'm too stupid to know words like that."

"You just did it again," he said.

"Did what?"

"Put yourself down."

"Of course. I do it all the time. What's that have to do with that deprecating bit?"

George sighed. "Now you're putting me on."

"Of course, I do it all the time." Huge chunks of her laughter bombarded the telephone forcing George to hold the receiver away from his ear. Then she confessed, "I only do it because I love you, George. I think you're the good man that's hard to find."

"Do you want to have dinner some night while your mother is gone?"

"Are we lonesome, George?" she cooed. "Now I ask you, why would I take time out from my busy schedule to help you out just because my mother's not available? You never ask me out when that old woman's around."

"I've been afraid you'd be so taken by me you'd stop looking for a more appropriate man."

"I'm more afraid I'd break my mother's heart when you fell for me."

"Let's stop sparring. You're right on the mark about my being lonesome. Help me out will you? Go to dinner with me."

"Sure. I'll go just to make my mother jealous. But I can't until Thursday. I'm breaking in a new cleaning crew. If you can wait until then, I'll pick you up in the truck, and we'll go to Sammy's."

"That dive?"

"Even though you may have to kick a few bikers out of the way to get a seat, the food's great. By now you know, George, you wanna eat with Gert? You go to Sammy's. You want to dine with the elegant Catherine, you take her to the Ritz."

George laughed and said, "Sammy's it is. I'll dig up a leather jacket and some ripped jeans."

"Don't forget the shades."

After George hung up, he headed directly to the bedroom hall and climbed the pull-down stairs to the attic. If he still owned a pair of Levis, they'd be packed away in the old trunk where Grace used to store the clothes that they never wore but were too good to throw out. There amongst some of her dresses that he hadn't been able to part with, he found the jeans. Further rummaging produced his father's old leather vest that Grace took because his father insisted. It was expensive and his father seldom wore it. George held it out and studied it. He was amazed at the perfect condition though it had to be sixty years old. He smelled the leather. The faint aura of his father's pipe tobacco still clung to the material.

George sat down on a box and began laughing. It would certainly piss off the sour old tyrant if he knew his near eighty-year-old son was going to wear his vest to a bar loaded with motorcycle jockeys. Or would it. The old man was no stranger to taverns. The vest had probably seen far

139

worse places than Sammy's.

After he gathered up the vest and jeans, closed the trunk and returned to the living room, he was still smiling to himself. Not only was he going to upset his father, he was going to shock the heck out of Gert with his get-up.

On Thursday night when Gert honked for him, in addition to the Levis, George had wrapped a blue bandanna around his head. To keep warm, he wore an old surplus World War ll bombardier jacket over his vest and white-sleeved undershirt. Glancing at his image in the full-length hall mirror, he smiled and gave a thumbs-up. Now if he'd only get the same reaction from Gert.

When he opened the door, the truck was filled with Gert's ear-shattering laughter.

"What's with the outfit? I thought I had a dinner date with George Konert, not Willie Nelson!"

"You don't like it?"

"I love it. It's the real George. If only my mother could see you now she'd drop out of the competition, and I'd have you all to myself."

Sammy's wasn't anywhere near as seedy as George had imagined. The decor was 1930's roadhouse complete with knotty-pine bar, jukebox and pool table. The customers were normal, well-behaved citizens casually dressed like Gert in slacks and sweaters. To George's surprise, he was the only person in the place dressed like a biker. In fact, compared to the other patrons, he looked like a man who got lost on the way to a masquerade ball.

Another eye-opener was the food. There was a huge salad bar, and George couldn't remember the last time he'd had a T-bone as tasty and tender as the sixteen-ounce he put away. Gert's fried cod looked equally good, and each meal included a mountain of French fries. Then came the biggest shock of all. The price. The whole bill without a senior citizen's discount was forty bucks including his two beers, Gert's Pepsi and the tip.

While they were eating, a parade of people stopped by the table to say "hi" to Gert and, he was sure, to check him out. Each time Gert introduced him, she would say, "This is my friend, George."

The innuendo in her voice and her radiant smile somehow suggested they had a much more intimate relationship than the reality of the situation. A burly, bearded lumberjack type named Chad came to the table and said, "You're a lucky man, George. Take care of this little woman." Before he walked away he slapped George on the back and almost broke his teeth when his jaw snapped together from the force of the blow.

He glared at Gert. "Why are you leading these people astray?"

In her sweetest voice, Gert said, "You are my friend, aren't you George?"

"You know what I mean."

"It's so nice to have a boyfriend again that I got carried away." She gestured to a few couples slow-dancing to the jukebox music in a small area near their table. "Want to dance, boyfriend?"

George threw his hands into the air. "Aw, come on."

"Just thought I'd ask."

That night as he was taking off his bandanna and vest, George raised his fist and yelled, "Yes!"

With Gert's help, he'd conquered another winter day. George the Mole was out of his hole. He liked that. "George the Mole was out of his hole." Only eight more days and Catherine would be back. The bed beckoned. It was time to sleep. "George the Mole was out of his hole."

CHAPTER THIRTEEN

FALLOW FIELDS

Years ago one April afternoon when Jill and Anne were pre-teens, George came home from Kerr and found Grace and the girls dancing in the driveway. He stopped the car in the street to watch. They twirled and hopped and giggled. Sometimes they joined hands and circled. Other times they freelanced, each following her own instinctive tribal beat. Were they not recognizable members of his own family whooping it up, he'd have thought they were a small band of Indians overloaded with firewater or locoweed.

When the gyrations ended, and they were laughing and gasping for breath, he pulled into the driveway, and rolled down the window. "What the heck are you doing?"

"It's a sun dance, Daddy," Jill said. "We're celebrating the arrival of Spring." Then the three started again.

Later when they were alone, Grace told him, "We were praying the Sun God would bring good weather soon so you could work in your garden and become human again."

"Am I really that bad?"

"The truth? You've been driving us nuts the last few weeks. We can't stand you any longer."

***

It was income tax day, April fifteenth, and George was leaning against his hoe in the garden grinning as he recalled the incident. On such a sullen day, he was probably the only non-senile seventy-nine-year-old man in America with a grin on his face.

Each spring while the kids were home and for many years after they left, he could expect a reprise of the "Please God, Restore George's Lovable Personality Dance." He never knew exactly when the "spirits" would move Grace to perform. The routine usually occurred after work on the first decent day of early spring when winter's demons held him in a visegrip. He'd be ready to turn into the driveway when he'd spot her, gyrating and puffing like a steam engine. While the ceremony was never an artistic triumph, it always made him smile and gave him the strength to limp through the remaining weeks until he could plant some early beets, snow peas, radishes and lettuce.

This spring when the first warm weather appeared and the ground was dry enough to work, he called Doug Wembley, the son of his farmer friend, Tom Wembley. Though Doug was now in his early twenties and busy on the Wembley farm, he still agreed to roto-till his plot for the pittance George paid him. Hiring someone was nothing new. After he turned sixty, Grace insisted he hire someone to handle the backbreaking labor because it was taking too much out of him. "You don't need to have a heart attack over some stinky cabbage."

At first, he scoffed at her suggestion. Then his old tiller died, and the Wembleys agreed to help. From there it was easy to convince himself it was cheaper to hire out the job each year than buy a new machine. When he made his decision known, Grace said, "By the time you die, George, you may be a halfway intelligent individual."

Gardening was always a year round avocation for George. Blueprinting his sixty-by-forty foot plot began during the winter when he detailed the location of each row. By January the seed catalogs began arriving--Jung's, Henry Field's and Harris' Seeds. In total, the catalogs were the source of all knowledge for an avid gardener; their wisdom the equivalent of the Bible to a believer. From the moment of their arrival, George wore out the pages studying them. He kept them in the wicker basket by the easy chair so he could easily take one to read while he was eating meals or sitting in the bathroom.

Once his head was crammed with facts and his notebook full of plant characteristics, George would sit down at the kitchen desk and try to decide which varieties would grow best in his clay soil. Instead of falling back on old standbys, he liked trying some of the new hybrids. Some worked well like Improved Detroit Dark Red Beets. Some failed miserably like the year he planted Super Sugar Daddy Snap Peas and ended up with a few stunted vines and a half-dozen pea pods.

By late February or early March he was ready to order. Consulting his list of varieties and the quantities needed, he compared the cost of the seeds he'd selected and picked the best buy from among the several companies he'd chosen to place orders. Saving a few bucks on his seed order was part of the enjoyment.

Once George retired, vegetable gardening forced him into a predictable cycle that he both wanted and needed. Like a trainman and his watch, he always knew where he was by consulting his garden. After the winter brainwork, he would wait for the boxes of seeds to arrive through the mail. When they were all accounted for, he'd call the Wembly boy to complete the tilling, and if the weatherman cooperated, George could begin his planting. Next came the strained back and aggravated knees period caused by sowing and weeding. Usually the healing season came about miraculously and coincided with the arrival of the summer harvest. Finally, at the end of the crop year, the fall cleanup occurred. Then it was winter and time to begin the cycle over again.

Most of the time as soon as the ground was ready in early April, he was itching to begin his fieldwork. Not this April. Though his seeds had arrived and his "tiller" had been hired, he felt the same reluctance toward gardening he felt the summer Grace was dying. Naturally, the reasons differed. When Grace was dying, he was depressed and not eager to put in all the effort. Now with Catherine in his life, he wanted to spend every moment with her sharing meals, watching TV, or playing gin. Any hours spent gardening were hours he couldn't be with her. He was torn. Although he still relished the idea of his garden, he loved the reality of Catherine. At his advanced age, he had to carefully consider his activities to be sure he was selecting the choicest morsels of time and energy. He didn't want to stuff himself at the buffet and spoil a gourmet feast.

Two weeks ago when April arrived in Carlisle sunny, dry and warm, and his knees didn't hurt, his ancient ties to the earth were too strong to break. He began exercising his fetish for straight rows by planting seeds like beet and peas whose sprouts wouldn't be wiped out by a late frost. April in southern Ohio was also early cabbage planting time. Over the winter he'd decided to plant a few plants for luck despite the previous year's glut. After all, the excess cabbage turned out to be fortuitous. Hadn't it

145

brought Catherine and him together?

Grace always razzed him about his meticulousness. Consulting the specifications on his clipboard, he'd tape measure the width of each row according to his plan. Beets for example, were planted in rows eighteen inches apart and one-quarter inch deep. To guarantee proper spacing, he'd measure, drive wooden stakes into the ground at the end of each row and connect the stakes with string. Using the line as a guide, he'd carefully hoe a furrow along it to make sure the seeds were sown straight and at the proper depth. When the seeds were covered with dirt and tamped down, he began the process all over again for the next variety.

Funny, he wasn't the least nit-picky about any activity other than gardening. He certainly never demanded a well-kept house. Why would he? That was Grace's fetish. Everything had a place, and he and the girls were taught to respect the order of things. Cooking? Food prepared simply and served family style suited him just fine. Clothes? Casual was his choice for the office or a night out. If the creases on his pants weren't sharp or if his shoes were a little scuffed, it didn't bother him. He knew if he was too disheveled, Grace would nag him into neatness.

But in the garden he was fastidious, and he knew the reason why. Raising vegetables was his means of artistic expression. While friends of his painted, wrote creatively or played the piano, he gardened. To George, leaf blight was a smudge on his canvas, a weed a discordant note. He needed to eradicate these recurring imperfections before they spoiled his masterpiece. Other artists were restrained only by their lack of passion for hard work and the limits of their talent. For George to create something of value he had to battle Mother Nature with all of her whims and quirks.

George knew Grace never fully understood the deeper layer of feelings generated by his garden.

"You suffer all that backbreaking labor for what?" she asked. "To duplicate produce I can buy at the Farmer's Market for less money? You're so focused on that plot of dirt you're oblivious to the children and my needs." Then with a flip of her head, she added, "When I'm dead and buried you can grow all the darn vegetables you want. Right now I'd be happy if you'd spend more time with me."

Despite all her reservations, each April she still did her silly dance, and he, of course, never took her forewarning seriously until she began to die. Then no matter how he might wish he'd heeded her words, it was too late.

From today's perspective, he and Grace were a perfectly matched couple. Each had flaws that chipped away at the bliss that was the supposed ideal for marriages of their era. But harmony didn't make their partnership work. Friction did. Grace was outspoken. He was too passive. For thirty-seven years, her sharp tongue kept him from slipping into a comfortable seclusion and boring her to death. Looking back, he realized this was a ploy she used to get him more involved with her emotionally, and he was glad she did. Sometimes, the same sword could prod him to the edge of rebellion. When he'd had enough, he'd tell her to shut up. Then he'd feel chagrined and apologize which usually brought a smile of forgiveness.

On those rare occasions when ill-tempered utterances escaped his mouth, he'd feel immediate guilt. Also panic. Because he knew his outburst would be the catalyst for Grace to gather her forces for an inescapable verbal donnybrook. A skirmish she intended to win.

When the sides disengaged and an uneasy truce was declared, George buried his dead and tended to the wounded. He'd moan, "Just once, I'd like to win an argument with you."

She'd smile, "Forget it, dear. It'll never happen."

147

In the years after the children left home, they mellowed. Scrapping became a less appealing method of keeping their attitudes in sync. When Grace held her tongue, and he listened for the meanings behind the words she used, their life together was more relaxed. Also with his retirement approaching and their energy waning, the prospect of spending their time fighting seemed ridiculous.

Once while driving to a favorite breakfast place in a nearby village, Grace kissed him on the cheek and said, "You actually heard exactly what I was saying."

George grinned. What he'd heard her say was, "I just love the omelets at the Egg Basket."

He'd replied, "They taste better because you aren't cooking them. That's why I like to take you to breakfast." That's when she kissed him, and he realized, probably for the first time, that making a woman happy wasn't such a difficult thing.

When they returned to Carlisle, she'd taken him by the hand and guided him to the bedroom where they made love. Though delighted, he was mystified. The last time they went to the Egg Basket nothing like that happened. What were the magic words going to be the next time?

Other changes came about during this time. George, with her urging, agreed to use all four-vacation weeks for what they were intended. Vacations. No longer would she allow him to pocket most of his vacation pay and spend a week in a rented cottage on some nondescript lake in Ontario. Usually this meant Grace bought the food, cooked the meals, and made the bed. Also, since most of the facilities weren't clean enough to suit her, she'd scrub, sweep and polish until the cottage met her standards.

George meanwhile was attempting to fish, a sport he neither liked nor understood. When he wasn't on the lake, he would be pawing the ground waiting for Grace to finish one of her tasks so they could have some "fun" together.

After her vacation proclamation, they divided the four weeks into long weekends with Jill and Anne, a winter Caribbean cruise, a week at a resort, either in Florida or Hilton Head, and a car trip in the summer to different locales to "see the countryside." At first, it was hard for each of them to adjust. George wasn't sure he could leave his garden for even a long weekend. Grace worried about household matters before they left and often while they were gone. Then there was the money.

George said, "We can't afford these expensive trips."

"We can't take it with us."

And, damn it, she was right, as it seemed she always was.

George finished planting the last half row of leaf lettuce, washed off his pointed hoe under the spigot and trudged to the basement door to put his tools away.

Then he hobbled upstairs and fixed lunch. He considered taking his sandwich and beer to the porch except it was cool, and he'd need a jacket. The living room couch made more sense. Eating, or perhaps it was the beer, plunged him into a reminiscence.

In the spring when he turned sixty-five, he retired from Kerr. He'd been tutoring his successor, young Bill Sundvold, for more than a year. It was his intention to have Bill's transition into George's superintendent's job be seamless. Kerr had been loyal to him. It was unconscionable to retire leaving a void. Thus in early March when he was convinced he wouldn't be missed and Bill could handle his job, George walked into the office of the Vice President of Manufacturing, and said he was through.

In April, the Friday after Easter, management threw a big party in his honor. All the hoopla made George uncomfortable. Still he was flattered by the speeches praising his role in the company's development and the kind words of his peers. When his gold watch was presented and his comments demanded, he walked slowly to the podium with Grace at his side.

After giving thanks for his gift and wishing everyone well, he ended his speech by saying, "Over the last forty-three years, I never doubted that working for Kerr was the second best decision I ever made." He smiled at Grace and placed his arm around her. "My best decision is standing beside me. While I'm sure there'll be times when I'll miss my job and particularly all of you, I'm mostly excited about spending the next forty-three years with my wife."

As he took Grace's arm and guided her through the handshakes, "good luck's" and pats on the back, he had a lump in his throat.

Two weeks later the gynecologist found a lump in her breast. Additional tests detected more tumors in other parts of her body. With little enthusiasm but much determination, she began chemotherapy. The next year in January she died.

George cried. Whenever he relived their last year together and her valiant efforts to survive, he habitually burst into tears. At first, the only notable change was her hair. Each morning she'd comb huge hunks from her head until she was nearly bald. Once when they were crying together about it, she raised her reddened eyes to his and defiantly announced, "I'm not going to spend my last days looking like this, George. Let's spend some of our retirement money on a wig. So they went together and picked out a short, straight blonde one although her hair had been gray for fifteen or more years, and for a few months she looked so stunning he had trouble realizing she was deathly sick.

Then that summer as the cancer progressed, she began losing weight and complaining of more and more pain that only the drugs the doctor prescribed could relieve.

His days were full caring for her, cooking her meals, helping her bathe. On warm evenings when the house seemed too oppressive for both of them, he'd help her get comfortable on the porch chaise. At least they could enjoy the shadows and be cooled by the gentle breeze. Then he'd move a chair next to hers and hold her fragile hand. "I love you so much, Grace," he said through tears.

Sometimes he'd slip out of bed at daybreak while she was sleeping fitfully and explore his garden. He didn't have a burning desire to work. It was more of an escape from the reality occurring inside the house. On his forays, he discovered enough cabbageworm, corn borer and tomato hornworm damage to seriously limit the harvest, but he didn't much care. Nor did the weeds choking his beets receive his attention. Ironically, the garden gods were good for some crops, delivering just the right amount of moisture, heat and coolness to create an exceptional crop of lettuce and green beans. Rather than pick them, he told the neighbors to help themselves to anything that looked good to them. "I'm not going to waste time in the garden when I want to be with Grace," he said.

In the fall and early winter, Grace's pain was so severe she was constantly sedated. Although he wanted to be with her, to talk with her, and wait on her, she seldom gave any indication she knew he was around. When Hospice finally took over his duties, he found solace in returning to his garden for the late fall cleanup. Ripping out dead plants and burning them at the back of his lot helped him.

After her death and for the next ten years, he relived the horror of her dying on a regular basis. Whenever he thought about weaning himself of the bitter memory, he refused to chance it. What if his joyful memories drifted away with the sad ones? So to stay comfortably connected, he returned to his garden, periodically cried and began conversing with Grace.

He removed his shoes and fluffed up the couch pillows. His hand roamed through his thinning hair. This morning, while he was planting lettuce, he'd had a revelation. His relationship with Catherine had been blooming for six months, and that was exactly how long it had been since he last spoke with Grace.

CHAPTER FOURTEEN

MANURE

The Fourth of July had passed and the kids had been out of school for a month and a half when George saw the Coleman punk pounding on Sean O'Hara from next door. At first he thought it was typical teenage roughhousing until he saw Coleman haul off and throw a fist at Sean's head. Sean ducked under it, but George had seen enough. He came limping across the lawn waving the three-prong cultivator he'd been using to loosen the soil in his flowerbeds.

"Hey, cut that out," he hollered. "Somebody's gonna get hurt."

The three boys froze.

"Coleman, you and your friend get on home." He pointed in the direction of the pale blue ranch three doors away. Yanking his thumb toward the O'Hara's, he said, "In the house, Sean."

Sean didn't need any additional encouragement and ran off. Nor did Coleman's crony. He was halfway down the block. By contrast, Brad Coleman took a menacing step toward George and said, "You can't make me."

George flared. He shook the cultivator at him and said, "How'd you like this thing stuck in your butt."

Coleman widened the distance between them and muttered an obscenity. George raised his weapon over his head like a demented warrior. The kid gave George the finger and hightailed after his friend.

When he was well past the point where George could effectively deal with him, Brad yelled, "I'm gonna get you, you old fart."

George laughed and rattled his cultivator at him.

The Colemans had been living in the old Tice house for the last several years. There were three of them. The father, a fat hairy lout, usually sat on the front stoop in the summer like a Buddha in a ribbed undershirt drinking a beer and glowering at anyone who passed. Unlike her husband, the mousy, slightly built mother was friendly enough whenever George ran into her at the grocery store. Brad, their only child, was thirteen or fourteen and the closest thing to a delinquent the neighborhood had to offer. From George's perspective, he was a first class pain. On several occasions, George had watched him bully Sean, who was the same age but a full head shorter. Prior to today he never intervened. The other time he yelled at the punk was when he'd caught him pushing little Jimmy Alexander around. Like today, he'd taken great pleasure in sending the cur home, yipping.

When Mike O'Hara came home from work that afternoon, George invited him over for a beer and to report on Brad and Sean's altercation. Using the porch as a sort of screened-in beerstube/sportsbar was a recent development. The revival occurred at the end of the previous summer when he and O'Hara resolved their

154

differences.

Before she became ill, he and Grace used the porch constantly during the warm, muggy summers. Whether they were sipping pre-dinner cocktails, eating supper or watching late-night TV, the porch was a haven between the stuffiness of the house and the mosquito-infested garden; a sanctuary of swooping swallows, cricket wing sounds and, after dark, blinking firefly sparklers. Then Grace died and except for an occasional nap, the porch fell into disuse. An evening there without Grace was too painful for him.

"What are you going to do about that bully pounding on your son, Mike?"

"Nothing. As much as I'd like to see him punished, I'll bide my time. Sooner or later he'll do something so I can have him arrested." He pounded his fist into his palm. "Or better yet, be able to sue his old man."

"That's the difference between lawyers and retired factory superintendents. You're like a cat waiting for the perfect time to pounce. I learned from Jake. I'd rush him now like a bull."

"The kid's a scourge, but I don't have a case."

"You don't need a case to talk to his parents."

"I'd be wasting my breath. The mother's a handwringer and the old man thinks his son is perfect. He'll stick up for Brad, and she wouldn't say 'shit' if she had a mouthful of it."

George shook his head. "Any wonder he's a delinquent? By the way, Brad said he's going to get me. Whatever that means."

O'Hara handed George his empty can and started for the door. "One thing about Brad. I'll bet he tries."

At 5:30 the next morning George threw on his gardening clothes and walked to the fenced-in vegetable garden with his hoe and plastic basket hoping to find some ripe tomatoes. Something was amiss. The gate was open and muddy footprints covered the mulched path. Upon entering he noticed some of his green beans had been trampled. He was livid. Even as he packed loose dirt around the stems to prop them into an upright position and watered them with the old sprinkling can, he knew they'd never make it.

From the beans, footprints traveled to the far end of the garden. Pain stabbed his gut as he tracked them to the tomato patch. He shook his head in disbelief. Every one of his plants, eighteen in all, had been pulled out by the roots and thrown into a pile. Tiny green globes still clung to the broken stems. Fallen green tomatoes lay on the ground smashed and oozing. His whole crop for the year was destroyed.

There was no hesitation. He knew exactly where to go. Despite the hour, he marched to the Coleman's and rang the bell. After a few seconds he pushed it again and kept his finger on it until he heard activity on the other side of the door. When it opened, he found himself facing the patriarch dressed in his boxer shorts and ribbed undershirt. He also wore the blurred look of someone startled out of a sound sleep.

George screamed at him. "Last night your son raided my garden and ripped up all my tomato plants."

The man blinked a few times.

"I said your delinquent son destroyed my garden, and if I get my hands on him I'll kill him."

Now more alert, Coleman took a step toward George and yelled, "Old man, you touch my kid, and I'll ream you a new asshole." The effort triggered a spasm of coughing. He spat a gob of mucus past George into the spirea. "Get out of here."

George didn't back down. "Then you better keep that little punk out of my yard, or you'll get him back on a stretcher." George started down the steps. At the bottom he turned and said, "I'm calling the police."

"Go ahead. I'll say Brad was home all night.

Never left his room."

George hadn't considered proof. "You and I both know he did it."

Coleman sneered. "That's what you say, old man."

As he was walking home, he continued to burn. He loved his fresh ripe tomatoes, and so did the neighbors he supplied. But his predicament went far beyond the loss. He needed to punish the kid for his vandalism, but how? He felt helpless, frustrated and angry all at the same time. Worst of all, he knew the brazen little bastard would return, and he wasn't ready for him.

After breakfast, while he napped on the porch his dreams were filled with elaborate plots for revenge. When he awoke, he had a plan. Creaking to his feet, he headed to the bedroom hall, pulled down the attic stairs and slowly hauled himself up the narrow treads. It only took a moment to find the object of his search exactly where he'd stashed it a few years before. He tucked it under his arm, backed down the stairway and returned to the porch.

The deer rifle and scope were in mint condition despite the years of disuse. For George, the fun went out of deer hunting when Charlie Nevin, his hunting partner, died suddenly. Even before that his arthritic knee made climbing into the tree blind and sitting in the cold so painful he'd intended to quit anyway. When Charlie died, he saw no point in breaking in a new partner.

Sitting on the porch he polished the stock and cleaned the barrel with an old towel. His exhilaration surprised him. The gun felt good in his hands. Shouldering the weapon, he peered through the sight until the cross hairs zeroed in on a large black crow cawing at the top of one of the silver maples. He squeezed the trigger and listened for the click. He chuckled. If the rifle had fired, and he'd hit the bird, there wouldn't be anything left but a few feathers. Instead, it was still cawing. It had little appreciation for its continued existence, or that only the absence of a cartridge in the chamber had spared its demise. George was now ready for Brad Coleman.

That night George peered out the window until darkness enveloped the garden. He turned off the lights as if he were going to bed and slipped out to the porch. With no moon and a backdrop of tall trees, the blackness was total. He took a seat and waited.

He knew Brad would be coming, if not tonight, then some night soon. He stroked the rifle. His heart accelerated in anticipation. Periodically, he placed the gun to his shoulder, squinted through the night scope and scanned the garden. In the infrared world of reddish light, every detail was clear.

Ten o'clock.

Eleven.

Eleven-thirty. Then he heard a sound. He placed the rifle to his shoulder and watched. It was the destroyer. George's hands tensed on the rifle as he saw him enter the garden. George rose. His voice pierced the night air.

"I know that's you, Coleman, and I've got you in the sight of my deer rifle. I'll count to three before I fire." The boy tried to lie low. "Don't squat behind the fence. By the time I stop shooting you'll look like a Swiss cheese. But I'll give you more of a chance than you gave my tomatoes. I'll count to three before I shoot. Run, you little shit."

The kid stood up. "One!"

Brad sprang from the garden and turned toward his house.

"Two!" By the time George said, "Three," the kid had cleared George's yard and made it behind O'Hara's house. George was ecstatic. He dropped the rifle to his side and headed into the house laughing.

For the next few nights, George waited for Brad's return. He never showed.

On the weekend when he and O'Hara were having

their beer, George told him the whole story. "God, I wish I'd seen him running away. You really bluffed him."

"Who was bluffing? He was gone before I hit three."

"You're kidding, aren't you?"

"Maybe. But he did kill my tomatoes. An eye for an eye. As my attorney, I want you to know I'm not done yet. This time I'm going after the father."

O'Hara raised an eyebrow, "You're going to shoot him?"

"Better than that."

"What could be better than that?"

"Just what I'd expect from a lawyer. You won't do a thing to bridle the menace. Then you encourage me to shoot his father." George grinned. "You must be hard up for defense work."

That afternoon George phoned his farmer friend, Tom Wembley. "Tom, do your pigs still make manure?"

"More regularly than me."

"Good. I need a ton of hog manure, the riper the better. Delivered."

The voice on the other end said, "That'll be quite a pile, George. Are you sure you want that much?"

"It's not for me. Load up your largest dump truck and deliver it to 3124 Fremont. That's three houses east of me."

"Whose house is that?"

"You don't want to know. It's a good-neighbor gift."

"I see! And I suppose you want this good neighbor to receive his *gift* in the wee small hours?"

"You got it. Dump it on the driveway."

"You old scamp. This will cost you."

"In a war, money's no object."

"Thursday night okay? Betty is staying at her sister's. It's easier for me to handle covert operations when

159

she's gone."

"Thanks, Tom. You're a good friend." He hung up the phone and headed for the porch. Anticipation rippled his insides. When he reached his destination, he fell back onto the chaise.

While he dozed, he dreamt of old man Coleman. It's the Friday morning after. George sees him opening his garage door wearing only his undershorts and gut stretched undershirt. Coleman stares at the pungent pile. He scratches his head. Once the dunderhead assimilates what's happened, he's fuming. He steams toward George's and pounds on the door. George lets him wear out his fist before opening it. Coleman looks ridiculous standing on the stoop in his underwear. The hairy oaf screams obscenities and accuses him of dumping the manure.

"I don't have any idea what you're talking about."

Coleman's bloated face is purple. He screams, "I know you did it, old man."

Before slamming the door in the man's face, George laughs. "That's what you say, Coleman."

On Friday morning after a hurried breakfast, George made out a grocery list and headed for the store in his car. He couldn't wait to see Mt. Manure. Easing up to the Coleman's, his heart fluttered. A six-foot high volcanic cone of fresh manure with a twenty-foot diameter base covered the concrete driveway. Tire tracks from the garage to the street bisected the outer edge of one side. Coleman must have headed to work without dealing with the mess. Rolling down the window George inhaled a long draft of barnyard air. The stink made his eyes water.

That evening about five-thirty, instead of driving, George decided to walk to Catherine's for dinner. Hobbling past the Coleman's house, he watched Brad and his father, wearing swimmer's nose plugs, shovel manure into wheelbarrows and transport it to various spots around their yard. Their efforts hardly dented the pile. Even when his lawn had been transformed into a barnyard, Coleman would still have to pay someone to haul the rest away.

He lingered hoping his appearance would help old man Coleman put two and two together and acknowledge his revenge. Maybe even confront him. When Coleman stopped shoveling to mop his forehead, George's pulse raced in expectation. Coleman glanced at him.

George stared back defiantly.

Coleman picked up his shovel and returned to his task.

CHAPTER FIFTEEN

COMPOSTING

In late August when George came in from harvesting his pole beans, there was a message on his answering machine. The machine was a recent acquisition. "Why would I need one of those contraptions?" he'd said to Jill whose constant harping was the primary stimulus for his purchasing the thing in the first place. "I'm never gone."

"You're gone a lot. If you're not in your garden, you're out flitting around with Catherine. I can never find you." The message on the machine proved her point. Her voice said to call her cell phone right away, which irritated him. She was rich as the Kennedys, and he was stuck paying for a long distance call. If she hadn't sounded distressed, he'd have waited for her to call him back.

"Jill Palmer," she answered in her usual clipped business-like way.

"It's your father. What's up?"

She began sobbing. "Oh, Daddy, the most terrible thing has happened."

"You lost your job?"

She continued crying.

"You weren't in an accident were you?" Finally his patience gave out. "I'm an old man, Jill. What in hell is the problem?"

"Stewart died last night."

"Oh, no!" The force of her announcement sent him reeling. "I can't believe it. What happened?"

"He's been sick for a long time with that dreadful hereditary disease." She spoke through her sniffles. "It finally got the best of him."

"What hereditary disease? I didn't know Stewart was sick."

"Of course you did."

"I did not."

Jill began sobbing. "All I know is one minute I'm married to the most loyal, considerate and loving husband any woman could have. The next he's gone. I need you with me, Daddy. You and Anne are all I have now."

"I'll call the airlines and get a flight," he said. "I may have to stay with you a few extra days. The fare's cheaper if I stay over a Saturday night."

She groaned. "Oh, Daddy! I already bought your ticket. You can go home whenever you wish. Can you make a one-fifteen flight today?"

"I'll try."

"Good. Carlos will pick you up at O'Hare." Through tears she said, "I love you, Daddy."

After hanging up, George drove to Catherine's to cancel his dinner date for that evening. After expressing her sympathy, she asked, "Wasn't he a young man?"

"Probably Jill's age, around forty-five or so. They were married for at least twenty years."

"What did he die from? A sudden heart attack?"

"Jill said he had some hereditary disease. I never knew a thing about it. I'm not surprised, though. I never had a feel for Stewart. When he and I were together, I struggled to carry on a conversation with him. I never knew his interests or pet peeves, and I'm sure he never knew mine. We could be in a room together for hours and never speak. The only time he showed a spark of life was when Jill was present, and I usually acted like a suitor vying for her hand. I made it awkward for Jill. She had to handle the situation with kid gloves."

George sat down on the couch and stretched out his leg. Catherine sat next to him and put her arm around his neck.

"I shouldn't say this about the dead, but I never cared much for Stewart. I always wished my daughter had married someone else." He patted Catherine's hand. "I want to be a comfort to Jill, so I need your help. How do I keep my feelings from getting in the way?"

"Just treat her like a woman who's lost someone she loved. Your feelings for him aren't part of the equation. Anyway, she's your daughter. She's probably always known how you felt."

He brightened a bit and said, "You're right. I'll just focus on Jill and try to be useful."

"Good. She needs her father, George. You'll know what to do when you see her."

He kissed Catherine. "Too bad you can't come along to guide me."

"I wish I could."

When he arrived at O'Hare, Carlos was waiting for him at the gate. He took George's carry-on luggage and guided him toward the baggage claim area. "How's my daughter doing, Carlos?"

"She called me this morning at seven and told me her husband died and not to pick her up for work until noon. Does that answer your question?"

"Unbelievable. I don't know why she drives herself so hard. When her mother died, I was totally out of commission for weeks, and her death was expected."

"If you ask me, Mrs. Palmer's in shock. She acted like she was in a trance."

The limousine ride gave George time to reflect. Though he had been less than enthusiastic about Jill marrying Stewart, he'd never mentioned anything to either Jill or Grace about his concerns. He assumed because Grace was silent on the subject she felt as he did. Even with Jill's long history of dating men that didn't meet his standards, Stewart seemed least suitable of all. Dull and unambitious, he was an auditor for an accounting firm until he quit working ten years ago to become Jill's househusband. He was a dimmer on Jill's shining light. From the beginning, a zero. At times acerbic. At times blah. In George's eyes, he was an actor portraying one of the walking dead.

Now that Stewart was gone he wondered about the exact depth of their relationship. Since he'd often wished she'd leave the guy, he couldn't imagine Jill loving him. Still, outwardly she seemed to care a great deal about Stewart, so George couldn't decide if her solicitous behavior was a facade or not. Was it a cover-up to preserve a merely comfortable relationship she was unwilling or unable to end, or did she actually have deep feelings for him? George suspected the former but couldn't rule out the latter either.

He looked out the tinted window at the freeway traffic slowing around them. Soon they'd be picking up Jill. He cleared his mind so he could focus all of his attention on her immediate needs. He fretted. What could he say to comfort her? He recalled Catherine's words. "You'll know what to do." At the time she spoke them, he was sure he'd be able to handle the situation. Now he wasn't so sure.

He watched Jill walk down the sidewalk toward the limo. Her normal pert, energetic stride seemed leaden. "My God, she looks miserable," he said out loud.

Carlos opened the car door, and she collapsed onto the leather seat.

"Hi, Daddy," she said and immediately burst into tears.

Sliding toward her, he gently wrapped her in his arms and pulled her limp body to him. Over and over he rocked her and whispered, "I'm so sorry, honey."

He continued to hold her as the limo slowly pulled away from the curb and snaked its way through the crowded streets to the even more jammed Lake Shore Drive. They crept past the bustling beaches and sidewalks loaded with joggers and in-line skaters, and he continued to cradle her.

Finally she slipped from of his grasp and rummaged through her purse for a tissue. She dabbed at her eyes. "Was the flight smooth?"

"How did he die?"

"The death certificate will say cancer. Of course, he really died from that ghastly M.E.N. disease he inherited from his father. When we were married, we knew the prognosis. Even so, it still doesn't seem fair."

"M.E.N.?"

"Multiple Endocrine Neoplasia. The disease that killed his father."

"His father died before you were married. Your mother told me he had cancer. She never said a word about Stewart having a hereditary disease."

"I told Mom all about it...how we wouldn't be having children because Stewart wanted the disease to end with him. His disease was no surprise. She never told you?"

"She never said a word about it."

He fell silent, too hurt to share his thoughts with

Jill. Why would Grace hold back on him? Did she think he'd forbid the marriage? Sure, she knew he didn't care for Stewart, but she should have known him well enough to know he'd try to change his attitude toward Stewart if he'd known about his disease? He'd willingly do that for Jill. Instead, she'd let him imagine all sorts of negative thoughts about the two of them. It was a cruel act to let him assume they weren't having children because Jill was selfish and self-absorbed with her career, or that they were too caught up with a flashy lifestyle to bother with a family.

"I wonder what other secrets she took to her grave?" George said aloud. "I can't believe it. All these years, letting me wonder . . . ."

"Like, why aren't we having children?"

"Exactly."

Jill patted his hand.

George's face reddened. "I'm embarrassed. I'm supposed to be doing the consoling here." He placed his arm around her shoulder and began caressing the outside of her arm.

"You are, Daddy. Just being here with me. You're the most genuine person I've ever known. You may not say the right thing all the time but the words you utter match the intent in your heart. That's what I admired about Stewart. He never said anything for effect. Many times he'd remain silent rather than say something hurtful."

"Is that why he was usually quiet around me?"

She paused. "Once in a while, I suppose. You weren't exactly his cup of tea. But he knew I loved you, and he wasn't going to say or do something that would interfere with our relationship." She squeezed his hand. "When you were here over Thanksgiving, he was just starting chemotherapy. Stewart asked me not to tell you because it would spoil your visit. He wanted us to have a good time. Besides, he was feeling so sick he preferred being alone."

167

She began crying again. "He only took those awful drugs to appease me. He knew the inevitable. I just wasn't willing to have him give up yet. That was my big mistake."

George smoothed her hair. "I wouldn't let your mother give up, either. I've regretted it ever since."

Jill took his hand and sandwiched it with her other. "We have a lot in common, don't we Daddy?"

"Yes, except for one important difference. You're young, and I'm not. This is terrible for you, but once you get past Stewart's death you have your whole life ahead of you. I don't have as much to look forward to."

"What about Catherine?"

He smiled. "I do look forward to her."

They rode on in silence. As the traffic thinned, the vehicle picked up speed. When it turned onto the side street leading to the condo, Jill kissed her father on the cheek.

"It was selfish of me to let Thanksgiving go by without telling you Stewart was in a critical stage. Maybe you could have made some peace with him."

"I would have tried."

"I know, and I'm sorry."

He shook his head. "Why didn't your mother tell me about his disease?"

"Only she knows, Daddy."

About eight that night Carlos picked Anne up at O'Hare and dropped her off at the Condo. When Jill opened the door they fell into each other's arms and cried.

Later, after Anne freshened up and Jill changed out of her business clothes, she called a cab and the three of them left for a late pasta dinner a Nino's. Although George had napped in the late afternoon, he was still exhausted. All through dinner, he could barely keep awake. When Jill and Anne began sharing female things, he gave up trying and let his eyes close. He had hoped to hear them unveil some private pieces of their lives. For nostalgia's sake, he wanted to hear them mouth Grace's teachings or hear his own words echo from the distant past. These were splendid, brilliant women. He wanted to be thrilled by their insights. Instead, as he dozed off, he heard them discussing appropriate clothing for Stewart's services.

Out of the haze he heard Jill say, "You always knew about Stewart's disease, didn't you Anne?"

"Of course. Mom told me before you were married."

"Daddy says he never knew."

"That's strange."

George opened his eyes. "It's worse than strange. It's the meanest thing your mother ever did."

The next few days passed quickly. Jill handled all of the arrangements for the memorial service. Stewart had requested his body be cremated, so there wasn't a chance his bad genes could inflict pain on another living soul. The logic was nonsense, Jill said, but the symbolism was fitting. She honored his wish.

The service was preceded by a visitation and was well attended. Bret had flown in the night before and stood with Jill, Anne and George. They greeted a few of Jill and Stewart's social friends and a horde of people from her company. Jill was on automatic pilot, greeting everyone, accepting their hugs and introducing them by name to the family.

George's mind wandered as he shook the hands and immediately forgot the names of the people moving through the line. He tried to remember Grace's visitation. Had he gone through this torture? Probably, but he was damned if he could remember. His knee was throbbing, and his brain wasn't functioning. He was about to tell Anne he was going to sit down and rest awhile when a recognizable face in a light blue dress took his hand. "How are you holding up, George?"

"Catherine! What are you doing here?"

169

"Gert released me for the day. I thought you could use some support."

"Oh, I can, I can. After the service, I'll need even more." He turned to the others. Jill was in full embrace with a large, purple chiffon clad matron so he turned to Anne and Bret. "This is my friend, Catherine. She came all the way from Carlisle to be with me . . . us."

Anne put her arms around Catherine and said, "I've been wanting to meet you ever since Dad first told me about you at Christmas. I'm so glad you came. Thank you."

"I wasn't sure it was proper for me to come, but my daughter, who is totally improper, insisted."

"Being compassionate has little to do with propriety."

"That's profound," George said. "Where did you hear that?"

"From you, Dad. When I was a teenager."

"That's one pearl of mine I'm really glad you remembered."

After George introduced Catherine to Bret, George grabbed her hand and dragged her over to Jill. Catherine spoke her condolences and hugged Jill before the surging line moved her out of the way.

George said, "What a mob. I suppose I should get back in line and do my bit."

"And I should go into the chapel and let you do it."

When the memorial service ended, George took Jill's arm and guided her up the aisle. Bret and Anne followed. They stopped in the foyer so Jill could slip off to a mirror and do a makeover on her tear-stained face. George went to the men's room.

When he reentered the foyer, he caught sight of Catherine, Bret and Anne standing in a tight circle, talking. Anne waved. "Get over here, Dad. Catherine is going back to her hotel."

George grabbed her arm. "You're not going back to Carlisle tonight?"

"No, first thing in the morning. I just wanted to say goodbye before I left."

Anne said, "You can't go. If Jill feels like it, Bret and I are taking Dad and her to dinner. We'd love to have you come with us."

"I wouldn't want to intrude, but I'd enjoy getting to know you better." She smiled at George. "That is if George agrees."

"He doesn't have anything to say about it," Bret said.

"Of course I want you to come." George stepped toward Catherine, intending to kiss her. She gently fended him off by placing her hands against his chest.

"It's okay. These two have seen kissing before."

"But they haven't seen you kiss me."

When Jill returned, Anne asked if she'd like to go for some dinner. "Can we go back to the condo for awhile and then decide? I'm wrung out."

"Of course. But we all have to eat something."

"Then I'd rather go out and be with all of you than be home alone."

"We're certainly not going to leave you alone," Bret said. "If you don't want to go out, we'll carry-in."

Anne grinned. "It's times like these I wish I'd learned to cook."

"Me, too," Jill said.

George shook his head. "Let's go back to the condo, and I'll cook."

"I think I've just found the strength to go out," Jill groaned.

***

At the restaurant, they began dinner by holding

171

hands and saying a prayer for Stewart. Then they prayed for Jill. She sobbed through all of it, but afterwards said she felt much better. "Lighter somehow. More at peace."

Throughout the dinner, with the exception of Anne who continually attempted to draw her out, Catherine stayed on the fringes of the conversation, content to be a smiling observer. As the flow of wine added decibels to the get-together, Bret asked George, "How did you and Catherine meet?"

"Gert, her daughter, and I made a trade. Gert got a cabbage. I got Catherine."

Catherine's face turned red. "He's a great kidder. The truth is we met at my daughter's house. George was returning fifty cents for the cabbage he sold her a few weeks before."

"Don't tell me you've taken over our vegetable route?" Jill asked.

"A man's got to make a buck any way he can."

"He pulls his little wagon . . ." Catherine began.

"With the yellow wheels?"

"Yes, and gives away his produce. He's the most popular person on the street."

Sometime before dessert, Anne and Bret began talking about their recent trip to China, and how they hoped they'd be going again in the next month or so. George tuned them out because they were always off somewhere and their endless travelogues bored him. He excused himself to find the restroom. When he returned, they were still on the same subject. Fortunately, before he was forced to listen the waiter showed up with the bill.

They all piled into Bret's rented SUV and drove to Catherine's hotel. "I can call my driver and have him take you to the airport in the morning," Jill told her. "It's no trouble."

"That's very nice, Jill, but I'd feel more comfortable taking a cab."

"When you come with Daddy the next time, then."

At the hotel, Catherine thanked Anne and Bret for dinner and hugged Jill. When George started to follow her to the door, she raised her hand and stopped him. "Stay with your family, George. We'll get together when you're back home." She kissed him on the cheek.

Driving back to the condo, Bret said, "That's one fine lady."

When Jill and Anne voiced their agreement, George didn't comment. He was watching the passing lights through the window and smiling.

George, Anne and Bret remained with Jill a few days longer. When Saturday morning dawned, and Anne and Bret flew home and Jill returned to work, he realized there wasn't much reason for his being there. Plus, Carlisle was beckoning. A week was a long time to leave a garden in the growing season. Weeds would have to be dug and lettuce picked before it bolted. Plus, he missed Catherine.

That evening as they dined in on deli sandwiches, he asked Jill, "If I fly home tomorrow morning, will you be okay?"

"I'll be fine, Daddy. I always knew I'd have to deal with Stewart's death. I had twenty years to get used to the idea. Some days will be tough, I'm sure. But, I have a few close friends, more work than I can handle to keep my mind occupied, and I can always call my father."

"From the time I retired until your mother's death, all I did was garden and watch her waste away. When she died in January, it was freezing, and I couldn't hide in my garden. I needed something to distract me so I thought about getting a job at McDonald's."

"You told me that before, Daddy."

"Still, I hope you realize there's more to life than your work. I set a poor example by missing a large portion of your childhood wrapping myself up in work. Anne's too. I worry about your job being an addiction." He

173

rubbed his hand on the sleeve of her blouse. "And that's my sermon for today."

"I hear you, Daddy. After I'm feeling better, I'll put my mind to delegating more and developing some new interests away from my job. At least I'll try."

After she cleared the table, Jill came up behind him, placed her arms around his neck, and kissed him on his bald spot. "Maybe I'll even take up cooking."

"A daughter that cooks. That would be novel."

The next morning as he was leaving she said, "I couldn't have survived this week without you, Daddy, and Anne and Bret, too, of course." Tears came to her eyes. "My family is so precious to me."

He kissed her and said, "It will take some time, but you're going to be just fine. The All-Powerful, All-Knowing Father decrees it."

Two-and-a-half hours before his flight, Jill called a cab. When the doorman notified her of its arrival, she told her father, "Keep your fingers crossed for Anne and Bret."

"Why?"

"Their China trip. They're matched up with a little girl. One of these days they'll get the word and bring her home. You'll be a grandfather."

George stared at her. "I don't know anything about it. Why doesn't my family tell me these things?"

She shook her head. "We talked about it at dinner the other night. Catherine knows all about it. You must have been dozing or in another world."

"Maybe the men's room."

"The cab's waiting." She pushed him toward the door and thrust a hundred dollar bill into his hand.

"What's this for?"

"I was going to say cab fare and prepayment for a lot of phone calls. Now I'm thinking it should go toward hearing aids."

He protested.

"Take it and go, Daddy. I love you."

"I love you more, even though you're part of the conspiracy that's always keeping secrets from me."

***

Just after Labor Day Anne called. "We just heard from the agency, Dad. Bret and I are going to China Sunday morning."

"That's nice. Have a good trip."

"Dad, pay attention! We talked about it at Jill's. Aren't you excited?"

"Why would I be excited? I'm not going to China."

"Oh, Dad, stop teasing me. You know perfectly well why we're going. We're adopting a little girl. I can't believe it's really happening!"

"Of course I'm kidding. Prospective grandfathers say any old dumb thing to mask their anticipation. When do you get back?"

"If all goes well, two weeks from Friday."

"I have nothing better to do that Saturday than hold my new granddaughter . . . and her mother. Have Martha fix lunch. Catherine and I will be taking a little drive."

CHAPTER SIXTEEN

SPROUT

While Anne and Bret were off to China, Carlisle experienced its first killing frost. Although George, with help from the TV weatherperson, had anticipated it and picked some immature sweet peppers and cucumbers and a peck of green tomatoes he hoped would ripen in brown paper sacks, the rest of the garden was decimated. Bean plants drooped and hills of zucchini lay in grotesque death poses. In a few weeks all would be brown, and he would be carting off the dead vines and plants to the compost pile.

The one exception was the late cabbage. It was hardy to frost and the green globes stood sentinel over the plant cemetery. Today he'd picked three, one for Mary Alexander, one for O'Hara and one for Gert. George liked giving cabbage away because, as long as he had other vegetables to eat, he shunned the stuff.

Except when he gardened and knew he was helpless

to Mother Nature's onslaught, George saw no virtue in patience. He just observed his seventy-ninth birthday for heaven's sake. Waiting for anything important was a luxury he couldn't afford. Thus he was becoming crankier and crankier each day waiting to hear from Anne. On October fourth, after three weeks of agonizing anticipation, her call finally came.

"Bret and I are back from China, Dad. You have a beautiful new granddaughter."

"What took you so long? I could have died and never seen her." He placed the phone on the table, wiped his eyes and blew his nose. When he picked up the phone again, he said, "Sorry, a little congestion. Is everyone well?"

"Bret and I are exhausted."

"I meant my granddaughter. I assume she's fine?"

"She's fine Dad."

"Good. I've really been on edge waiting for you to return. By the way, I know you told me, but I forgot her name."

"It was Kwai Le, but we changed it to Lily."

"Kwai Le Lambert. Lily Lambert. I think I like Lily better."

"You'll love her, Dad. She's the sweetest little thing, with jet-black hair and a heart-shaped face as perfect as an open flower. The name Lily seemed just right for her. Guess what her middle-name is?"

"George?"

"No, silly. It's Grace."

"Oh!" he said. "That gives me goose-bumps. If only your mother were alive."

"She'd be pleased, wouldn't she?"

"Thrilled. So, when can I see my Lily?"

"Bret and I are really messed up from the jet-lag. Could you give us a day or two to get adjusted? How about Tuesday?"

"Tuesday's fine. Now don't fuss over us. Catherine and I won't stay long. We'll just hold Lily and leave."

"Ha! Holding her is like eating potato chips. You can't eat just one. You'll get your mitts on her, and I'll never get rid of you. I'll have Martha prepare a nice lunch."

After he cradled the phone, he had a sudden chill. Ever since Anne told him they were adopting a Chinese child, he'd worried about her acceptance. Living in a small mid-western town, George's exposure to Asians was limited, but he remembered how the Japanese were treated in California during the war. He didn't want his granddaughter exposed to any lingering prejudice.

***

Late Tuesday morning when he and Catherine arrived, Anne ushered them into the study. After Martha finished serving coffee, George scanned the room.

"Where's Lily?"

"She's sleeping. She's not on much of a schedule, yet."

"Can we peek at her?" Catherine asked.

"Sure, she's upstairs in our bedroom. Can your bum knee handle it, Dad?"

He scowled at her. "What bum knee?"

Standing over Lily's crib, Anne and Catherine grinned maternally.

George studied her and whispered, "She's so small."

Anne placed a finger to her lips and motioned them from the room. They returned to the study. Catherine sat on the couch with Anne while George sat across from them on a leather recliner. Once they were settled, Anne began telling them about the trip and the details of the adoption.

"We flew to Hong Kong and were met by two young women from the International Social Services. They would be our guides and interpreters the whole time we were in China. They were invaluable. After two days of R&R in Hong Kong, they led us to Guangzhou where all of the foreign adoptions take place. Guangzhou is a big city, about six million people, and the capital of Guangdong, which is China's most prosperous province. It was once called Canton, like in Cantonese food."

"I'll bet you were excited," Catherine said. "Did they take you right to the orphanage so you could see Lily?"

"Oh, no," Anne said. "We checked into a posh hotel on the Pearl River and toured the city while we waited for the ministry to contact us. Three days later we were given an appointment to complete the final paperwork. Up until then, we only knew we were matched with a healthy year-old little girl. We knew her Chinese name, and we'd been sent a grainy black and white picture of her.

"The Chinese venerate age so they like adoptive parents to be older. In the US, forty is too old to adopt a first child. In China, it's just right." Anne laughed. "You'll have to excuse me. I'm so delirious my mind races in every direction at once."

George pulled at the handle of the recliner footrest and raised his feet to ease the pain in his knee. Keeping his eyes on Anne as she excitedly related her experiences, he smiled to himself. Instead of a life dedicated to wasting time on life's non-essentials, his younger daughter was turning out exactly like he hoped. Look at her. All radiant and babbling like a trout stream. Wasn't he wise? As he'd always predicted, once she had kids, Anne would be a whole lot happier. And, of course, so would he if he could ever get her to shut up long enough so he could meet his granddaughter.

George coughed to get Anne's attention.

She ignored him. "When we met with the Mandarin-bearded ministry official, he helped us complete the final paperwork. Then he said, 'Many female babies are left to die. Yours was placed on the doorstep of an orphanage in a cardboard box.'

"Later after explaining the final procedures and telling us about the orphanage, he asked, 'Are you satisfied with your match?'

"In unison, Bret and I replied, 'Yes!'

"He smiled, wished us well and left the room.

"Shortly after the official left, a sinister looking little man gestured for us to follow him. We hesitated. He became extremely agitated which made us even more unsettled. We weren't too excited about following some crazy man in a strange country. Fortunately, one of our guides showed up and explained the man was driving us to the orphanage.

"Within minutes after our arrival, a caretaker came tap-tapping down the hallway carrying our child. Lily looked exactly like her picture, only she was far more petite than I expected. In her high-pitched voice, the caretaker said something in Chinese.

"I looked at our interpreter, who said, 'She wants to know if you wish to hold your little girl.'

"I was so overcome with emotion I began crying. I held up a finger for her to wait a second until I could compose myself. Finally, I held out my arms. When she handed Lily to me, I thought all of the air would go out of my lungs. I said quietly, 'Lily, Mamma's here,' and held her tightly to me.

"She pulled away to look at my face. Her eyes moved back and forth, taking in this person who looked and sounded so strange. Then I handed her to Bret. She fussed so much he handed her back to me.

"That evening after spending the remainder of the

day chasing around the city getting papers notarized, we ate at a restaurant in the hotel. All through dinner Lily sat quietly on my lap eyeing Bret and me. As we were about to leave, she said the first word we'd ever heard her say, *'amma'* mama in Cantonese."

George began tearing.

Anne smiled at him. "I always knew you were an old softy, Dad."

Catherine put her hand on his. "He is, isn't he?"

"You women! You don't even know the difference between crying and watery eyes."

"I think we do, George," Catherine said.

"Since the officials wanted us to get used to each other before leaving, we spent an extra week relaxing and splashing in the hotel pool. During this time we found out Lily not only could walk, but she babbled incessantly and sang tuneless songs. In preparation for her adoption, someone had taught her *amma* and *baba dada*. We also learned before she went to sleep, she'd say something over and over that sounded like, *'goya, goya, goya'*. When we asked our interpreter about it, she chuckled, and told us it meant *good girl*, a phrase the caretakers probably used at bedtime in the orphanage.

"That night when she went to bed we said, *'goya, goya.'* She looked up at us and giggled."

"What a wonderful revelation," Catherine said.

"And so here you are," George said impatiently.

Anne said, "Getting out of China and flying all that way with a child was a nightmare. But, you're right. We're here, and I've been rattling on long enough. Let's go upstairs and see if Lily's awake. Sometimes she'll lie in her crib with her eyes wide open and not make a peep. I can't tell from the monitor if she's asleep or awake. If she's still sleeping, we'll have some lunch and play with her later."

George watched as Anne and Catherine climbed the

spiral staircase. When they returned empty-handed, George said, "She can't still be asleep. Doesn't she know her grandfather is waiting to meet her?"

Anne said, "She's worth the wait, Dad."

She ushered them into the dining room and seated them. After filling their glasses with ice tea from a pitcher placed on the sideboard, she headed for the kitchen to tell Martha to serve lunch. Upon her return, she plopped down at the end of the table between George and Catherine.

Martha entered carrying a tray with three luncheon plates each holding a chicken-salad sandwich cut into quarters. The sandwiches surrounded a handful of lattice-work potato chips and a dainty fruit-cup filled with apples, peaches and grapes. "It's beautiful, Martha," Anne said.

"It certainly is," Catherine added.

George winked at Martha. "I'm looking for a good wife that cooks. Are you interested?"

Martha nodded.

"You're too old for Martha, Dad."

"Hey!" Catherine entered the fray. "Does that mean I'm some oldster?"

"Oops!" Anne said.

George said, "I can answer that."

Catherine glared at him.

"Sorry, Martha," George said. "Offer rescinded. I'm only allowed to play with girls my own age."

While they ate lunch, Anne continued talking about the adoption.

"All of Lily's caretakers were female. In fact, I don't remember seeing any men at the orphanage. Consequently, Lily may be a bit shy with you, Dad. She was nervous with Bret at first."

While they were finishing lunch, rustling sounds came over the monitor.

"That's Lily." George stuffed the remainder of an almond cookie into his mouth. "Can I get her?"

"I don't think that would be wise. You may scare her."

"How could Lovable George scare anyone?"

Anne tried a different approach. "When was the last time you changed a dirty diaper, Dad?"

He held his nose. "You get her. We'll wait. What's a few more minutes?"

Taking the plate of cookies, he followed Catherine into the study.

While he waited, George drummed his fingers on the arm of the chair. His foot twitched. Catherine was saying something, but he had no idea what. He was trying to remember if he was this excited when either of his children were born. Despite all the risks of childbirth he concluded that he was a lot more blasé about becoming a father. It was no big deal. A man got married and spawned a few kids. Becoming a grandfather was far more nerve-wracking, especially when he'd given up all hope of ever becoming one.

He looked over at Catherine. She was smiling at him. "What?" he said. "Did you say something?"

"Nothing important. Anyway, I wouldn't want to jar you out of your reverie."

Anne stepped into the room holding her daughter. She'd dressed her in a bright red dress, tights and white high-top shoes. Lily surveyed the smiling strangers before clutching her mother's neck with both arms and hands.

Anne said softly, "Lily, this is your Grandpa and his friend Catherine. They've come all the way from Carlisle, Ohio to see you." She buried her face in Anne's neck. Anne kissed her and turned her so George and Catherine could see her face. Lily scrunched her eyes shut.

"She's still sleepy," Anne said as she bent down and stood Lily on her feet.

She clung to her mother's leg.

George reached out his arms. "Come see your

Grandpa, Lily."

She moved behind her mother. Anne said, "Give her some time to get used to you."

"Can't wait any longer." George took a cookie from the plate and waved it at his granddaughter. "Lily want a cookie?"

Anne protested. "Hey, that's bribery."

"Whatever works. I could drop dead before this kid warms up to her Grandpa." He stretched out his left hand. Lily's face brightened. Clinging to Anne's leg with one hand, she slowly stretched her other hand to George.

He beckoned her to him. She took a step toward him still gripping her mother's slacks. Motioning for her to take the goodie, he said, "Lily, here's your cookie."

While he held it out to her, George observed the tug-of-war playing out in her little head as she furtively glanced at the sweet cookie and searched her mother's face for permission. Finally, she took a step toward George.

Anne urged her on by saying, "Lily, go see Grandpa."

He moved from his chair to kneeling on one leg and waited. Finally, she came to him, grabbed the cookie from his hand and toddled back to Anne. She peeked at George as she nibbled on it.

"It's a start," George said. "Before the day's over she'll be sitting on my lap."

Later, as the day wore on, Lily stayed clear of him. By contrast, she quickly warmed up to Catherine as Anne predicted and eventually sat on her lap. George felt rejected, but kept his feelings from showing.

When they were about to leave for the trip back to Carlisle, George saw Catherine and Lily snuggling on the couch. Not willing to be left out, he sat down next to them and began touching Lily's little fingers and stroking her arm. Lily didn't shrink from his touch, but held fast to Catherine foiling any attempt to shift her to his lap. Over and over as he pointed at Catherine and then himself, he said in a soft voice, "Catherine loves Lily, and Grandpa loves Lily."

This latest tactic also failed, so George pulled the last arrow from his quiver. *"Goya, goya, goya."* he said.

Lily turned her head and stared at him. A smile spread across her face. Then she rolled from Catherine's lap onto his. Tears formed in his eyes as he held her gently to him. She pulled away and patted his face with her tiny hands.

"Bampa," she said.

***

A week later on a cool late October evening, he joined a get-together of six retired men from Kerr at one of Carlisle's blue-collar bars. George had a standing invitation to join the old geezers for a sandwich and beer, but since he'd been squiring Catherine his attendance had slipped. He preferred her gentle companionship to rehashing the past with them. Tonight, he had a purpose. He wanted to fill them in about Stewart's death, give them a Catherine update and tell them about Lily.

He sipped on his beer and waited for a lull in the conversation. When one occurred, he grabbed the spotlight. "My younger daughter, Anne, just returned from China where she adopted a little girl."

A tough old codger who'd been the head of maintenance at Kerr and was known as Cement Head Hamilton because he'd lived through a bullet in the head in World war II, said, "Why would anyone want one of those slant-eyed bastards? During the war we shot at them for target practice."

A searing pain seized George's gut. He never cared much for the crusty SOB. Now he absolutely despised him. Rising from his seat, he yelled, "You're talking about my granddaughter, asshole."

"When I was fighting in Luzon, those little shits threw rocks at us. If they'd had guns, they would've shot us just like the rest of the yellow-bellies."

Whitey Kurowski tried to intervene. "You were fighting the Japanese, Hamilton. I'm sure some of the local Philippine kids got involved, but the enemy was Japan. Anyway, the Chinese were on our side."

"Japs, Philippinos, Chinks. They're all slant eyes. I can't look at one today without puking."

Kurowski said, "You must be throwing up all the time. The United States has millions of Asians."

"Shut up, Whitey. Anyway, the Chinese aren't on our side now. They're Commie's. I wouldn't want no Commie in my family."

George glared at the man. "Hell, your family doesn't even have humans. Just dogs for kicking and sheep for screwing!"

Now Hamilton was on his feet at the other end of the table. "You were never in the war, old man." He took a step toward George. "I'd love to beat the shit out of a draft-dodger."

In the back of his head, he heard Jake say, "Take him now, George. You can do it."

Pushing a chair aside, he raised his fists and started toward Cement Head, but the others clamored to their feet and formed a buffer.

Amused patrons turned to watch. A waitress came running with the bartender close behind. He said, "Gentlemen, we don't want any trouble here. If you don't settle down, you'll have to leave."

Everyone except Cement Head and George returned to their seats. While the bartender eyed them, the two men continued standing toe to toe glaring at each other. Finally, Hamilton sat down and said, "Sorry, we'll quiet down."

"It will be a great day when your big mouth shuts

for good, Hamilton," George said. "I'll come to your funeral just so I can piss on your grave."

George reached into his wallet, pulled out a fifty and slammed it onto the table. "I'm going home. Pay my tab and buy everyone a drink but Cement Head."

He grabbed his jacket, threw it over his arm and glowered at Hamilton one last time. Then he stomped away.

George couldn't wait to escape. In addition to the abject stupidity of the man, he was equally upset with himself for getting into a shouting match with him. But as long as he was barking at the idiot, he should have hammered him as well. He was fumbling with his car keys, when the picture of two geriatric specimens slugging it out toe-to-toe flashed before his eyes. He broke into laughter. If a bullet couldn't stop Cement Head, how could he?

He opened the door and muttered, "But how could a baby be a Communist, for heaven's sake?"

The next day George took Catherine to lunch at the Tower Deli. While they sipped cups of matzo ball soup and nibbled at their shared corn-beef sandwich, he told Catherine about the encounter. After chastising him for letting the man get under his skin, she said, "I understand your fears for Lily. But it's a different world now. Our generation is about gone and all that hatred is going to die with us. Today's young people don't have any feelings about World War ll. How could they? They weren't even born yet. She'll be accepted. You'll see."

CHAPTER SEVENTEEN

DEEP FURROWS

George peeked at the bill the waitress tucked under his coffee mug and told Catherine, "For a moment when I was upset with Cement Head last night, I actually saw myself as a young man again. Not only was the testosterone pumping through my veins to the point I was going to bop him, but the actions I was contemplating seemed perfectly normal. Why is it the passage of time doesn't alter our perception of ourselves?"

Catherine laughed. "I know what you mean. I still think I'm young and cute until I look in the mirror and see the effect gravity has had on my body and face. I'm just one big sag."

"You look good to me."

"You're going blind."

"Wrong. While a lot of my body parts don't work too well anymore, my eyes still do."

"Then I accept the compliment."

"And you know the best part of your looks? You don't look bionic.   Some women have had so much cosmetic surgery their eyes have a look of perpetual surprise. They have these tight little butts and firm breasts. It just ain't natural. Now you, Catherine, on the other hand have . . . ."

"Let's not go there, okay?"

George laughed. He reached across the table and took Catherine's hand. "Do you ever worry about how much time you have left?"

"Every day. Not that I dwell on it. I just can't escape thinking about it. When you're older, so many things remind you of death. An acquaintance dies of cancer. For a week after, I think every new pain might be a tumor I should have looked at because early detection could save my life. But, I'm too embarrassed to go to the doctor because I know deep down it's probably nothing. Then that pain disappears and is replaced by a new pain. Now I wonder if the new pain is the one that'll do me in. Like I said, I don't dwell on it, but I can't escape it either."

"I've been through what you're describing, but it was years ago. Truthfully, from the time Grace died until I met you, I rather hoped, or more accurately, didn't really care if I died. Now I think about dying all the time. Sometimes my thoughts take the form of gallows humor, but usually I struggle with a feeling of overwhelming sadness. The thought of not being with you just gets me down."

Catherine lifted his hand and kissed it. "That's the most romantic thing any man has ever said to me."

"Pretty unlikely source, huh?"

"Not at all, George. Not at all."

Leaving the deli and walking to the car, he said, "You know what scares me more than death?"

"Tell me."

189

"Having a stroke or losing my mind like the lady across the circle from my house. She's such a sweet old soul, but some of the time when I visit her, she's really out of it. Please make me a promise. If I get Alzheimer's like Mrs. McConnell I want you to shoot me or run me over with a car before I make you and my kids miserable."

"What if I'm the one with the disease? Will you do that for me?"

George clutched her arm and guided her into the open car door. "No. I'll visit you and bring you vegetables and hope you can still make chocolate chip cookies like Mrs. McConnell."

Although George had neglected his neighbor for years after Grace died, for the last fourteen months or so ever since his excursion with the wooden wagon full of cabbage, he'd religiously checked up on the poor soul. Not that gorging on the fresh-baked chocolate-chip delicacies she always gave him had anything to do with his neighborliness. He just felt better knowing she was all right. About once a week, he'd traipse across the cul-de-sac carrying a shopping bag full of whatever vegetables were available and make a trade for cookies. Each trip was a revelation because he never knew which Mrs. McConnell would be home.

About a month ago, when he climbed the stoop and peered through the screen door, the gnome-like creature was in her kitchen and most likely baking. He pounded on the door to announce his arrival.

"Mrs. McConnell. It's George."

"Whatever you're selling, I don't need any. Go away."

George paced the small patch of concrete before pounding again. No answer. He stared through the screen, and saw she hadn't moved. He shook his head. She was going to let him rot outside her door. Finally, in frustration he opened the screen. "Mrs. McConnell, I know you're busy, so I'm letting myself in."

There was still no response. He walked slowly down the hall and entered the kitchen. "Don't be startled, Mrs. McConnell. I'm bringing you some vegetables."

He placed the bag on the table. Seeing her witch-like, permanently stooped body sliding cookies from the oven reminded him of a fairy tale. As she shuffled past him, she peered at George, her face a blank screen.

She set the steaming tray on the counter and removed her oven-mitts. A confused half-smile crossed her lips.

"Hello. I'm somebody," she said with good humor. "Do I know you?"

"I'm George from across the circle. I brought you some vegetables." He pointed at the bag.

She studied it for a moment and peeked inside. "Well, aren't you nice. You need some of my chocolate-chip cookies."

George watched as she pulled a canister loaded with cookies from the counter. She took out two of them, opened another container, and removed several more. There were twenty or more identical vessels scattered around the room. Each, George presumed, was filled with cookies. After several additional openings and closings, a cookie pile formed in the middle of the table. She eyed the pile, and then started opening and closing drawers.

"You're looking for something. Can I help?"

She shook her head and continued searching. When her gaze landed on George's bag of vegetables, she said, "There it is," and hoisted it from the table. She carried it to the sink and rudely emptied the contents.

George cringed as his tomatoes and cucumbers mingled with her dirty dishes and baking utensils.

Returning to the table, she proceeded to fill the now empty bag. Then she proudly presented him with it.

They moved toward the door. As he was swinging

open the screen, she said, "I hope you like the cookies...uh...I'm sorry, I've forgotten your name."

"It's George. And I hope you like the vegetables."

"Vegetables? I love vegetables. Do you have some?"

George shrugged. "I put them in your sink."

"Really? I didn't see you do that." While he retreated down the walk, she called after him, "Come again. I'll make more cookies for you."

A week later, right after the delivery truck dropped off her groceries, George returned with another bag full of tomatoes, beans and two medium-sized zucchinis. When he knocked on the screen door, she tottered down the hall to let him in. Her housedress was covered by a pink checked apron speckled with flour. As he expected, she was baking. He followed her and the cookie scent to the kitchen where he jettisoned the bag on the table. She peered inside.

"Lovely. Tomatoes and squash. Oh, and some beans, too. You're so nice to me, George." As she brushed past, she gave him a little hug. "I'll bet you'd like a cookie? They're fresh baked."

"Of course, I would. That's why I'm here."

She beamed. As the spatula scraped hot cookies from the sheet, she transferred them to a plate and set them in front of him. She asked, "Would you like some coffee, George? I'm afraid all I have is instant."

He nodded and began to rise from his chair. "Would you like some help?"

She placed her hand firmly on his shoulder. "I'll do it. You eat."

He watched as she filled the teakettle, set it on the stove and turned on the gas burner. Slipping into a chair next to George, she took a cookie from the plate and started munching it.

"I see you're having one, Mrs. McConnell. I didn't

think you ever ate cookies."

"I seldom do. Just have them around for company--and the neighbor man."

George laughed, "You mean me?"

"You'll do."

George raised his head and sniffed. He smelled gas. Turning, he saw that no flame was showing beneath the kettle. Springing from his chair, he reached for the knob and turned off the burner. Then he hurried to the back door and opened it. When he returned to the table, he searched her face for some realization of the potential danger. There wasn't any. She just smiled and pushed the plate toward him.

"Mrs. McConnell, don't you realize we could have been blown to kingdom come with the gas on like that?"

She patted his arm. "Soon enough, George. Have another cookie."

"Does it always do that?"

"Does what always do what?"

"The pilot. It didn't work. Is it typical or rare for that to happen?"

"I usually light it with a match. I guess I forgot with you here."

He shook his head. "That's dangerous. I'm going to call the gas company and get it fixed."

She patted his arm, again. "There, there, George. Let's not let a little gas spoil our party. It will be fine."

Moving from the table she began foraging through a drawer until she found some wooden matches. She raised the box in triumph for George to see. Then she turned the burner knob and attempted to light a match. She failed several times before lighting one. "Now I'll boil that water for our coffee," she said as she stuck the match under the burner and the flame flashed across the range from under the pot.

"Oh, my God," George gasped.

"If you don't like the smell, George, take the cookies to the porch. When the coffee's done, I'll bring it out, and we'll have a nice talk."

He took the plate of cookies and settled into a dilapidated wicker armchair. Sharp cane ends jabbed at him from all directions. He moved to the couch. It was much the same, but by leaning forward he could avoid all but a few cruel stabs. The cookie plate lay within easy reach on the glass-covered wicker coffee table.

When Mrs. McConnell arrived with two steaming cups, she arranged them on the table and sat down next to George. He picked up his cup and sipped. He choked back a laugh.

He watched her take a taste. She exclaimed, "My, my! This coffee is a bit weak. I like mine stronger than this, don't you?"

I like mine with coffee, he thought. "It's fine, Mrs. McConnell. Next time use a little more coffee."

"You're exactly right, George. I'll do just that."

***

Their relationship had a long history, one that was more neighborly than close. Perhaps that was why he always thought of her as Mrs. McConnell, not Alice. When Grace was alive, the two women shared those things that housewives share, and men aren't privy to.

In 1964, he and his wife built the house across from her at the end of Fremont Street. As he recalled, Grace said Mrs. McConnell's son had been drafted out of college and subsequently killed in the Korean War.

After that, or maybe because of it, she and her husband became estranged. One evening, her husband came home from work, told her he'd accepted a promotion at GE, and left town without her or their teenage daughter. A few months later, after George and his family moved into their new home, the daughter was gone, too. Grace found out she'd left for California to do her "sixties" thing. From what George remembered, Mrs. McConnell and the daughter never had much contact thereafter.

When George turned fifty, Grace threw him a surprise birthday party. Along with many of their social friends and some of George's associates from work, she invited a few special neighbors–the Martin's from next door and Alice McConnell.

Prior to the big event, he'd been feeling morose. Fifty was ancient, not young like it seemed now. Looking back, his feelings most likely came from a combination of events--his daughters were thriving in the world without him, the corporate ladder he'd been climbing didn't reach to the next level and his football knee forced him to endure constant pain. Whatever the reason, his fiftieth birthday spawned a week-long depression.

After most of the guests had paid their respects and tried to raise his spirits with the traditional 'over the hill' black humor, George eased into a soft chair and began sipping his fourth Cabernet. As he brooded, Mrs. McConnell, who'd appeared a bit tipsy upon her arrival, joined him and began sharing the stored wisdom of her many years. Sitting on the wide arm of his chair, she leaned back and fell against him. As he moved to the far side to accommodate her bony structure, she slipped into the chair with him. They were stuck. Rather than try to extricate himself, he resigned himself to her presence.

Out of the corner of his eye, all he could see was her blue-gray hair and bright red lipstick. She began philosophizing. Until then, George hadn't remembered exchanging more than a few words with her. Now she was hell-bent on a full-blown dissertation. He chose to be gracious and listen, at least until Grace discovered his plight and rescued him.

"So, you're depressed, George," she slurred.

195

"Thash too bad." She let out a cackle and snuggled closer. "Well...get used to it. It doesn't get any better."

"This is supposed to make me feel good?"

"Why do you expect to feel good? Life is sheep dung."

"Mrs. McConnell!"

"When you're past sixty like me, birthday boy, you'll understand. You'll think fifty was a walk in the park."

Attempting to plant a kiss on his cheek, she banged her nose on his cheekbone. She tried again and succeeded in splashing lipstick all over his ear. Their laughing caused heads to turn. Thinking her audience needed an explanation, she said, "Just trying to make the old guy feel better."

George rolled his eyes.

She inched back onto the chair-arm and sat smiling at George. She patted his arm. "Feel better, George?"

George did feel better. A great deal better.

After the party and after she'd downed several additional bourbons, George walked her across the cul-de-sac to her home. The trip was memorable. Mrs. McConnell clung to his arm and boisterously sang "Happy Birthday" as they staggered to her house.

The next day a plate of chocolate chip cookies covered with tissue and tied with a red ribbon showed up at the door. A little card tucked inside read, "For the nice neighbor man. Happy Birthday and Thank You."

***

Whenever George visited her, Mrs. McConnell was in the kitchen. Baking cookies was the glue that held her gradually crumbling existence together. It also formed the basis of their friendship. George enjoyed her cookies and their "little talks." When she was lucid, her lapses amused him. When a serious breach caused her to treat him like an intruder out to do her harm, he worried about her future.

It was the last of September, a time when the heat of summer had given way to autumn. It ushered in Southern Ohio's finest weather. George crossed the street to drop off a small bag of pole beans and a few turnips.

When he rang the bell, she didn't answer. Assuming she was in the kitchen, and it might take a while for her to open the door, he paced the stoop. He rang again. Still no answer. His concern heightened as he stepped from the stoop and began walking around the house toward the back, glancing through the windows as he passed. He saw nothing. As he rounded the rear corner of the one story ranch, he came upon the porch. There he squinted through a crack in the closed jalousie and saw a form sprawled on the wicker couch. The pink apron identified the body as belonging to Mrs. McConnell. He opened the door and moved closer. She didn't appear to be breathing.

"Mrs. McConnell, are you all right?"

No movement. He poked at her gingerly with a finger, not wanting to startle her if she was sleeping, not wanting to know if she was dead. He shook her shoulder. Her eyes snapped open. The breath went out of him.

"Is that you, George?" Then indignantly, "What are you doing in my bedroom? You're not getting any ideas, are you?"

Keeping a straight face, he said, "You're on the porch, Mrs. McConnell. You took a nap."

She struggled to sit up. "I guess I did." She looked at him and broke into a grin. "I'll bet you thought I was dead."

"It never occurred to me. I was waiting for you to wake up so I could give you some vegetables."

She rose unsteadily, smoothed her cotton house dress and cackled. "You thought I died, and it scared you. Poor boy, you deserve some cookies."

Over coffee she said, "I'm always scaring people. Remember how the young people used to avoid cutting through my yard to get to the next subdivision? They were afraid of me. Once in a while I'd yell at them just to exercise my lungs, but I didn't mean anything by it, and I never yelled at Jill and Anne. They were nice children, and Grace was good to me. I'd feel bad when I'd look out the window and see them give my yard a wide berth just like the others."

She searched George's face for an answer. "Why did I do that, George? I love children. I didn't want to be the neighborhood meany." Her voice trailed off. "They're all gone, now."

George reached over and took her gnarled hand. "I know."

Two weeks later a killing frost flattened his garden. No more produce to take to Mrs. McConnell. He went to see her anyway although he soon wished he hadn't.

"Who are you?" Her voice was harsh.

"George."

"I don't know a George. Go away. I'm waiting for my son to take me away for a visit."

"You mean your daughter?"

"I don't have a daughter."

George stepped back to assess the situation. He'd seen her confused before, but he hadn't seen the fear darting in her eyes. He wasn't sure what to do. His first thought was to whisk her away to a place where she could be watched over, protected. But he didn't have any authority, and lacked the skills to influence her. A home would be the right place for her, but that decision rested with her daughter, wherever she might be.

On one of her lucid days several months past they'd talked about her living elsewhere, perhaps in a retirement home or with her daughter. She'd been adamant. "I'll never leave my house. Giving up my independence just to squeeze a few more days from the calendar makes no sense. They'll have to carry me out, George." Since his feelings matched hers, they'd sealed their agreement over a warm cookie.

***

George was cleaning the debris from his garden during a mid-October warm spell when he heard an explosive clap of thunder. He looked up at a cloudless sky and scratched his head. It had sounded like thunder or a sonic boom. He bent back to his task, carefully piling plant remnants on an old bed sheet so he could drag them off to the woods and place them on his compost pile.

The sheet was fully loaded when he glanced across the circle and saw flames shooting out her kitchen window. Slapping the flat of his hand against his forehead, he hustled off to the house to call 911. Later, as the sirens screamed up Riverside Boulevard and then his own street, he felt weak-kneed. Tears the size of raindrops filled his eyes as he watched a cloud of smoke waft over her house. He could smell it; oily, putrid. Not the autumn odor of burning leaves he loved so much.

The fire truck moved into position and firemen in yellow slickers began racing around hauling hoses. From his stoop, he watched two of them axe the front door and go inside. He had an urge to be helpful, to be part of the mission, but he refrained. Logic told him a raging house fire was no place for an old man.

When the activity slowed, he crossed the street. A fireman stood near the truck wiping sweat from his face with a towel. George tapped him on the shoulder. "Gas explosion?"

"Yep."

"Was the old lady in there?"

"Yep. We dragged her out, and they're trying to

revive her now.   Personally, I don't think it's gonna happen."

George wrapped his arms tightly against his chest to quell the pain of a thousand knives tearing at his stomach.

"She's a friend of mine. Can I see her?"

"You don't want to. She's not a pretty sight."

George didn't persist. Leaning against the truck, he watched the firemen pour water onto the flames.   Grey steam hissed as the stream hit the roof.   Then two brawny firemen wheeled the gurney with the covered figure on it into the yard and lifted it into the ambulance.   When her body was secured, the vehicle snaked its way down the curvy street, unhurried, sirenless.

The scene left him numb. He stood and watched until the last thread of smoke disappeared into the bright sunlight.   The remaining firemen were peeling off their wet, sooty rubber outfits and throwing them on the back of the truck when George finally trudged across the circle to his house.

He needed a beer.   Stopping at the garage refrigerator he retrieved one and carried it to the porch. He gazed out past the bare earth and piles of dead plant material in his garden and focused on the colorful woods beyond. A cool breeze made him shiver.   Once he was sprawled on the chaise and the brew had found its way down his parched throat, he directed his thoughts toward Mrs. McConnell. Though shocked at her death, he didn't feel sad, or angry or guilty. In a way, he felt relief.

He recalled the minister who officiated at Grace's funeral saying he should be joyous. Death had put an end to her suffering. Despite his words he'd felt nothing but misery. Until today, he'd always thought the minister was full of it.

A smile crossed his lips. At the time, he'd been too self-absorbed with his sorrow to comprehend what the clergyman was telling him. Now the message made sense, because joy was exactly the emotion he was feeling for old Mrs. McConnell.

CHAPTER EIGHTEEN

DORMANCY

Every year since Grace died, George dragged himself to the attic about the second week of December, plopped into a cobwebby old living room chair and peered at all the dusty cardboard boxes that held the artificial Christmas tree and a lifelong collection of ornaments. Because decorating for the holidays was Grace's passion, he hadn't actually opened any of the boxes in fourteen years. This year he decided to give it a try.

Grace always said decorating for Christmas was a joint project. She was the brain and he was the body. She knew where she wanted every decoration to go so she assumed the supervisory role. He was the carton carrier, tree raiser and light stringer. When he finished his tasks, he watched her fondle the ornaments, until she'd found just the right place for them on the tree. Each one was loaded with sentiment and memories important only to her.

Seeing her joyfulness was a bit hollow, because he knew he was on call to perform any unforeseen tasks and to carry all the empty boxes back to the attic. His real reward came when all the decorations were in place and Grace was satisfied with her efforts. Then she would sit on his lap with her arms around his neck and smother him with kisses.

George raised himself from the chair and laid the long carton that held the artificial tree on its side. He tugged and pulled at the tree parts until he had them all out of the container. The green prickly pile mystified him. He realized he didn't have a clue how the damned thing went together without her, so he began stuffing the fake limbs back into the box. When he was finished, he scratched his head. He had a problem. What was he going to do with the two small branches that no longer fit in the container?

He picked up some boxes of ornaments and returned to the chair. Carefully unwrapping each one, he admired it for a moment before rewrapping it and returning it to its place in the container. Then he did the same with another...and another. After awhile a few tears streaked his face and his sadness made him question why he was up there in the attic amongst the ghosts.

When he had examined the last of the relics, he returned the ornament boxes to their carton. Next he sorted through the strings of lights. As his frustration mounted with each tangle, it dawned on him that despite his good intentions he was about to make a futile and physically exhausting mistake. At his age, it was suicide setting up a tree and decorating it, and without Grace's direction he'd screw it up for sure. Even if he did get the job done successfully, he'd just have to tear the whole mess down after the holidays and haul everything back to the attic.

George stood up and carried the strings of lights back to their carton. Shuffling to the attic door, he turned off the light and closed the door behind him. As he slowly descended the stairs, he congratulated himself on making another in a long line of brilliant decisions.

George was not the Grinch. He actually liked putting out effort for some parts of Christmas. Like shopping. While he disliked the clamoring crowds and the piped-in Christmas music, he enjoyed rising to the challenge of finding the perfect gift. Shopping for his daughters and Bret was difficult. They already had everything. Finding a gift for Catherine was less trying because she had so little in the way of things. She'd like anything he bought her. Lily and Gert were the easiest of all. At her birthday party in October, Lily's greatest joy came from ripping up the brightly colored paper. Gert liked shirts with printed sayings. The cruder or funnier the saying, the more precious the gift was to her.

This morning when he awakened George was already depressed. Nothing in the gray, rainy early December weather offered him any relief, nor did finishing the breakfast dishes, reading the paper or straightening up the downstairs. It was nine o'clock. There was nothing left to do until dinner with Gert and Catherine.

He clicked on TV. Oprah. Click. Jerry Springer. Click. He'd like to castrate the SOB! The Cooking Channel, Shopping Channel, Nickelodeon. More clicks. He sighed and turned off the set. A visit with Mary Alexander would be fun, but when Rachel started first grade, Mary began working part-time in an accounting office. He hadn't talked to her since summer. If only he could have a beer with Mike O'Hara or walk across the street and chow down on a few of Mrs. McConnell's cookies, it might relieve his funk. But Mike was defending the unwashed, and the cookie lady was gone.

He wasn't tired, yet he pulled his feet up and laid his head on the cushioned armrest. It was pathetic, he thought, when the most exciting thing in his life was taking a nap.

Then a thought struck him like a slap along the side

of the head. Eighteen months ago when he wouldn't have minded joining Grace, and he was estranged from his neighbors, it was natural to feel lifeless and depressed. But not now. He had reunited with his daughters and been given the gift of Lily. He'd built new relationships with Mary Alexander and her kids, the O'Haras and especially Catherine and Gert. Was he too myopic to see his blessings? He stared at the ceiling and followed the plaster crack that ran from over the hall door diagonally to the corner by the TV. If he squinted, he could almost count the fine spur tracks that veined off the main line. Eventually his eyes closed, and he fell asleep. When he finally rose from the couch, it was nearly noon. He didn't feel like fixing lunch or calling Tom Wembley to see if he wanted to play cribbage, and he sure as hell didn't want to count ceiling cracks again. Only one thought had any appeal. He picked up the phone and dialed. When Catherine answered, he said, "After I go to the store, can I come over this afternoon and be with you? We can talk or play gin or something."

"I'd like that. Come as soon as you can."

"Being with me all afternoon and night won't drive you crazy?"

"I always feel good when you're around, George."

"Me too."

How strange and wonderful to be a human, he thought. The moment he hung up his depression was gone. Even his body responded to the conversation like it had received a shot of cortisone. It was also crying out for food. He opened the fridge, made a huge ham and cheese sandwich and wolfed it down. When he finished, he left the dishes in the sink and hobbled up the stairs to shower, shave and dress for the store and Catherine.

Later, while he was walking to his car carrying a small bag of groceries from the supermarket, he spotted three small boys huddled behind a pickup truck. They were smoking. As he got closer, he realized the one in the red jacket and baseball cap was Kevin Alexander. He debated confronting him. Instead he kept walking to his car and deposited the bag on the back seat. Just as he was about to slide into the car, he whirled around and headed directly for the group. When Kevin spotted him, he flicked away his cigarette and started to run.

"Kevin," he yelled. "Stop running and come here."

He stopped dead in his tracks and stared at George. The other two boys disbursed. With his head bowed, Kevin came slowly toward him. George tried to keep his composure, yet he had no idea what to say or do. A twelve-year old smoking was such a small transgression, yet in the paradigm of the Alexander family it was a further indication that Kevin was marching to a far different drummer than the rest. Maybe he had an opportunity to impact the little kid's life in some small way. Kevin was standing in front of George, eyes examining his shoes, hands in his pockets.

"I never smoked, Kevin, but I've buried a lot of friends who did. It's a horrible habit."

Kevin's eyes stayed focused on the ground. "Yes, Mr. Konert."

George scratched his head. Telling a kid he was going to die fifty years later if he smoked wasn't going to cut it. He tried again. "When I was young, the only kids that smoked were hoodlums."

"Yes, Mr. Konert."

Still no good. "When I go by your house, I'm going to stop and tell your mother I saw you smoking. She and your father can figure out what to do with you."

George turned and began walking toward his car. Kevin chased after him.

"Please don't, Mr. Konert. I promise I'll never smoke again."

George kept his back to Kevin. He couldn't turn

around until he could control the grin that had overtaken his face.

"I promise. I promise." Kevin was crying now. "I've never done it before. I was just doing it because my friends were. Please don't tell my mom."

When George reached his car, he pulled the handle and opened the door. He turned to Kevin and asked, "How did you get here?"

"I walked."

With no expression in his voice, George said, "Hop in. I'll drive you home."

When they reached the Alexander's, he said, "What have you learned today, Kevin?"

"Don't smoke?"

"You already knew that. What I hope you'll learn from my not telling your mother what I saw is the power of a promise. You promised me you won't do stupid things you know are wrong." George pointed to his chest. "I promise I won't tell your mother because I believe you are sincere and won't break our trust."

"I mean my promise, Mr. Konert."

"You're a good young man, Kevin. Now get out of here. I've got a date."

A half hour later he was pounding on Catherine's door. She opened it and took his coat to the closet. When she returned, he startled her by pulling her close to him and kissing her.

"What brought that on?"

"I don't know. I just know I was waiting all day to do it."

"Do it again, then."

That night after the dishes were cleared and placed in the dishwasher, George and Catherine carried their coffee cups into the living room and sat on the couch. While they chatted, Gert excused herself and disappeared into her bedroom. When she reappeared, she was wearing a red long-sleeved blouse and neatly pressed black woolen slacks. Her hair was nicely combed, and she had on makeup. She moved to the hall closet and pulled out a new short winter coat. Struggling into it she announced, "I'm going out for some fresh air."

Catherine watched her leave the house. As the truck roared away, she said, "I don't know where that girl goes every night."

"If you ask me, she probably has a lover."

"Oh, George. Don't be silly."

CHAPTER NINETEEN

RIPENING

In January, Anne invited George to Bret's birthday party. She also insisted he bring Catherine and Gert. He told Anne, "Catherine won't need to be charmed into coming, but Gert will. In fact, I'll be shocked if Gert even considers the offer."

"Use your sales skills, Dad. You can do it."

To his amazement, when he phoned Gert and asked her if she would like to ride along, she accepted immediately. While he was hanging up, George stared at the receiver in disbelief. Was every woman unpredictable?

Early Saturday morning, he pulled into Gert's driveway and climbed the familiar three steps to the door. At the first ring, Gert opened it. He clutched the doorframe to steady himself and gawked at her.

"Good God, Gert! You're wearing a dress."

It was a black number with muted tan vertical

stripes that minimized her blocky figure and emphasized her height. She looked stunning. Her short hair was curled and framed her round face. She was even wearing lipstick. George continued gawking until Gert giggled and pirouetted for him.

"What do you think, Georgy Boy?"

"You look fabulous. You should get dressed up more often."

"Maybe I will. I'm tired of you always preferring my mother. I need some positive attention, too, you know."

He stepped toward her. She moved back. He continued pressing forward. Then he wrapped her in his arms and hugged her. Slowly he could feel her strong hands on his back, and then she was holding him to her. When she broke away, he saw tears in her eyes.

She excused herself to find Catherine. When they returned Catherine was wearing the same attractive blue outfit she'd worn to Stewart's funeral. She kissed him on the cheek and said, "Doesn't Gert look nice?"

Before he could answer, Gert interrupted, "Please Mother, we've already discussed that."

"I was only saying..."

George caught Gert's eye and frowned at her.

"Thank you, mother, for saying how nice I look."

In the driveway, George held the car doors while Gert climbed into the back seat and Catherine slipped into the front next to him. Over Gert's and Catherine's objection, George turned left at the end of the street and took a shortcut through a subdivision to miss the traffic that always clogged Riverside.

When his choice of routes worked smoothly, he crowed, "See what having a man at the wheel accomplishes. If one of you were driving we'd still be tied up at the Wal-Mart light."

"You were lucky," Catherine said.

"Do I hear the voice of envy?"

"Just drive George."

A few minutes later George turned onto the freeway, brought the car up to speed and set the cruise control. While they were breezing through the rolling farmland north of Carlisle, George reached over and found Catherine's hand. She responded by covering their two hands with her other one.

From the back seat a voice said, "Come on you two. You're making me carsick."

When they arrived at Anne's and everyone had said their 'hellos' in the foyer and drifted into the living room, George was in for his second surprise of the day. A male stranger was standing next to Jill.

"Hello, Daddy. I'd like you to meet my friend, Curtis Axelson."

George blinked. In one recent phone conversation, Jill mentioned she was dating someone, but he hadn't expected her to drag him to a family gathering so soon. Stewart had only been dead five months.

Curtis smiled at George and extended his hand.

Suddenly George felt foolish. Why was he, of all people, concerned about propriety? Wasn't he the one who told Jill to stop working so hard and have more fun? Wasn't dating fun? Instead of being critical, he should be happy for her. Though George always felt Jill's taste in men was suspect, if she thought enough of Curtis to bring him to Anne's, he should at least respect her decision.

George shook Curtis's hand and said, "I've heard so much about you, it's a pleasure to finally meet you." George glanced at Jill. She was rolling her eyes.

"Word travels fast in this group," Curtis said. "This is only the fourth time Jill and I have laid eyes on each other."

"Really!"

Out of the corner of his eye, George spotted relief.

Anne was carrying hors d'oeuvres from the kitchen, and Lily was tagging along with her dolly.

"It was nice meeting you, Curtis." George pointed at Lily. "I see my granddaughter over there and need to say 'hi' to her."

"No problem, Mr. Konert. We'll talk later."

George turned away from him and beckoned to Lily with his finger. She avoided his gaze and toddled after her mother. He chased after her, hoisted her off the floor and hugged her. She squealed to be let down. He wasn't doing much better with her than he was with Curtis.

After another of Martha's exquisite lunches, Anne put Lily down for a nap and the group divided up and played charades. The highlight of the game was everyone laughing at George's tantrum when his team of Gert, Bret and Jill failed to guess the Grand Canyon.

"You guys are really dumb. For the first word, didn't I point at my chest for grandfather and stand peering over the edge of a chair back like I was looking down into a canyon? You kept saying 'chest--down,' and 'black hole,' all kinds of stupid answers. I really got the short end of the stick with this team."

Late in the afternoon while George was sitting on the couch next to Catherine, Lily walked past. He motioned her toward him. She hesitated. Her dark eyes darted around the room then back to George. Clinging to her doll, she toddled toward him. He patted his thighs. She studied him. He patted again. "Come to your Grandpa, Lily."

She climbed onto his lap. When she was settled, and her dolly was safely in her arms she said, "Bampa."

He gave her a little squeeze and smiled at Catherine. "Isn't she a sweetheart? Lily loves her Grandpa."

Lily's eyes followed his. "Catin," she said, and wiggled from his lap to Catherine's waiting arms.

"How do you like that? You're not even related."

When Lily eventually trotted off, George asked Catherine if he could be excused to get something to drink. "Do you want anything?"

Catherine shook her head and waved him off.

George carried a beer to where Curtis was sitting and plopped down across from him in a matching wing chair. After taking a swig, George said, "Living in Chicago, I suppose you like the Bears and Cubs?"

"Actually, I'm not much of a pro sports fan. When Michael Jordan was playing, I enjoyed watching the Bulls on TV, but I don't follow them anymore."

"No sports?"

"I play racquetball all winter, jog three days a week and have a five handicap in golf. Does that count?"

"I suppose. I have an old two iron in my garage that I use to swing at the chipmunks that burrow under my porch, but I've never hit one. Jogging's out. Ever since I hurt my knee playing football in college, I haven't been able to run."

"I noticed your limp. Jill says you were a star halfback."

"I could have been, but I wasn't nearly the hero I told her I was. I made up some great bedtime stories when she was little."

George rubbed his hand over his left knee. "Let me ask another question."

"Jill told me to expect the third-degree."

"What do you do for a living?"

"I own a technology company. We make--"

"Don't even bother to explain. The only thing I can do on the computer is play Yatzee with some neighbor boys. I presume you do pretty well?"

"We don't starve."

"We?"

"I have custody of my two teenage boys, Kyle and Peter."

"You're divorced?"

"For three years."

George stroked his chin. "Hmm. There's a lot of that going around lately."

"Mr. Konert, my ex-wife is a serious substance abuser."

"Oh! There's a lot of that..."

"Going around lately, too."

George smiled at Curtis. "I'm really bad at this. I appreciate your putting up with my bumbling. You're a nice guy. Just make Jill happy, okay?"

"I'll try. As I said earlier, we barely know each other, but I'll let you in on a little secret. I think she's terrific."

"We have that in common." George placed his drink on an end table. "Out of curiosity, how did you meet?"

"I actually met Jill five years ago when she came to my company to consult. I always remembered how impressed I was with her high-energy and insightful recommendations." He laughed. "Plus, she is very good-looking."

"Why thank you, Curtis, " Jill said as she came up behind her father.

"I'm telling your father about how we met."

"Can I join you?" Without waiting for an answer, Jill sat down on the floor and sat cross-legged at George's feet.

Curtis continued. "When Jill's associate tipped me off about her husband's death, I called and asked her to dinner. It was too soon to call her, but I had to let her know I was interested. To my surprise, she accepted my invitation."

George smiled down at his daughter. "Good for you, Jill. For once, you actually took a sage old man's advice."

"When Curtis called, I told him I'd go out with him because you said I had to. Isn't that right, Curtis?"

"Ever since then I've wanted to meet the man that tells Jill Palmer what to do."

Jill laughed. "I'm glad you two are getting acquainted. Has he passed your inquisition, Daddy?"

"So far, Jill, but I do have one more question for him."

"Go ahead, Mr. Konert."

"Do you garden?"

"No, sir. I'm afraid I don't."

"Not even a tomato plant?"

"Nope."

George frowned. "He doesn't even garden. You certainly can pick 'em, Jill."

"One gardener in my life is enough."

"You're probably right."

Curtis stood up, extended a hand toward Jill, and pulled her to her feet. When their eyes met and lingered, George smiled to himself. At least Jill picked one he liked this time.

George went searching for Anne. He found her in the dining room setting the table.

"I'm still full from lunch. Are we going to eat again?"

She laughed. "Have you forgotten? You're here for Bret's Birthday Party."

"I know that."

"Well, have we had it yet?"

"Not that I recall."

"So there you have it. By the way, Dad, you were great at charades."

"I was so frustrated. Everybody laughed at me."

"That's what was so great about it."

After chatting with Anne for a moment longer, George spotted Catherine playing with Lily and her doll on the couch. She said, "Do you realize how bright your granddaughter is? Watch."

She touched the doll's shoes. "What are these, Lily?"

"Shoes."

"And this?"

"Dwess."

"Now Lily, your dolly's dress is the same color as my dress. Can you tell me what color it is?"

Lily studied Catherine's dress. Then she touched the doll's dress. He could almost see her little brain computing. "Boo," she stated and looked intently at Catherine's face.

George and Catherine clapped their approval. Lily beamed and clapped, too.

Catherine looked up at George. "Please do me a favor, George. Go check on Gert. She's not exactly in her element here."

"Don't sell your daughter short. She always finds a way to have a good time."

He glanced around the room. When he didn't spot Gert, he began a room-by-room search. She wasn't in the dining room or library. Walking down the hall, he heard muffled laughter. He followed the sounds. Nearing the game room, he heard Gert roar, "I don't care if it is your table, Bret. Your butt is mine." The outburst was followed by the distinctive clack of billiard balls.

George entered the room and watched.

Gert was bent over the table lining up a shot. "Hi George. You're just in time to see your son-in-law contribute to Gert's retirement fund. By the way, Bret, I'll take the stripes."

She slammed the nine-ball into the corner pocket spinning the cue ball into a perfect position to make the fifteen. When she completed the run only the solid balls and the eight ball remained.

"Very impressive," Bret said. "But how do you expect to make the eight with me playing defense?"

"Tigers wait until their prey screws up. It's only a matter of time before I pounce."

Bret asked, "How did you learn to play so well, Gert?"

"My father's bookie worked out of a pool hall. From the time I was little, he took me with him on his Saturday morning outings. Mother was so naive. She thought we were bonding. I didn't mind covering for my father. I loved playing pool."

Bret stopped shooting and studied her. "You're kidding, aren't you?"

"No, it's all true. Now I stay sharp playing in a couple of bars where I hang out."

"But you don't drink," George said.

"Right, but I make a lot of money hustling drunks."

George laughed. "Do you ever give a straight answer?"

"Only if I can't think up a crooked one."

It was easy for George to see why Catherine might have gravitated toward her other daughter. Gert was so different from her. However, something concerned him more than her choosing Marianne over Gert. How could Catherine not have realized her husband was such a lowlife? Or if she did know, why did she accept it? He smiled to himself. It was a good thing the guy wasn't married to Grace. She would have known he was a louse and done something about it.

Bret sank a few balls before missing a straight-in shot to the left corner, then watched helplessly as Gert nailed the eight ball.

"Ca-ching!" she said. "How the money rolls in. Want to lose again, Bret?"

"Sure, after I get George and me something to drink. Want a coke or something?"

"No thanks, I'm trying to get down to a svelte size fourteen."

While Bret was gone George said, "You're an excellent pool player!"

She gave him a disgusted look. "Aren't you overstating the obvious?" Then she whispered, "I'm going to take a dive these next few games. Bret's such a neat guy. I want him to like me."

"He's such a good guy he'll like you whether you beat him or not." Then he asked, "Gert, do you think you'll ever be interested in finding a man?"

She turned crimson and continued to whisper, "I found one, George. Oops, Bret's coming back. I promise I'll tell you about him. I need your advice."

At four they gathered around the huge dining room table. All except Lily, who at Anne's urging had dutifully taken a nap and was still asleep. "Just like her grandfather," Jill had said.

Bret gave thanks for the gathering and blessed the food, which judging by the Shrimp Louie appetizer waiting for them, gave promise of being sumptuous. By the time they'd consumed Martha's endive salad, roast duckling with wild rice dressing and green beans with almonds, there was much groaning and tummy rubbing. However, when Martha returned with a carrot cake and forty-two lit candles everyone recovered to sing "Happy Birthday" to Bret.

Following dinner, George needed a nap, so he limped to the couch in the study. When he awoke, it was dark. He turned on a table lamp and looked at his watch. He'd slept over two hours.

Returning to the living room, he observed a tableau. Jill was talking with Curtis, Gert and Bret were laughing over something one of them said and Lily was sitting between Anne and Catherine on the couch. They were reading her a story. He stood for a moment unnoticed. Then Gert spotted him and announced his entrance,

"Heeeere's George."

He puffed out his chest and walked down the two steps. Then he announced, "I hate to be an old poop, but it's eight-thirty, and I think we should get on the road."

His statement was a catalyst. Everyone rose and began their goodbye hugs.

When Gert offered to drive, he didn't resist. Besides being sleepy, he was well aware of his failing night vision. Catherine insisted he sit in the front, so he would have more legroom.

Once the lights of Columbus faded behind them he heard a faint buzz emanating from the rear.

"She's out like a light, Gert."

"Are you sure?"

"Maybe this would be a good time to tell me about the 'him' you've found."

"I can't risk Mom hearing about it now. I'll meet you for coffee tomorrow morning at the Green Parrot. Ten okay?"

"I'll be there."

Following the lights of a few passing cars, a smile formed on his lips. His world was changing. While it was too soon to call, he liked the way Jill lit up when Curtis was attentive to her. Then there was he and Catherine, and Gert finding someone. Who said winter wasn't the mating season? He closed his eyes. Soon he was asleep.

When the car eased to a stop and the steady drone of the engine shut down, George woke up. He blinked open one eye and peeked through the windshield. They were in the driveway of Gert's house.

"Home sweet home," Gert said.

He collected himself. Creaking from the car, he opened Catherine's door. When she stepped out, she clutched his arm for support. Then they kissed goodnight. By the time they parted, Gert was already standing by the front door.

"Do I need to throw water on you lovebirds to break you up?" Gert said. "Come on, Mom. It's time for bed."

***

The next morning when George arose at six he found a dusting of snow on the stoop. He swept it off the steps with a broom before he walked to the street to get the paper. After two slices of whole-wheat toast with apricot jelly and a cup of instant coffee, George took the paper to the couch to read. About nine he shaved, showered and put on the new gray wool sweater Catherine insisted he buy over his objections. At 9:45, he drove to the Green Parrot.

Entering the noisy hash house, he searched for Gert. He looked at his watch. He wasn't that early. Where was she? He found a booth in the back where he could keep an eye on the door.

"You want coffee?" the waitress asked as she cleared away the debris from the previous occupants.

"Not now. I'm waiting for someone."

"Just send up a flare when you're ready," she said as she hurried off.

When Gert finally arrived, George waved her in for a landing, and they ordered.

"Now tell me about this guy," George said.

She fiddled with the miniature creamer and poured the liquid into her coffee. "His name is Walt. He's been running one of my cleaning crews for about a year. He's very intelligent, and he's the most dedicated manager I have. Pitches right in and works with the crew. They respect him and work hard for him. We like each other a lot. Mom doesn't know it, but we go out for dinner and movies sometimes."

"Sneaking out on your mother like a teenager, huh? Isn't that kind of silly?"

"Probably, but I can't tell her yet. Walt and I have

220

some issues to work out."

"You can't tell her you're dating someone?"

"I can't tell her we're talking marriage."

"Gosh, Gert! Sometimes I don't understand you at all. You rescue your mother from the Poor Farm and welcome her into your home, yet you don't have the decency to tell her you're serious about some guy. When are you going to tell her, after you have a couple of kids?"

Gert took a swig of her coffee. "I don't need to trouble her with my problems. I've already caused her enough grief."

"Grief. You saved her life for cripes sake."

"You don't know the whole story, George. I'm a recovering alcoholic."

"I never suspected that."

"I've been dry for fifteen years. I know I won't have a relapse. I can even hang out with my cronies at bars and not be tempted. But, Walt's also an alcoholic, and he's only been dry for a year. He still needs AA several times a week. He's a much bigger risk."

"That would concern me."

"If I told my mother, it would worry the heck out of her. In addition, Walt has two grown boys. One is an engineer in Massachusetts. He's fine. The other lives in Carlisle. He's hooked on drugs and sucks up to Walt whenever he needs money. Walt feels guilty and tries to help him just like my dad did. Dad gave me a lot of family money for booze when I was drinking."

"Some father! He was supporting your addiction."

"Dad never considered consequences. Walt knows he's doing the wrong thing, but he can't seem to stop. He says it's hard to write off his son."

"Aren't there groups he could get involved with that would help him deal with his son's problem?"

"Sure."

"Why doesn't he?"

221

"He says he's not ready."

"You do have a problem. Still, I think you should let your mother in on it."

"There's more. Another problem is Walt works for me. How can I have my husband work for me, George? My mother's life has taught me an important lesson. Bad things happen when you give up your independence, so I'd never give up the security of owning my own business or take on a partner."

"Help him get another job."

"And lose my best manager?"

"You have a point. Is there more?"

"Probably," she said sadly. "I just haven't identified it yet." Gert finished her coffee and pushed the empty cup away from her. "I better get back to the grind."

George was thoughtful for a moment. "I don't have answers for you, Gert, but I do have some general advice. See if Walt can overcome the big obstacles in his life before you marry the guy. Take your time. You don't want to get hitched and find yourself trapped in a bad relationship."

"You know, I was thinking the same thing myself. Thanks, Georgy Boy."

Gert signaled the waitress for the check. "There's another serious problem."

"Another one?"

"My mother. If I marry Walt, and we're all jammed together in my little house, everyone will be miserable."

George patted Gert's arm and cooed, "There, there, Missy. Don't worry your little head. George Konert can take care of that little project for you."

"I thought you might."

Later that afternoon as George lay on the couch pondering his conversation with Gert he realized marrying Catherine was not a new idea. He'd been thinking about it for some time. He'd weighed all the issues. He loved her.

His kids thought she was terrific and Gert was his buddy. Even though Catherine couldn't contribute much financially, he wasn't concerned. He had enough money to comfortably support them both if the 'two can live as cheaply as one' proverb was close to true. He'd even considered the eight-year age difference. If he died before her, his assets would take care of her for the rest of her life. Sure, it might eat up his daughters' inheritances. Big deal! They didn't need any of it anyway.

Considering everything, it should have been easy to blurt out a proposal, but he hadn't. Then again, he sure as hell ought to have some plausible reason for waiting, but he didn't. Marrying Catherine was not something to procrastinate over. After all, how many viable years would they have together? Five, six, maybe ten at most. Anything beyond that was pure luck. Too soon the nursing home would beckon or worse yet, the mortician.

CHAPTER TWENTY

GRAFTING

The first two weeks of February in Ohio were brutal. It seemed like every night the temperature dipped below zero. The wind howled endlessly, often blowing powdery snow into blizzard conditions. The entire winter in Carlisle was one of the coldest winters in history and still George was unaffected. He had Catherine. In an earlier time, he'd be deep into a mid-winter funk, passing the time doing garden planning and moaning to Grace about having no place to go, and because the snow was piled high on the driveway, no way to get there.

Now he kept the driveway clear of snow so he wouldn't miss a moment with Catherine. Tonight, she and Gert had invited him to dinner at her house. For the last month, being alone together in the evening had become the norm. After dinner, Gert would get cleaned up and go out. George assumed she and Walt were working on their relationship, which he presumed was progressing faster than his and Catherine's. Tonight he'd make a conscious effort to get back into the lead.

He and Catherine were sipping coffees in the living room. "With Gert out every night, I'm worried," she said. "She's an alcoholic, you know. My worst fear is she's drinking again."

"You worry too much. Why don't you ask her where she goes every night?"

"I'm not going to do that."

"Then I guess you're not going to find out."

A few days later she confronted Gert and learned about Walt. She also found out George already knew about him. In the car going to Fantini's, she was livid. "Though I'm relieved Gert hasn't fallen off the wagon, I can't understand why you didn't tell me about Walt. I endured enough secrets and lies during my marriage to Floyd to last a lifetime. Now you're doing the same thing to me."

He shrugged.

She glared at him. "Of all people you should be aware of the pain secrets cause. You hated it when you realized Grace kept information from you."

"It was up to Gert to tell you about her love life. Not me. Anyway, for whatever reason, she asked me not to say anything, and I wouldn't betray a trust."

"How will I ever be able to trust you if I think you're keeping secrets from me?"

They arrived at the restaurant. "Stop thinking it," he said too directly. Embarrassed by his abruptness, he said, "I'm sorry. Let's go inside and talk some more."

When they were seated at a table, George grinned. "I'll make you a deal. If I'm keeping a secret from you, I'll tell you. I'll say, 'Catherine, I'm keeping a secret from you.' That way, if I don't say anything, you'll know I don't have a secret. How's that?"

A smile made its way across her face. "That's the

most ridiculous thing I've ever heard."

"Oh really. Let me show you how it works. 'Catherine, I have a secret I'm keeping from you.'"

"Sure you do!"

"I do have one, and I want to share it with you right now."

She covered her ears with her hands. "What if I don't want to hear it? I'll make you a deal. When I'm ready to hear your secret, I'll say, 'George, I'll listen to your secret now.' How's that?"

"I'm tired of playing." George formed his mouth into a pout. "I wanted to surprise you with a proposition, and now it's spoiled. Oh, what the hell! Catherine, will you go on a Caribbean cruise with me next week? I want out of this weather, and I think we'd have a good time. I have a hold on a one-week Eastern Caribbean trip out of Miami on the 23rd. Yes or no."

"Yes."

"That was easy! I'll confirm it in the morning."

They both began laughing. After the giddiness wore off, Catherine asked a bunch of questions about clothes, meals and what they might be doing each day. George explained the itinerary and detailed a typical day at sea as well as what to expect in port. After that he described their staterooms.

"We each have one? Don't staterooms hold more than one person?"

"Sure. Usually they have twin beds, but some ships push them together and make them up as queens."

"Wouldn't it cost less if we shared one?"

He stared at her. "Of course, but it never occurred to me you'd like that."

"Why not? I'm a healthy, slightly past middle-aged female. I think it might be quite enjoyable to shack up for a week with a dude like you."

George blushed. "Catherine!"

"Maybe I should have kept that thought a secret. Do you think?"

George recovered quickly. "I'll use the savings on a mini-suite . . . with a queen-size bed."

***

Looking back, the whole time he and Catherine were planning the cruise and for the first few days on board, he never had an inkling his knee would flare up. In fact, those first nights together were magical. They traded smiles and clinked wine glasses across the small dining table as the waiters served course after course of fabulous food. Following dinner they strolled hand-in-hand on the promenade deck, the sea breeze gently blowing their hair, the moon lighting their way. Some nights they'd make a trip to the top deck for a slow dance to a Glenn Miller tune. Finally, the best part of all, when they returned to the suite, he'd slide next to Catherine under the cool white sheets and find joy in remembering what happens between a man and a woman when they love each other.

It was late afternoon on the fourth day that he and Catherine boarded a rocking tender after wandering up and down Front Street in St. Maarten. It bounced and bucked like a rodeo horse as it ploughed through the waves to the ship. When they finally tied up to the mother ship, George helped Catherine out of the tender and onto the platform that formed the base of the gangplank. As he was stepping over the side, a sudden searing pain pierced his knee. Falling backward, he was caught by a burly young man standing behind him. "Whoa, old man!" he said.

He wanted to kill him for the geriatric slur except the guy helped him off the tender and up the gangplank to the ship.

Catherine took over from there. With her help, he made it up the elevator and down the narrow hallway to their stateroom. He opened the door and fell onto the bed.

"Damn!" he said. "Why did this have to happen?"

Catherine sat down next to him and attempted to soothe him by patting his hand. "I'm sure you'll feel better tomorrow."

He raised himself until his shoulders rested against the headboard. Then he pulled his good leg onto the bed leaving his other one dangling over the side. "I know this leg. It takes a long time to heal when it flares up this bad. It must have been gathering fluid for days, and I was too distracted to notice. Unless the ship doctor has some miracle cure, I'm out of commission until we get home." He moved his leg and grimaced. "Will you call him, please?" He studied his knee. Since he last looked it had ballooned even more.

The ship's doctor was very cordial and absolutely no help.

"Ice packs and Tylenol," George moaned after he left. "I didn't need him for that. I thought he might drain my knee and give me a shot or at least suggest how to get to the dining room for dinner tonight. I'll have to have room service. You'll be sitting alone."

"Actually, I'd like a night off from playing dress-up," she said. "I'll have room service, too. We'll order a bottle of wine and maybe watch a video, and we'll worry about tomorrow when it gets here."

After a sleepless night George felt worse in the morning. He was worrying about leaving the ship to catch the plane two days later when the steward brought their breakfast. He said in his Italian-flavored English, "Last night after I serve you dinner, I find a wheelchair for Mr. Konert. You want it for rest of trip? Also I think about Saturday when you disembark. I get someone to push you to the airport bus while I carry your bags."

Catherine said, "Oh, Gino, that's wonderful. You saved us a lot of worry."

"Then you want the wheelchair?"

228

"No," George said from the bed.

Gino stared at George and shrugged. He looked at Catherine.

"Yes, we certainly *do* want it," she said smiling at the steward. "Thank you very much."

Avoiding eye contact with George, he said to Catherine, "I bring it to the cabin when I pick up breakfast trays."

"That will be perfect."

After he left, George mocked her, "That will be perfect, Gino. That won't be perfect, and I will not be wheeled around like some of the crippled old coots on board this ship. I'm not spending one minute in a damn wheelchair."

"Yes you are, George Konert. I won't let you spoil the rest of the trip moaning."

"I suppose you think I'll feel better doing wheelies!"

"You don't get it, George, do you? You're not in charge anymore. I am. You're going everywhere I go except the ladies room."

"What about the men's room for me?"

"Don't drink any beer. We'll work that problem out when we need to."

She put on a stern face. "Any more questions?"

He eyed her. There was no mistaking her determination. "No questions."

Despite his pain, the remainder of the cruise was an eye-opener. Whether Catherine was wheeling him around the deck, helping him dress for dinner or playing bingo, she was revealing pieces of her personality he'd never noticed, or she'd never shown him before. The new Catherine was direct, voiced opinions and was borderline assertive. She was becoming remarkably Grace-like.

Seeing her taking charge, George wondered what happened to the milder version. It was only his curiosity that raised the question. He had no desire to resurrect the old Catherine. Not when he was enchanted by the new one.

***

George was half-sitting, half-reclining on his couch, his left knee propped up on a pillow and an ice pack stinging the skin on his leg. Since the cruise, he'd spent most of his time in the same position, despite the cortisone shot in his knee and the anti-inflammatory drugs prescribed by the doctor. In the past, when he stayed off the leg a few days and used ice, he'd feel better in a week or so. Not this time. He was hurting as much after three weeks as he was on the ship.

This morning when Catherine came over to fix his breakfast and help him get cleaned up, George recalled the time several years before when he'd consulted with his orthopedic surgeon. Dr. Perry told him he was a good candidate for a knee replacement when he couldn't stand the pain any longer. Confronting George with the prospect of knee surgery had ticked him off. "I'll never feel that bad," he'd said.

Dr. Perry didn't answer, but seeing his patient wince as his foot hit the floor after getting down from the examining table and watching him limp from his office forced him to say, "I hate to tell you, George, but you'll be back."

George shifted positions so Catherine could fluff up his pillows. For three weeks whenever he moved or tried to take a few steps, his knee felt like a thousand daggers were piercing it. It took all his courage to get to and from the bathroom. At night, it throbbed so much he couldn't sleep. Between the pain and sleep deprivation he was rapidly going looney.

Catherine was sitting at the end of the couch. "It's obvious your drugs are not working, George."

"You're right, and I've got to find some relief. I'm so desperate, I'd let some surgeon cut off my leg--even sharpen his knives for him."

"Wouldn't it be better to reconsider having a knee replacement?"

"Probably. But I don't know a thing about the procedure. When Doc Perry first described the operation, I never took him seriously and didn't listen."

"He'll explain it again."

"Even so, I hate the idea of a sawbones messing with my leg. It scares me. After all, I've been living with this deteriorating knee for almost sixty years. It's a known quantity. Despite Doc Perry's con job, surgery's risky business. If he makes one miscalculation or his knife slips, I'm an invalid. Besides, I knew a guy who had the surgery and never got rid of the pain. What's the sense of that?"

"George, I'm not minimizing the risk, but I know Dr. Perry has an excellent reputation as a surgeon."

"I'll bet he carries malpractice insurance."

Catherine got up and kissed him on the forehead for reassurance.

"It just occurred to me why you're so eager for me to be hacked up. You're hoping I'll get an extra whiff of anesthesia that sends me off to dreamland permanently. Then you can sue his behind and get millions."

Catherine contorted her face into a witch's expression and rubbed her hands together. "He, he, he. I'd never do such a thing."

"Ha!"

"Your daughters would sue, and we'd split three ways."

"Get out of here and leave me to my misery."

"Can you manage without me?"

"No, nor do I want to. I love you. Though I could do without your maliciousness."

"In that case, we'll get through this together."

231

After Catherine left for home, George continued weighing his options. Since the first night of the cruise, he absolutely knew without reservation he was going to marry Catherine. But he didn't want to contractually sign up for the gig until he was fully recovered. The way he was progressing, he needed the operation because the knee wasn't going to get better without it. However, a replacement was a long drawn-out process. Assuming he had the surgery, he couldn't marry her and have her sitting home twiddling her thumbs while he was holed up in some convalescent home learning to walk again. That could be months. What if he died recovering?

Then there was Lily and his daughters. He wouldn't be able to travel, and they were so busy they couldn't be visiting all the time. Talking on the phone was a poor substitute for a hug.

And what about his garden? If he had the operation, this year would be the first in almost sixty that he'd fail to plant one. Of course, if he didn't have the replacement there was no assurance he'd feel good enough to garden this year, anyway. After all it was already mid-March. He became misty eyed. What if he was never able to garden again? He couldn't imagine a summer without one. Better to be dead, he thought.

For a time, his musings took his mind off his pain. But lying in one place so long took its toll. His chest and upper back began cramping. He moved. His knee made him cry out. Despite his reservations, he only needed one assurance from the doctor to move ahead with a replacement. If it was successful, he'd be pain free.

Monday came and Gert drove Catherine and him to Dr. Perry's. They listened as the doctor explained some alternatives to a replacement. Then he described the procedure itself, why he'd be donating his own blood and answered some of George's questions about rehab and the usual length of recovery.

George interrupted him. "I'll be able to work in my garden without pain?"

"Not this summer, but you'll be knee deep in cabbage next year."

"Okay, Doc. Let's get it over with."

CHAPTER TWENTY-ONE

FULL BLOOM

By the time the surgery was scheduled for late May, George's knee felt better. He shared his second thoughts with Dr. Perry at the pre-op exam.

"It's still not too late to cancel."

George groaned. "You're a big help."

Doctor Perry shook his head. "The MRI shows your knee's a mess. You tell me it hurts all the time, and I can make it better. I've explained the risks, the post-surgery regimen and what to expect during the recuperation period. I'm not some salesman peddling replacements. You have to decide if you're desperate enough to want to move your leg without pain, because you're the one who has to sign the consent form."

"You know I've already made the decision. That doesn't mean I couldn't use some reassurance."

Dr. Perry patted George on the back and said, "The

surgery's a good decision, George. I know there'll be times over the next few months when you'll be cursing me, but after that you'll be so pleased you'll want to send me a box of expensive cigars."

"Does Medicare cover cigars?"

"Don't be silly. Medicare doesn't even pay me what the operation should cost."

George reached across the desk. "In that case, Doc, give me the damn form."

***

The next week when Gert and Catherine drove him to Central Hospital for the operation and helped him check in, he was more anxious than he expected. Somewhere deep in his gut an impulse jolted him. Could this be the last day of his life? As Gert pushed his wheelchair to the surgical area and Catherine walked beside him, he held onto her hand.

"Your hand is clammy, George," she said. "Are you that uptight about the replacement?"

"I'm not worried about the replacement. I'm scared as hell about not living through the surgery so I can use it."

"Oh, George. Doctor Perry has done hundreds and hundreds of successful knee surgeries. Do you think he would operate if it was life threatening?"

"Yes. It's not his life."

"I'm not worried. I trust Dr. Perry, and you're having a regional not a general anesthetic. You'll be fine, and Gert and I will be here the whole time, won't we Gert?"

"Any guy that's tough enough to survive a meal with me at a biker bar, is certainly going to survive this teeny operation."

George laughed. "That was just fun. Something tells me this isn't going to be fun."

235

When they arrived at the surgical wing of the hospital, a nurse took the wheelchair from Gert. Hugging George before leaving for the waiting room, she said, "Good luck, Georgy."

The nurse pushed George toward the operating room. Walking along next to the wheelchair, Catherine held his hand. When they reached the end of the corridor, the nurse said, "I'm afraid this is far as you can go."

Catherine removed her hand from his and kissed him. "I love you, George. See you in a few hours."

"I hope so," he moaned.

Following surgery, as he lay in the recovery room, he saw Gert and Catherine peek through a crack in the curtains that surrounded his bed.

"Now that we know you're fine, we'll leave and let you rest," Catherine whispered.

"Come back soon," he thought he said, but wasn't sure.

Closing his eyes, he made a pleasant discovery. He was free of pain. It hadn't registered on him yet that he was still numb from the spinal. He glanced about. Drawn curtains surrounded his bed, and instead of feeling claustrophobic, he liked the privacy. No nurses to bug him with their annoying questions. Just silence. He yawned and rubbed his eyes. It was time for a little nap.

It seemed like only ten minutes had passed when a cheery female voice said, "So, you've decided to wake up, have you? I've been in and out checking your vitals. You've been sleeping like a baby."

"I woke up because my knee is killing me."

"Oh, that's normal. The anesthetic is wearing off. Are you hungry? I'll see what you can have."

"I want to be pain-free. Doc Perry promised."

"You can have another pain pill around nine."

"I don't want a pill, and I don't want food. I want what I was promised."

"You've got to eat a little."

"I won't eat anything. It'll just go in the garbage."

The nurse left shaking her head, and he dozed off.

A pain from his knee snapped his eyes open. A pink-clad woman with a white nurses cap perched on her short gray hair was standing over him holding a tray. She looked to be about his age.

"What happened to the other nurse?"

"That was me, Sonny. I aged. Would you believe I went from forty-six to seventy-six in the time it took me to get your tray?"

He groaned. "Time does fly around here, doesn't it?"

She placed his tray on the table and peered at him. "You're hurting from your surgery, aren't you?"

"Yes, I am. Thanks for asking. A few minutes ago when you were younger, you didn't seem to care."

She smiled. "I'm Gladys. I'm a hospital volunteer."

"I figured you weren't a nurse. You're too kind."

"They're so very busy and short staffed, but all in all they do an excellent job for the patients here."

As she watched over him, George pushed the button that raised the head of his bed so he could sit with the food table over his lap. Lifting the metal cover from his plate, he frowned and glanced up at Gladys.

"You can only have a soft diet today," she said.

"Does anyone live after eating this stuff?"

"I haven't lost anyone yet."

George took a bite of Jello. "I grew up liking this stuff, Gladys. It still tastes pretty darn good."

"I'm glad. But I don't make it, honey. I just deliver it. I'm just grateful I can help out. They cured my incurable cancer in this hospital twenty years ago." She tucked a sprig of white hair back under her hat. "I could do more than just deliver meals. I have lots of experience.

Sometimes I think I know as much as some of the paid help."

"I'll bet you do. They're lucky to have you here."

"Keeps me busy, too. When you're old you need to keep busy."

"That's very important. That's why I garden."

She walked to the door and waved.

He raised his voice. "You're not going to transform into the mean nurse again, are you? My knee feels better when you're like this."

"That's my gift, young man. Now I have to make the others feel better."

After dinner, Catherine returned and sat in the chair next to his bed. As he drifted in and out of sleep, she told him she'd called Anne and Jill to tell them he was fine as well as returning calls to Mike O'Hara and Mary Alexander who were concerned about him. When visiting hours were over at eight-thirty, she slipped out of the room. George was snoring.

The next morning Dr. Perry came to check on him and perform a few perfunctory taps and pokes. While he hovered over George, he said, "When I got inside your knee, it was worse than I expected. But it's going to be fine. I covered all the worn spots on the ends of your tibia and femur so you won't have the pain of bone rubbing on bone. I also realigned it."

George moaned, "You must have missed something because it still hurts a lot."

"That's normal. I cleaned up a lot of mess in there."

"Normal! Normal! Normal! I've only been here a day, and I'm already sick of hearing how normal all this pain is!"

"George, the knee has to heal. I'll prescribe some pain pills for the next 30 days. Take them as needed. I doubt you'll need a refill. By the way, George, the nurses will have you up walking this afternoon."

"You've got to be kidding!"

"If you're going to get back into your cabbage patch, you have to start your therapy right away." He pulled a chair over to the bed and sat down. "As long as we're on the subject, I'll go over your rehabilitation and recovery. As it looks now, you'll be here three to five days or until I'm sure there's no infection or other complication." He smiled. "I was going to say, that's normal, but I know that irritates you. Before you're dismissed, you'll have a decision to make. Many times I release patients directly to their homes if there's someone to help them around the clock for a week or two. Could one of your daughters stay with you for a few weeks?"

"Nope. Jill's an executive in Chicago, and Anne's caring for my new granddaughter in Columbus."

"What about the attractive lady who came with you to my office and was here yesterday? You haven't gotten married again have you?" Dr. Perry seemed to think that was outrageously funny.

"Not yet." George smirked.

The doctor raised an eyebrow. "The other option is a rehabilitation facility where the staff manages your therapy, feeds, bathes and helps you get to the toilet. If you go that route, you're generally home in two weeks; earlier if your knee bends to ninety degrees."

George thought for a few moments. "I'd better go to rehab. I don't want to stick Catherine with all that responsibility."

"No matter where you go, the harder you work with the therapist and use the continuous passive motion machine, the sooner you'll be back into your regular routine, including driving and gardening. We'll begin using the machine today." He patted George's shoulder. "When you get home, you may need a walker or a cane for a month or two. Also, you should know, a few patients report pain for up to a year."

"Now you tell me."

"I said a few patients. My guess is George Konert will be harvesting tomatoes a year from now."

***

For the next two weeks, at the Rathke Rehabilitation Center, George worked with two physical therapists, Diane and Sue, who he insisted on naming Pip and Squeak because of their diminutive stature. He doubted either of the good-natured young women weighed more than a hundred pounds, yet they could tug and pull his body and leg with the strength of a heavyweight wrestler. Although the stretches and lifts in the regimen they taught him caused immense discomfort, he pushed on because each day he could see progress.

After two weeks when they released him to Catherine's care, he was right on schedule. As he stood with his walker at the front door of the Center with an arm around Pip on one side and Squeak on the other, he thanked them for their help.

Pip said, "It was our pleasure. You're probably the hardest working patient I've ever seen. You'll be doing anything you want in no time."

"And to think Dr. Perry said you might be a problem," Squeak said.

"He said that? You get what you give. If he was as nice to me as you two, I wouldn't give him any problems, either."

"But he did a great job on your knee."

"He was supposed to," George said, and slowly pushed his walker to Catherine's waiting vehicle. With the therapists' help, he struggled into the front seat.

He'd been home just a few days when casseroles began arriving from the neighbors. On Friday Mary

240

Alexander sent one with Jimmy who'd grown a foot since George last saw him. "What grade are you in now, Jimmy?"

"I'm a freshman, Mr. Konert," he said in his new deep baritone.

"Next summer I'm going to need some help with my garden. Are you interested in a paying job?"

"Can I make enough to buy a skateboard?"

"As long as you're dependable and they cost under a few hundred bucks." George thought a moment. "Skateboards? I don't like skateboards. The punks at the shopping mall try to knock the old ladies over with them. I can't understand why they haven't killed someone. Isn't there something else you want to work for?"

"Baseball camp."

"Now there's something I'd be proud to finance." George stuck out his hand. "Shake pawdner?"

"Just let me know when you need me. I'll be ready to work."

"That's the attitude I like in my men." George threw his head back and laughed. "You know what, Jimmy? Let's start right now. It's still not too late in the year to plant a few tomato plants."

"I know how to plant them. I've helped my dad do it. You dig a hole with a spade, get the dirt all broken up, pull the plastic away from the plant and stick it in the ground, dirt and all. Then you water it in."

"That's it. One way or another, I'll have some plants here by tomorrow morning. Be here at noon. Tell your mom to feed you or you can grab a sandwich here. Then you can plant them all by yourself without any supervision. Later you can pull off the suckers, weed and pick them. It will be good practice for next summer, when I can help you. Five bucks an hour okay?"

"I could do it for practice, Mr. Konert, but . . . ."

"It's settled. Five bucks an hour."

241

George had the young man help him to his feet, "By the way, how's your brother?"

Jimmy scrunched up his nose. "Kevin never changes. He's always the same."

"By that you mean?"

Jimmy held his nose and rolled his eyes.

"Okay, then how's Rachel?"

"She's in first grade and has a boyfriend."

"And you?"

"My mom says she doesn't expect much from me. I'm a teenager."

"Well I do. Work hard on your schoolwork and keep your nose clean. You're a good kid, and I want you to stay that way." George extended his hand and Jimmy shook it. "Tell your mother thanks for the dinner and say 'Hi' to everyone for me. I'll see you tomorrow at noon."

"I'll be here, Mr. Konert, and I'll impress you."

Several nights later, when he and Catherine were eating the beef stroganoff Cheryl O'Hara prepared, he began to laugh.

"What's tickling you?"

"It's all these casseroles. The last time I received this many Grace had just died."

"So?"

"Most of them were from single women."

"What's your point?"

"Don't you know single women send meals to get a foot in the door so they can sell the rest of their wares? Casseroles are their loss leaders."

"Oh, George, they were just being kind."

"They were peddling. Haven't you ever taken a single man a casserole?"

"Let's change the subject."

George sat back in his chair and grinned.

***

He'd been home a month. Virtually every day, he received a call from Jill or Anne checking on his progress. Most days their call and Catherine's visit were the highlight, because the dog days of late July kept him inside in the air-conditioning. He hated being cooped up, but the heat and humidity made the porch unbearable. Still he would have enjoyed the firefly nights and surveying his domain from the chaise if it were possible for him to get up and down off it.

While staying inside bothered him, seeing giant weeds growing behind the wire fence where his garden should have been absolutely depressed him. The lone exception was the small weedless patch where, according to Mike O'Hara, Jimmy's tomatoes were thriving. He'd never lived in this house when there wasn't a full garden of vegetables growing in that space. In his mind, a tidy garden and his well kept home were one and the same, an integrated living area. Now a major feature was missing like a kitchen or toilet. Fortunately, Mike had been mowing his grass. Otherwise the rest of his yard would have looked like a vacant lot.

Since he'd been home, Mike had been over a lot. It seemed like most afternoons when Mike got home from work, he'd be sitting in George's kitchen drinking a beer and shooting the breeze. One Friday, he showed up with a package. It was a long skinny corrugated box. He handed it to George.

"What's this?"

"It's a token of my esteem."

"What did I do to deserve your esteem?"

"You're a wonderful neighbor."

George rattled the box. Hearing an object bang against the side, he tore at the end. When the box opened, a long piece of wood slid from the package. He stared at it. It looked like a damn walking stick. What in hell did he need that for? Glancing at O'Hara, he saw his neighbor waiting expectantly for his reaction.

Without much enthusiasm, he said, "It's very nice, Mike. Thank you."

"I hope you like it. I went back into the woods, and cut the branch from a green ash. That's what they make baseball bats from. Then I whittled and chiseled it into the shape I wanted, sanded it smooth and put five coats of shellac on it. I know you probably won't need to use it, but I thought it might commemorate your surgery."

George felt like an idiot. He picked up the stick and examined it. The workmanship was spectacular. He couldn't fathom all the hours Mike had put into making it.

"It's the most beautiful walking stick I've ever seen. Actually I may need to use it for a while. Then I'll buy a rack so I can hang it over the mantel."

"Don't do that. I'll make you one."

"You're too much. I'm sure fortunate to have you and Cheryl living next door."

"We feel the same way, George."

Following Dr. Perry's suggestion George stopped using the continuous passive motion machine at the same time he moved back home from the rehab center. Instead, he religiously performed the daily exercises his smallish friends had taught him. In addition, he visited Pip and Squeak on an outpatient basis three times a week so they could work his leg and ignore his playful moaning and bitching about how much they were hurting him. Eventually, his hard work paid off. At his next appointment with Dr. Perry, he could bend his knee a hundred degrees, and the doctor cleared him to drive. The reward was a concession of minor importance since Catherine kept him in food, supplies and companionship. The only time the old, gray sedan left the garage was when she drove him to the doctor and the therapists.

By mid-August he and Catherine were taking long

walks around the neighborhood. Other than soreness in some underused muscles, he felt great. For the first time in sixty years, his knee didn't trouble him. On one of their walks, Kevin came running after them with a bag in his hand.

"My mom saw you and wanted you to have some of our cucumbers." He pointed to the garden behind their house. "We grew them ourselves."

George took one out and examined it. "Very impressive. Nice shape. Good size. Not too large. You guys are getting good. They'll go great with Jimmy's tomatoes."

Kevin beamed.

"How are you doing otherwise? Like with some of the things we discussed the last time I saw you?"

"I think I'm more mature now."

George and Catherine both laughed. "Then I have a job for you. I already talked to Jimmy about it. Would you help me in the garden next summer? You'll have to follow my instructions, but I'll pay you."

"That would be cool. Can I ask my mom?"

"Of course. Tell her I want to hire you because you're a man of your word."

"I will, Mr. Konert," he hollered as he ran back to the house.

At one of his last appointments with Dr. Perry, he said, "If I'd known a replacement would make such a difference, I'd have had it done years ago. You're a miracle worker, Doc."

"Today, hip and knee replacements are so perfected they've become relatively routine."

"It still takes a good surgeon. You did a wonderful job."

"Thanks, but not all patients are as diligent as you. That's why you're happy with the results."

"Happy enough to bring you a box of cigars. What

245

kind do you like?"

"I was only kidding, George. Save your money. I don't smoke. But I sure like home-grown tomatoes."

"I'll get some to you right away. Next year, I'll also throw in a few cabbages."

A few nights later he and Catherine were playing gin rummy on the couch. While Catherine looked intently at her cards, he said, "You know Catherine, this knee thing has gone so well I'll bet I will be planting my garden in the spring."

"I'm going down with four."

"You're not even listening to me."

"A few minutes ago you told me to shut up and play cards. That's what I'm doing. How many do I get?"

"If you'd listen . . . ."

"I count 36. Write it down, George."

"If you'd listen, I have something important to ask you."

She began dealing the next hand. After sorting her cards, she said, "Wow, what a hand. Now you're going to get it."

He glared at her.

"Discard," she said.

George was becoming more and more agitated. Finally, he slammed his cards on the couch, and said, "Damn it, Catherine, I want to ask you to marry me!"

"That's very sweet George. Let's talk about it after I beat you."

"Grrrrr!"

When she'd won the three game set, she picked up the cards, slipped them into their box and placed the box in the end table drawer. Folding her hands in her lap, she looked up at him with an angelic expression and said, "Now what was it you were saying about marriage?"

"I should say I don't want to talk about it anymore."

"That's all right, George. It's taken you so long to

ask me, I've kind of lost interest."

"Be quiet, Catherine, I want to do this right."

"You're certainly off to a poor start."

They both began laughing. She moved closer and placed her arm around his neck and kissed him. Then she said, "What's the plan, man?"

"I'm going to ask for Gert's permission, which is in the bag, and then talk to Jill and Anne. Not that they'd object. They love you as much as I do. Still I owe them the honor of asking. To top it off, we'll honeymoon on a Caribbean cruise in February." He kissed her cheek. "As for the wedding details, I'll leave those to you." He searched her face for acceptance. "What do you think?"

"About what? I just heard an old man rattling on about asking permission and taking cruises. Didn't you forget something?"

"What? Oh, damn, I did. Catherine, will you marry me?"

"On two conditions."

"What are they?"

"You stop swearing so much, and when you're 100% you'll get down on one knee and propose to me."

"If you want."

"That would be so romantic."

"And a good test to see if I can still plant my garden."

CHAPTER TWENTY-TWO

GROWING SEASON

On the Sunday before Labor Day, Gert invited George to a backyard cookout. When George arrived, Catherine met him at the door, hugged him and kissed him on the cheek. Hand in hand they walked to the kitchen where Gert was chopping salad vegetables. He said, "Those are beautiful tomatoes, Gert. If I didn't know better, I'd have thought they were from my garden."

"They are, George. Apparently, your young tenant farmer gave them to mom when you were napping, and she borrowed a couple for us."

Catherine nodded.

"That's thievery," George said.

"Mother's finally learning. I was hoping she'd also steal some corn on the cob from the Farmer's Market, but I had to pay for it."

Catherine hung her head.

"And the porterhouse steaks?" George asked.

"What do you think, mother? Can you see yourself taking steaks from the meat counter at the butcher shop and racing down the street to a get-away car?"

"Hardly."

"I didn't think you were ready either, so I bought them, too."

George put his arm around Gert's waist. "Well, regardless of how you procured the ingredients, the menu looks terrific. I can't wait to eat."

"Do you need any help, Gert?"

She shook her head. "No thanks, Mother. This evening is the Gert Show. You and George sit on the patio and help yourselves to a lemonade."

As he shuffled past the counter, George counted four thick steaks piled on a platter. I'll bet anything we're going to meet Walt, he thought.

Yesterday, while taking their daily walk, he and Catherine decided the cookout was an ideal time to have George formally ask for Gert's permission to marry. With just the three of them present, Gert would get a kick out of it. Now George hesitated. He certainly didn't want to compete with Gert's plans.

A few minutes later when Gert joined them on the patio, George changed his mind. He set his lemonade on the small table next to his chair and smiled at her.

"What?"

He glanced at Catherine and went into his speech. "Gert, if you approve, your mother and I will be getting married next February."

Gert pretended to faint. Then she said, "Oh-oh! I-am-so-shocked-I-don't-know-what-to-say. I guess if you both want this, I won't stand in your way."

Her mother scowled. "Do you have to make light of everything?"

"I'm happy for you and George, Mother. I really am."

"Thank you, Gert," George said. "By the way, is Saturday, February nineteenth, okay for you?"

"It's fine. Why would I care when you lovebirds tie the knot?"

George winked at her. "You bought a lot of steak for the three of us."

She blushed. "I thought you might be hungry."

A half-hour later when Walt walked around the house and made his appearance on the patio, George was alone in the kitchen. He watched through the window as Gert introduced him to Catherine. He could see the tension. Tall and angular with a shock of reddish hair, Walt shifted from foot to foot as he spoke--a sure sign to George that meeting Gert's mother and eventually him was an ordeal to be endured, not enjoyed.

George made a decision to ease the man's pain. He banged open the screen door, easily navigated the three steps, and nudged Gert aside.

"You must be Walt. I'm George, the old curmudgeon that squires Catherine around." He stuck out his hand.

Walt took it and covered it with his left.

Like they do in church, George thought. Or AA.

Walt smiled. "I'm really pleased to meet you, George."

The breeze from Gert's sigh almost blew George over.

As the afternoon passed, George found Walt to be a mixed bag. Sometimes, he seemed to cower like a mistreated dog. George worried he'd taken one too many blows in life. Other times, he was talkative and oozed Irish charm and a bit of the blarney. Whatever confusing qualities he possessed became inconsequential when George observed his attentiveness to Gert. Seeing her glow from his devotion was reason enough for him to accept the man. While Gert was flitting around making sure everyone was content, she winked at George. He smiled. Though he wasn't so sure of the match, for Gert's sake, he hoped it worked. From the corner of his eye, he spotted Catherine. She was watching the sunset. Her head was tilted slightly to the left and a gentle breeze ruffled a few strands of loose hair. Then he noticed her hands folded reverently in her lap. He shivered. God, he thought, for our sake, I hope *we* make it.

***

Over the next few weeks, George talked with Jill three times. Once she called to see how his knee was doing. He called her the second time. Without revealing the reason, he told her he and Catherine wanted to visit her in Chicago before the fall was over. She seemed pleased and gave him some dates when she was available. After he and Catherine had settled on mid-October, Jill called the next day to notify him that two plane tickets were in the mail for the weekend of the seventeenth. Before he could protest her extravagance, she confessed, "I want you here for a special event on that Friday evening."

He hung up and called Catherine. "Jill must know about our wedding plans and wants to make a fuss over us. She's having some sort of shindig on Friday the seventeenth."

***

When they arrived in Chicago, Carlos met them at the luggage carousel and drove them to Jill's condo. About six-thirty, Jill burst into the apartment, ripped off her coat and gave them both a big hug. "I've got to hustle and change into something casual for dinner. We're meeting Curtis at a little bistro he and I love. His boys are coming, too. This will be such a special night."

251

"Are we dressed okay?" Catherine asked.

"You both look fine. Excuse me a second, I'll be right back." She dashed into the bedroom, and then reappeared with her blouse partially unbuttoned. "There's beer and wine in the fridge, help yourself."

George watched her vanish again. "Who was that woman who swallowed the dervish pill?"

"She's certainly excited."

"Jill's usually not hyper. This woman's apoplectic." He rose from his chair and walked to the kitchen.

In the refrigerator, he found an opened bottle of Chardonnay and poured a glass for Catherine. Then he grabbed a beer for himself and returned to the living room. As he handed Catherine the wine, he said, "Since she obviously knows we're getting married, I wonder why I'm asking for her permission?"

"It never hurts to do things right, dear."

At dinner, George chatted with Curtis and made friends with his teenage sons, Kyle and Peter. When he found out they were Bears fans, he chided them about how his Bengals would clobber their team when they met later in the year. After milking that subject, they discussed the upcoming baseball season and how his Reds and their Cubs would fare. When George glanced at his daughter and Curtis, they were smiling at him.

"What did I do?"

"Nothing. I'm glad you like the boys," Jill said.

"They're a treat. I never had boys to chat with at my house. I got stuck with girls."

"Was that so bad?"

"Not bad. Different."

Soon the whole table erupted into conversation. It only quieted slightly when the waiter arrived with appetizers. Between bites of curried shrimp, potstickers and fried mozzarella, George waited patiently to share his news. The salad and main courses offered him little opportunity, though. But, as they waited for dessert, there was a lull. He winked at Catherine and cleared his throat to make his announcement. Then he noticed Curtis throw a glance at Jill. She smiled and began clinking her wine glass. Good, he thought. They're reading my mind.

"George, Catherine, Kyle, Peter," Curtis began. "Jill and I have an announcement to make." Catherine put her hand on George's hand. "We want to get married, and we're hoping that you, our family, will give us your blessing." He searched their faces for affirmation. Jill waited expectantly.

George was speechless.

Finally, Kyle said, "Peter and I think Jill's the greatest. We're cool with it, Dad."

Peter nodded his agreement.

All eyes turned to George. Catherine squeezed his hand--hard. He gathered himself and said, "Catherine and I think it's terrific. Welcome to the family, Curtis." Then nodding toward Peter and Kyle, "And you boys, too."

"Congratulations to both of you," Catherine said.

The nuptial dominated the conversation through dessert, coffee and after-dinner drinks. They'd chosen Thanksgiving weekend for the wedding because the boys would be out of school. The ceremony would be restricted to family and held in the chapel at Curtis' church, but they'd have a large reception at his country club.

Though George was mildly disappointed, the more they discussed their event the less inclined he was to share his news.

When they were about to leave, George asked Jill and Curtis, "When can I start bragging about my two new grandsons? Fine young men like Kyle and Peter would make any grandfather proud."

"They don't remember their grandparents," Curtis said. "You'd like the idea of having a grandfather, wouldn't you, guys?"

"Cool," Peter said. "Grandfathers send lots of gifts."

"Peter!" his father said.

Catherine laughed. "That's grandmothers, Peter. We're the ones who give presents. Lots of practical things like school shirts and handkerchiefs and socks. Grandfathers don't have the patience to pick out gifts. They send money."

Kyle grinned. "Money's cool."

George spoke up. "I'm not going to stand here and take a bum rap for other men. I like to shop, and I have lots of patience. When I know you guys better, I'll find the perfect gift, like a Bengal's sweat shirt or a Red's cap."

Kyle glanced at Peter. "Yuk!" they said in unison.

The next morning after breakfast, Jill told her father, "I'm so glad you like Curtis and his boys. He and I feel so lucky to have found each other. I'm so glad you came to Chicago so we could tell you and Catherine in person."

He placed his arm around her shoulder and gave her a little squeeze. "Actually, there was another reason we wanted to see you."

"What was that?" A worried look crossed her face. "Your health is fine, isn't it?"

"I'm perfect, and my new knee makes me feel like a kid again. That's one of the reasons I wanted to come here and ask if you had any objections to my marrying Catherine."

She stared at him. "That's fantastic, Daddy. Why didn't you tell us last night?"

George paused, not wanting to say he couldn't get a word in edgewise. Instead, he said simply, "Last night was your party."

She threw her arms around his neck and kissed him. "I'm so thrilled. I've got to find Catherine and congratulate her." She started for the hall, and then stopped in her tracks. "I'll call Curtis. We'll have another celebration tonight."

When Jill was out of sight, George said under his breath, "Judging by your reaction, I guess you approve?"

George and Catherine flew back to Carlisle on Monday afternoon. When he was unpacked, he called Anne. Following his knee operation he'd talked to her almost every day, but lately he'd been so distracted with Gert's romance and his own plans he hadn't called her. Since she hadn't called him either, he wondered if something was wrong. With a touch of guilt, he dialed the phone. However, more than contrition caused him to call. He wanted to see Lily as well as share his good news.

When Anne answered, her voice sounded strained. "Sure, you can come up to Columbus for the weekend, Dad. Lily asks about you and 'Catin' all the time. She'll be thrilled to see you." Almost as an afterthought, she said, "And, of course, so will I."

"I'm coming for a reason."

"I already know. Jill called me."

"About our wedding in February?"

"Yes."

"And you approve?"

"Of course. I love Catherine. She's a great catch for you."

"Should we still come?"

"Please. I want to tell you about something, too."

After he hung up, he called Catherine. "Anne sounds strange. I hope she's okay." Then he added, "You don't suppose she and Bret are having problems?"

"I doubt whatever she wants to tell us is bad news. Haven't you noticed we're on a roll lately?"

When he and Catherine arrived on Saturday morning, Anne greeted them at the door. She looked pale and haggard. Though she hugged them both and congratulated them, he had the feeling she was just going through the motions. He sensed something was distinctly wrong.

He placed his arm around Anne's waist as they walked to the study. When they were seated, he said, "You don't look well. What's the matter?"

"I feel lousy."

"What is it? Flu or something?"

She laid back in the soft chair with her neck against the back, her legs straight out in front of her. She patted her stomach. "I'm pregnant."

George's thoughts were jumbled. His words escaped uncontrolled. "But you can't have kids."

"I guess I can."

"And you're fine? No complications or anything? You don't look good."

"Thanks, Dad!"

Catherine shook her head. "George, you're making her feel worse. She has morning sickness and feels rotten, for goodness sake!"

"Morning sickness that lasts day and night. All my life I wanted to have a baby, and now that I'm going to have one I'm wondering why."

"How far along are you, dear?" Catherine asked.

"Two months."

"You'll start feeling better soon. I guarantee it."

"That's what my OB tells me. I can hardly wait."

George interrupted, "But you and the baby are fine?"

"I throw up a lot, but your grandchild is doing fine, Dad."

"I'm going to have my very own baby George?"

Catherine grabbed his hand and pulled him to his feet. "Are we a bit self-centered, George?" She turned to Anne, "You stay here with your feet up. We'll find Lily."

"Thank you for understanding, Catherine. I can

barely find the energy to stand up."

Catherine pointed to George and whispered, "Men! What ninnies!"

They found Lily helping Martha bake cookies in the kitchen. Lily was covered with flour. When she saw George and Catherine, she climbed down from her stool and ran to them. Catherine hugged her and began wiping the flour from her hands, face and hair.

"I'm going to have a grandson!" George said to Martha.

"Or a granddaughter," Martha said without enthusiasm. "Would you mind doing something with my little helper so I can fix lunch?"

"I was just going to ask if we could borrow her," Catherine said.

She grabbed Lily's hand and guided her into the living room where she jumped up on the couch and said, "Story, Catin."

With George on one side and Catherine on the other, they alternated reading to her.

Then Bret came home from his half-day at the office. When he entered the room, Lily jumped from the couch and ran to him. "Daddy's home."

When he picked Lily up from the floor and raised her over his head, she squealed. Then he put her on his shoulders and walked over to the couch. "I understand I'm going to a wedding in February. Congratulations."

"Thank you," Catherine said. "And we're thrilled with your great news."

"My very own grandson," George said. "I can't believe it!"

She nudged him, "Shush George. You've gone bananas."

After a lunch which Anne didn't touch, George and Catherine decided to head home while it was still light.

"You don't need overnight company right now,"

Catherine told Anne.

They said goodbye to Bret and told Anne to take care of herself. The hardest part was saying goodbye to Lily. She was holding a book and crying.

***

One night in early December after Jill's Thanksgiving wedding, Catherine and George were having dinner at the Fish House.

She said, "I just received the best news today, George. Marianne sent a note saying she and her husband, Bob, and my grandchildren, Nicole and Peter, are flying here from Seattle in February. Isn't that the greatest? My whole family at our wedding."

"That's terrific. I'm so wrapped up with all my grandchildren, I completely forgot about yours. Does this mean that after we're married Nicole and Peter will be my grandchildren, too?"

"Of course, George."

From out of nowhere, he announced, "Catherine, I love you."

She gave him a quizzical look. "What brought about that tender sentiment?"

"Before I met you I didn't have a single grandchild. Now I have five and a four-ninths."

"And that's why you love me? You certainly are romantic, George Konert."

CHAPTER TWENTY-THREE

BLIGHT

George was on a high. For the first time since Grace died, he was enjoying winter. Funkless in January! That would make a great movie title, he thought. Or maybe it should it be Winter Wonderful. Whatever. He liked feeling up when the thermometer was down. Focusing on the roots of his euphoria, he realized that besides his painless knee his impending marriage buoyed him beyond his most far-out expectations. Being with Catherine on a daily basis simply enriched his life. So did his adult relationships with Jill and Anne and accumulating a gaggle of grandchildren. His joy encompassed all of these. But there was more. A spiritual feeling. Something ethereal. Hard to grasp, impossible to describe, but extraordinary.

He carried his musings from the couch to the refrigerator. After filling a glass with ice, he slowly poured a Sprite and watched the bubbles dance on the frigid cubes.

In May, he would be turning eighty-one. BC, Before Catherine, he would have been wary of making any plans at all. Dreams were for the young. If a man his age dared to look too far ahead, he would certainly find a nightmare. Now he was filled with optimism. Whereas, at times in the past his mortality might fill him with apprehension, today he drew satisfaction from drawing a longer straw than many men. He felt a trifle smug. He was healthy, willing to contest each day as it unfolded and about ready to order the seeds for next summer's garden.

Just two years ago, he saw Mary Alexander and the kids frequently. They were the first to fill the void caused by Grace's death. He loved talking with Mary and spending time with the children. But now Rachel was in school full time, and Mary was working. Although he seldom saw her, he vowed some Saturday morning soon he'd drop off some goodies to repay her for her casseroles. Maybe even have a chat.

He returned the empty glass to the sink. Changes, he thought. Always changes. It had been over a year since Mrs. O'Connell died. George missed looking after the old lady and eating those wonderful cookies. When he thought of her, he still hated the tragic way she died. But was it any worse than his old buddy, Tom Wembley, dying in three months from pancreatic cancer? One thing was sure; death hit the old ones fast.

Then again sometimes young people go just as quickly. Just two nights ago Brad Coleman and his friend Buzzy were killed when they got drunk on pilfered booze and Buzzy wrapped the car they'd stolen from his mother around a tree.

At first when George read about the accident, he decided to pass on attending the visitation. He'd never forgiven the kid or his fat, hairy father for covering for Brad when he ripped up his tomatoes. Why try to console someone he despised? Then he waffled. He had, after all, exacted his own sweet revenge. Maybe going out in the cold to make a showing was the proper thing to do.

When he arrived at Olson's Mortuary in downtown Carlisle Thursday evening, George was surprised at how few cars were parked in the lot. Generally, services for a teenager attracted a crowd. He pulled his overcoat up around his neck and headed for the front door. When he signed in, there weren't more than thirty names ahead of his and the visitation was half over. He hung up his coat and stepped into the short line behind a middle-aged woman. Glancing around the room, George didn't see the familiar faces of any of the neighbors. They couldn't all have had previous engagements.

As he waited in line, he spotted the closed casket. Then his eyes lighted on Coleman talking with a man George didn't recognize. Until this moment he always visualized Coleman sitting on his porch stoop in a ribbed undershirt, wearing shorts and a dour expression. He looked so different dressed in a neat blue suit, crisp white shirt and complementary tie. Perhaps George needed to imprint the sad-looking, cleaned-up version on his memory bank. His gaze switched to Mrs. Coleman. She was wringing her hands.

The man in front of him moved away. George approached. He wasn't sure what to expect.

"I'm sorry for your loss," he said.

The large man had tears in his eyes. "You're nice to come. Considering, Brad . . . ." His voice trailed off. He began crying.

Mrs. Coleman stepped forward and said through her own tears, "Mr. Konert, before we had Brad I miscarried so many times we never thought we'd have children. When I finally went full term, and I was handed a beautiful baby boy to look after, my joy turned to fear. I...we loved him so much we over-protected him. We were so afraid we'd lose him, we were paralyzed. You have children. You

261

understand."

George nodded.

"As he grew into a handsome young man, there were many times we knew we needed to discipline him-- that he was spoiled, out of control–but we couldn't." She put a protective arm around her husband. "We couldn't, didn't, ever say no to him. We knew we should, but we didn't." She stared at George. "You do understand, don't you?"

"In the end we lost him anyway," Coleman said.

She patted her husband's shoulder.

The man shook George's hand and said numbly, "Thank you for coming." Looking past George, Coleman focused on a young couple following him in line. "You're nice to come," he mumbled.

George moved away and sat down in a chair to catch his breath. Piped-in organ music played softly in the background as the overly sweet scent of a funeral bouquet wafted past his nose. After several minutes, he rose to leave. The few remaining people spoke softly to each other as they milled around.

***

Several mornings later his hiatal hernia woke him from a deep sleep. As he recalled the previous day's menu, nothing he ate should have provoked an attack. He hurried to the medicine cabinet and took an Alka-seltzer. The chest pain persisted.

When he opened the door to retrieve the newspaper, he was greeted by four inches or more of freshly fallen snow piled on his porch stoop and driveway. He wasn't too concerned because he enjoyed using the snow blower. However, he would be upset if the weather and his stomach misery conspired to keep Catherine and him from attending an afternoon movie and early dinner.

George decided to postpone breakfast until his stomach settled. He put on his fleece-lined parka, galoshes, fur cap and gloves. He found the snow shovel in the back hall, carried it through the house, out the front door and cleared the stoop. When he finished, he reentered through the front door and tracked through the house to the garage. As the overhead door opened, he was greeted with a vast expanse of snow covering his driveway. He started the snowblower on the first pull, and headed out the door.

Tacking into the fierce wind, George began clearing the driveway. As he completed a long swath, he felt a sudden pain. He clutched his chest. He swung the blower around and headed back to the garage. The agony intensified. Shutting off the motor, he left the blower by the edge of the driveway and opened the door to the kitchen. He sat down at the table, hoping his discomfort would subside.

When he started back toward the garage, a sudden flash of pain ran down his left arm. Now he was scared. He grabbed the car keys from the kitchen counter, backed the car through the snow and headed for Central Hospital.

His anguish continued.

He kept driving.

At the emergency room he parked, entered and collapsed.

***

George was aware of a misty, fog surrounding him. As he made his way through the haze, he could barely make out strange Gaudi-like forms. Figures floated about. None of them were discernable. It was clear he'd arrived at a place he'd never been to before, yet, he wasn't anxious. He felt calm and untroubled, like he imagined he'd feel if he'd been hypnotized. He sat down on a bench to rest.

A figure approached and sat down next to him.

After a moment, she opened a small bag and said, "Hello, George. Want a cookie?"

His eyes alighted on the familiar face. Her gnome-like body was transformed. She appeared as he first knew her.

"Mrs. McConnell, is that you?"

"It's me, Birthday Boy," and she planted a big kiss on his mouth. "Am I glad to see you. I want you to meet someone."

A young man in his early twenties wearing a khaki military uniform stepped from the mist to greet him. George stared at his strong jaw and crew cut. He looked exactly like the framed picture on Mrs. McConnell's piano. George grimaced. Hadn't he been killed in Korea?

"I've been wanting to meet you for a long time, Mr. Konert." He stood at attention as he spoke. "My mother has been telling me how good you've been to her."

"George, this is my son, Seth. Other than you, he's the love of my life."

"Don't let Grace hear you say that." He reached out a hand to the young man.

Seth shook it warmly. "Now that we've finally met, let's not wait so long until our next visit."

"I'll second that," George said.

"Gotta go now," she said. "We'll be seeing you, George."

"Don't go, Mrs. McConnell, Seth. Let's talk some more." He stared as the fog enshrouded them. There was only silence.

Another person approached. It was a teenage boy.
"Mr. Konert?"

The voice sounded familiar. "Yes?"

"I was hoping to find you here."

"Do I know you?"

"I'm Brad Coleman."

In this strange environment, all of George's old

animosity toward the young man had vanished. It helped seeing a familiar face. "I'm so pleased to see you, Brad. I hope your parents are doing better."

"I think they'll be okay eventually, sir. I appreciate your concern." He stooped down to speak to George at eye level. "I stopped by to tell you how sorry I am about tearing up your tomato plants. I know now how much your garden meant to you."

"Means to me."

"Of course."

"You can make it up to me by helping me grow some vegetables. Where do people garden?"

"I don't know, Mr. Konert. I've never seen a vegetable garden around here."

"That's terrible. I can't be where I thought I was." George reached up with his hand and Brad pulled him to his feet. "I'd appreciate having a guide. Would you help me find my way around this place?"

"It's the least I can do. Follow me."

George sauntered next to him into the haze. They were gliding along a wide esplanade. Vague figures slipped past them in every direction.

"I'll take over from here," a voice said as Brad faded off.

"Is that you, Jake?"

"None other. Jake Parrino at your service."

"You can't believe how great I feel seeing you again."

"I know. I'm Mr. Excitement. By the way, I almost bopped that Cement Head character for you, but around here they frown on that stuff."

"Thank God you never change, Jake."

"Nor you, George. I've kept an eye on you. You turned out just as I expected, and I'm envious of the way you've lived your life."

"You never had the time."

"It wouldn't have made any difference. I could never have been a George."

A lump formed in George's throat. "That means so much to me, Jake."

They kept walking through the haze.

"Where are we going, Jake?"

"You'll know when you get there." He laughed and smacked George in the arm, "You know I'd never lead you astray."

"Of course not."

All at once, two small girls skipped up to him, one on each side. One said, "Can we come with you, Daddy?"

"Jill? Anne?"

Jill grabbed his left hand and Anne the other. "Where are you going?" Jill asked.

"I don't know," he said. "Jake is leading me."

"There's no one leading you, Daddy."

George looked ahead. Jake had disappeared. "Then I'm sure glad you're with me." They walked on. "Remember the day when you were selling vegetables, and it began to storm? I was so scared something might happen to you. While you were safe at the Gill's playing Monopoly, I was scouring the neighborhood in the thunder and lightning."

"We know," Jill said. "We were worried about you too, Daddy."

"I didn't know that." As he studied each of his daughters, he was struck by a sudden thought. "There's something I don't understand. Why are you girls here?"

"Because we love you, Dad," Anne said.

Tears formed as he pulled his daughters to him. They were such a comfort, these daughters of his. But then like ice they slipped from his grasp and were gone. "Kids," he hollered. "Jill, Anne, don't leave me. I didn't tell you how much I love you."

He sat down on a nearby bench and placed his head

in his hands. The novelty of this strange place was wearing off, and he was becoming distressed. How does one leave, he mused?

A form, white-robed and hooded, eased onto the bench next to him. The figure slipped a hand around his back. George cringed.

"Don't get shook up, George. It's only me."

"Grace?"

"Of course, George. Aren't I always near when you need me?"

He broke away from her and peered into her dark eyes. The robe had transformed into the yellow and black suit he'd helped her pick out for her thirtieth birthday. Her brown curly hair was pulled back into a long ponytail. He wrapped his arms around her delicate figure and kissed her gently on the mouth. When he released her, he said, "I've missed you so much!"

"I know, George, and I love you, too. But don't get any ideas about joining me."

"Why, Grace. It's always been you and me."

"Not yet, George. Catherine needs to complete the finishing touches before I want you back." She smiled and kissed his cheek. "Bye for now."

"Where do I go from here, Grace? I need you." But she was gone.

He laid his head back on the bench and rested. A state of total comfort overtook him. He closed his eyes. The bench began to rise. Breathing became unnecessary as he floated upward through the clouds and fog. In the distance, he was aware of a bright shimmering light. He was moving toward it. As the light became brighter, George squinted through one eye and then the other. A white figure was hovering over him. He felt panicky and gasped for a breath. His voice came forth in a whisper. "You're not my wife."

"All you have to do is ask, my Prince," the figure

267

said.

"Who are you?"

"I'm your recovery nurse, Suzy." She tugged at the bottom of the blanket and smoothed it over his legs.

"Recovery?"

"I'm also your Fairy Godmother. Now that you're awake, I'll make your daughters appear. They'll explain." She turned and left.

George felt a foreign object filling his nostrils. Moving his eyes he spotted a tube in his arm attached to a bottle hanging from a silver stand. He was in a hospital room. But why?

He moved his hand to pull up the sheet. A pain tore at his chest. Instantly, he recalled blowing the snow, then driving the car with his chest hammering and pain radiating down his arm. He saw the entrance to the emergency room. Then blackness.

Jill came running to him with Anne walking close behind. Jill said, "We were so scared, Daddy. When they called, we thought we'd lost you."

"We've been here all night," Anne said.

"Why?"

"Quadruple bypass. Heart surgery," Jill said.

George stared at Jill. She was always so fastidious. Now she had mascara tracks trailing down her face, and her hair was disheveled. Her smart business suit was a wrinkled mess.

He turned his head. As he smiled at Anne, he noticed her maternity top. "No baby yet, I see."

"Three more months before you have your grandson. Thank God you'll get to know each other. I was so worried you wouldn't."

Jill sat down on his left and touched his arm gently while Anne carefully clasped his right hand. He turned his head from side to side to see them more clearly. "In my dream, I remember feeling terrible because you were both gone before I could tell you how much I love you."

"We know, Daddy. We heard."

Jill whispered to her sister, "You need sleep, and so do I." She squeezed George's hand and raised her voice, "Daddy, now that we know you're going to be fine, Anne and I are going back to the hotel. Catherine has been here, too. She'll be back later."

"Who?"

Anne looked at George with alarm. "You don't know who Catherine is?"

"Never heard of her."

"Dad, she's the woman you're supposed to marry next month."

"Why would I get married on February nineteenth? That's when my seeds arrive."

"You're not funny, Daddy. We thought for a minute you lost your mind."

"Anyone that gets married at my age probably has."

Jill and Anne got to their feet. Avoiding the paraphernalia surrounding George's head, they each bent over and kissed him.

Anne patted her stomach. "This has been a long, tough day."

"Go put my grandson to bed," George mumbled before closing his eyes.

CHAPTER TWENTY-FOUR

THE HARVEST

Two weeks after his bypass surgery George and Catherine were sitting at the kitchen table sipping herbal tea. George put his cup down. "There's absolutely no need to change the wedding date. I feel great except for the pain in my ribs and the fact that I get tired easily."

Catherine took another donut from the bakery bag and closed it before George could take one.

He glared at her.

"Your daughter, Marianne, and her family have plane tickets for February."

"They've already changed them to June fourth."

"That's the wedding, June fourth?"

"Saturday, June sixth."

"How do you know that works for my girls and Gert?"

"I checked with them. Anne likes it better than

February because the baby will be old enough to travel, and she hopes she'll be nursing. It's fine for Jill, Curtis and the boys as well."

George eyed her. He was mildly disappointed. There were reasons he'd originally agreed to February. He wanted to honeymoon on a Caribbean cruise when the weather in Ohio was at its worst. Carlisle was too nice to leave in summer. Anyway, where would they honeymoon in summer? At some cottage in Canada?

Mainly, he didn't like waiting until June for Catherine to move into his house. He wanted her with him every minute, *now*. He couldn't wait to cook with her and just watch her read or whatever, and have her share in his domestic life. Long before June as the weather warmed they could share a drink on the porch and watch the crab apple trees flower and the birds flit from tree to tree and the plants spring from the earth. More than anything, he wanted to share his bed with her every night and enjoy the warmth of her body next to his. Good grief, by June he could have cancer or another heart attack.

A sheepish grin crept over his face. "Catherine, we need to get married now. I'm busy June sixth."

"Doing what? Hoeing your cabbage plants? You're barely out of the hospital with a quadruple bypass. I don't care if we were supposed to get married in a week and a half. June is soon enough." Catherine raised her eyes to the ceiling. "Oh, Lord! Will he always be like this?"

"Then maybe you'll move in with me, and we'll live in sin?"

"I'd have to think about that."

The next morning after fixing a bowl of cereal with a sliced banana on top, George searched through the desk drawer where Catherine said she placed the seed orders he was going to send the day he had his heart attack. He found them exactly where she said they'd be. After checking the orders, he put on his heavy coat and cap,

271

wrapped a scarf around his nose and mouth and shuffled to the mailbox at the end of the driveway. He stuffed them in and put the flag up.

When he returned, he called Doug Wembley about tilling his garden. No one answered, so he left a message on the machine. As he thought about it, he hadn't seen Doug or his mother, Betty, since his friend's funeral. He was angry with himself. Even before his surgery, he hadn't phoned or checked up on them. If he'd been the one who died, Tom would have been seeing after Catherine and consoling his daughters.

Tom was always helping out his friends. Like the tilling. Even though his son, Doug, did the work, George always knew his friend had a hand in persuading Doug to do it. Now that Tom was gone and Doug was running the hog operation instead of working for his dad, he wouldn't have the time or the inclination to help George with his garden. In fact, George thought, it was an imposition to even ask him. He'd rent a tiller and let the Alexander kids do the backbreaking work.

Doug returned his call several days later on Saturday, and apologized for taking so long to get back to him.

"That's okay, Doug. I understand. It must be hard trying to fill your father's shoes. Especially since you don't have *you* to help like your father did. I always knew you'd eventually be managing the farm when your dad retired just like Tom took over from your grandfather. Tom died so quickly, you must be under a lot of pressure."

"I am awfully busy, but I'm not running the farm. I'm studying accounting at Miami University."

"Your mother's managing the farm alone?"

"Oh, no. We sold it to Consolidated. Neither of us wanted to spend the rest of our lives slopping hogs, so I returned to college, and she's in the process of moving into a condo in town."

"I didn't know." George stroked his chin. "I wonder what your father would think of your decision?"

"It was his idea. Before he died, he negotiated the sale. He realized he was the last of a dying breed and wanted us out from under it."

George wiped a tear from his eye with the side of his index finger. "That's Tom, thoughtful to the end. Do you know he played cribbage with me after my wife died to help keep my spirits up?" He sighed. "He was a great friend. I miss him."

"He thought a lot of you, too, Mr. Konert. That's why he left you a gift. I'm sorry I haven't gotten it to you yet."

"A gift?"

"The tiller."

"His Toro? Oh, Doug, I'm overwhelmed. I promise I'll dedicate my garden to Tom each spring."

"I'll tell my mother. She'll be pleased. One weekend soon, I'll bring it over. Sorry I can't till for you this year."

"You hit those books and become a great accountant. I can hire the neighbor kids to till, or maybe I'll just sit and admire it . . . or teach the tiller to play cribbage."

March slipped by without a setback. The pain from spreading his ribs during the operation had subsided, his seeds had arrived and Doug Wembley had delivered the tiller. He also scheduled a preliminary meeting with Jimmy and Kevin Alexander at their house to discuss how they were going to plant and tend the garden. After he outlined their duties and settled on their hourly rate, they ran off.

Mary came and sat with him at the kitchen table. She brought out a coffee cake and poured him a cup of coffee. It felt like old times.

"It's been too long since we've talked. How do you feel?"

273

"Great. I'm the luckiest man alive."

"I was shocked when I heard about your heart attack."

"No more than me. Ever since I found Catherine, I've ignored the ticking of the clock. The surgery was a wake-up call. Even though my cardiologist says I'll live a long time, I know any episode might be the last. I'm not so scared of dying. I just have reservations about leaving Catherine a widow for the second time."

Mary studied him. "Remember when you helped me with my marriage?"

"You were all out of sync over nothing."

"Exactly. Now, thanks to you, we've been back on track and getting along great. So I'm going to give you a dose of your own medicine and return the favor."

Mary topped off George's cup and pushed the coffee cake toward him. "Let's pretend I'm Catherine, okay?"

George nodded.

"I'm a widow and live with my daughter. I can marry a handsome man who loves me and who I love. Now there's some risk in that. He might pass away, and I'll feel terrible. Or I can choose not to marry him, and if he passes away I'll feel terrible. Either way I feel terrible, or either way I end up a widow living with my daughter. Now I ask you, where's the risk?"

George laughed. "You're good. You're very, very good."

"I should be. I learned from you." She reached across the table and squeezed his hand.

George took a piece of coffee cake and began munching. He had something else to ask Mary, but he didn't know how to begin. Lately, when he slept at night he'd been troubled by a persistent dream. In the dream, he was in bed with Catherine when Grace appeared and stood at the footboard and observed them. She showed no expression and said nothing. At each appearance, he wanted to tell her he hadn't forgotten her, that he still loved her and Catherine wasn't replacing her. But he couldn't say the words because they sounded hypocritical. After all, he did love Catherine, and in a way she was replacing Grace.

"You're awfully quiet," Mary said.

"I'm sorry. I'm having another problem." Despite feeling sheepish telling Mary about his dream, he blurted it out anyway. "So how can I love two woman at the same time? I'm not some gigolo."

"Of course, you're not. You love Catherine. You only love the memory of Grace, because that's all you have left of that relationship."

"But when Catherine moves in she'll scrape and paint and empty out closets and drawers that hold pieces of my marriage to Grace. I'm not sure I want to let go of them."

"They aren't the memories, George." She pointed to her temple. "You'll always have them tucked away up here. What may get thrown out are some of the little stimuli that bring them back and make them more vivid. Your job now is to make room for new triggers so you can get at the memories of Catherine you're storing away."

"Like every time I see a cabbage I remember the day I first met her?"

"You got it."

George stood up and moved toward the door. "Again, I'm indebted to you. When I was a lost old man three years ago, you took my vegetables and, in return, gave me a family to love and an understanding ear. That was one lopsided deal."

Mary wrapped her arms around him, "I'm not sure it wasn't an even trade. You raise wonderful cabbage."

That night when Grace stood at the foot of the bed she was smiling.

***

By the first weekend in April, George was feeling strong and itching to start his garden. There was only one thing holding back the operation. Two weeks of solid rain. The ground was a swamp that would suck the tiller down to the axle. Each day between showers George walked over the wet lawn to peer through the garden fence. The sight left him morose. Unless the sun came out and the wind started blowing, it would be May before he'd plant any lettuce or beets.

When Catherine came over to have lunch with him, he groused about the nasty weather. "If we were married, I wouldn't care about my garden. We could play gin, plan trips and have dinner out."

"Nice sentiment, George. But I don't delude myself. Grace did her dance every spring because she knew you cared more about your garden than any human."

George laughed. "The dance had nothing to do with gardening. It was a mating ritual. Let's see yours."

Catherine got up from the table and did a few pirouettes. "How's that?"

"Just okay. I think you need to incorporate a couple of fans like Sally Rand. Or seven veils."

"Thanks a lot."

Catherine began clearing the table and filling the dishwasher. George stood up and carried his glass to the sink. A clap of thunder rattled the house.

She shuddered. "I don't like thunderstorms."

"You don't suppose that was Grace telling us she's jealous?"

Catherine grinned. "Of me? Don't be silly. If anything she's relieved I've taken you off her hands so she doesn't have to worry about you."

He took her hand and guided her into the living

room where they sat down on the couch.

"I like being worried over."

"Of course you do, George. It's a male trait."

He pulled her to him so her head rested on his shoulder and closed his eyes.

"It's time for a little nap," he said.

When he awoke, he glanced at Catherine. Her head was still leaning against his shoulder, and she was asleep. He gazed at the newly patched ceiling and began mulling over a scenario that first appeared in his mind when the wedding was put off until June.

Catherine finally moved her head from his shoulder and stretched. He smiled at her and said, "Instead of waiting until June, why don't you move in with me right now? It's going to take you a while to get the house just the way you want it."

"George, I can't deal with that now. I'm half asleep."

"Well, wake up. This is too important to sleep through."

"The only thing that concerns me is what your children will think. I wouldn't want them upset with us."

"I'm eighty-one and just had open-heart surgery. You're seventy-three."

"Seventy-two."

"Whatever. Anyway, I don't give a damn what they think, do you?"

"I care, but not too much," she said.

They both started laughing.

To add weight to his argument, George said, "Maybe, if you moved out of her house Gert and Walt would work out their problems and get married."

"I'm not the problem. In fact, Gert told me this morning it's all over."

"Oh, no! She was so happy."

"Until he went off the wagon last week. He was so

awful to her, she had to fire him."

"Poor kid. She doesn't get any breaks."

"Not yet. But, if I can find someone as good as George Konert, there will be someone out there for Gert."

"Unfortunately, there's only one George Konert. Maybe I should marry both of you."

"It would be easy enough to do. We could just add Gert's name to the wedding invitations."

"On second thought, Gert's too young for me. I prefer older women." George patted Catherine's hand. "Now let's get back to discussing your moving in with me."

Two weeks later Gert and Catherine boxed her few belongings, loaded Gert's truck and found space to put them in George's house. By the third week of April, Catherine was supervising Gert and a couple of buddies as they tore up the house room by room, splashing paint on the walls and ceilings and wallpapering the bathrooms in an effort to transform twenty-plus years of neglected dinginess into a bright, cheery habitat. To complete the refurbishing, George agreed to new white shantung drapes for the living and dining rooms and red and white checked polished cotton curtains for the kitchen. After much moaning about the cost, they also purchased new Berber carpeting to replace the worn out flooring in the living room, dining room, hallway and the stairs leading to the second floor.

Even with the redecorating, having Catherine with him night and day was more of a joy than he'd imagined. Not only did he have a partner, he had a heat generator next to him in the bed after an absence of fourteen years. So what if she smelled of paint.

Buoying his already upbeat mood were the elements. The winds had been howling for a week, the sun had made frequent appearances and the rains had ceased. Even Good Friday when it often seemed to rain was pleasant enough to allow Jimmy and Kevin to share the tasks of tilling and raking George's garden in the morning. When they finished and while they relaxed on the porch drinking the lemonade and eating the roast beef sandwiches Catherine served them, George showed them his planting chart and outlined the next day's tasks.

"We're a team. I'll show you exactly what to do. You'll do the work."

"What are we going to plant?" Kevin asked.

With disdain, Jimmy said, "Look at the chart, Kevin. Mr. Konert has it all spelled out. Peas go here. Radishes over here in two short rows. The tomatoes go over by the peppers. It's all on the chart if you just read it. Right, Mr. Konert?"

"Pretty much," George said not wanting to contradict Jimmy's teenage declarations nor incite Kevin to insurrection.

Without a word, Kevin glumly studied the garden diagram. Suddenly, he brightened. "It says here that we plant tomatoes and peppers on May fifteenth. You're not so smart, Jimmy."

"Let me see that." Jimmy grabbed for the chart, but Kevin spun away from him.

"Whoa, guys! If you tear the planner there won't be a garden." George took the chart from Kevin and folded it up. "See why I'm in charge of this team?"

He motioned both to their seats and in a drill sergeant's voice said, "Tomorrow, our team will plant peas, carrots, beets, three kinds of lettuce, Swiss chard, onions and early cabbage." He studied his workers. "If there are no further questions, you're dismissed until nine in the morning."

After the boys followed him from the porch and scampered out the front door, he chuckled. He was such a good boss, and tomorrow he'd have the beginnings of a garden. He grabbed the doorjamb as he headed for the living room. It was wet with off-white paint.

***

June sixth was a month away. Catherine had booked the chapel at Carlisle College for the ceremony and the City Club for the reception. She obtained the services of the Chaplain from Central Hospital whom she and George had met and liked following his heart attack. Just last week she'd sent the invitations and made hotel reservations for Jill's family and Bret, Anne, Lily and two-month-old Gregory George Jackson.

In George's mind, Catherine ought to be done. Instead, George found her going through his closet. "What are you doing?"

"Checking out your suits for the wedding."

"I don't own a summer suit."

"Then we need to buy one."

"It's a waste of money. I'll die before I wear it again."

Catherine held up his good blue suit. "You can't wear this. It looks too heavy to go with my new peach dress."

"Wear a different dress. I'm not buying a new suit."

She sat down on the bed. Tears filled her eyes. "Why are you so difficult? All I want is for us to look nice for one day, and you give me grief."

George sat down next to her and put his arm around her shoulder. "I'm sorry. I just hate spending money on something I'll never wear again. Can't we rent a suit?"

Catherine pulled away from him, stood up and tucked in her blouse. "Sometimes in your ignorance you come up with the best solutions. Tomorrow we'll go and rent a summer tux."

"Aww, come on Catherine. Not a tux. I'll buy a new suit."

"Too late. Now you're wearing a tux."

Besides whipping his garden into shape, George had two prenuptial problems to solve in the next four weeks. He had yet to determine where and when he and Catherine were honeymooning, and he needed a plan to guarantee Catherine's financial security. She'd been left destitute by her first husband. Assuming he'd die first, he had no intention of letting that happen again.

The honeymoon proved the more difficult of the two. Since a summer cruise in the Caribbean was unappealing, he'd begun researching resorts in Canada and upstate New York. Many were full. Most were too swishy or catered to families with small children. Moreover, he still had a bad taste in his mouth from the time he and Grace picked out a resort in the Poconos and were served rotten fish. That was also the resort where their room was moldy, their tablemates were from Pittsburgh and the man persisted in talking with his mouth full of food and gesturing with his silverware.

"Catherine, what if we postpone the honeymoon until November or December, and then take a Caribbean cruise?"

She smiled sweetly. "So you can garden all summer?"

"So I don't have to eat dinner with a man who talks with his mouth full."

"Huh?"

"It's a long story."

She kissed him. "Whatever makes you happy. I just want to be with my man."

"Speaking of 'your man,' I'm going to the lawyer on Tuesday and have a trust drawn. When it's signed, you'll have income for the rest of your life and access to principal if you need it. How's that?"

"Have you talked to Jill and Anne about it? It's their inheritance."

"They're fine with it. By their accounting I don't have all that much, and they're comfortable with your using it up if you need to. I also made provisions for Gert. When we're both dead, Gert gets a third of whatever is left."

Catherine began sobbing. "Who would have thought a man selling cabbage for fifty-cents from a child's wagon could be so generous."

"I found the woman I love the day I gave the fifty-cents back. I learned a lesson from that."

When the day of the wedding finally arrived, George couldn't sleep and was up at five. Although he'd promised Catherine he'd stay out of the garden, he was too restless to sit around until one-thirty when he'd have to put on his monkey suit for the service. After scanning the paper and downing a bowl of Rice Chex, George padded down the steps to the basement. From there the lure of the earth was too great. He followed the siren song, walked across the grass and peered over the fence at his crops.

He was shocked. Five days before he'd paid Jimmy and Kevin to hoe and pull weeds. He'd supervised them at the beginning, and when they seemed to understand their duties, he retired to the porch chaise. The one time he'd checked on them, they were doing fine with the weeds between the rows. Evidently, they hadn't been as thorough with the nasty, green interlopers within the rows. The weeds were choking out the lettuce, beans and beets. Since he couldn't call the boys at such an early hour, and he couldn't stand the sight of the weeds, he'd have to pull them by hand, wedding day or not. He headed back to the house. Because squatting and kneeling were no longer an option with his knee replacement, he needed his folding aluminum and canvas stool so he could sit. He also grabbed his wide brim hat.

While George weeded the beets, he noticed quite a few Asian Beetles on the leaves. They concerned him. If he didn't do something soon, they'd ruin the greens, which he liked to eat even more than the beets. He trudged back to the basement and returned with a coffee can full of soapy water. Whenever he spotted a beetle on one of the leaves, he picked it off and dropped it into the can. After a row of hand de-bugging resulted in far too much effort, he decided he'd have to spray away the beetles.

When he finally finished weeding, he marched back to the basement and returned with his sprayer. Before beginning the process, he decided to check out the green bean and the pole bean leaves. He couldn't believe his eyes. They were loaded with beetle holes as well.

Next he checked out the cabbage. He didn't spot any beetles, but each of his perfect spheres was infested with cabbageworms. He peered at the sun bearing down on him and wiped the sweat from his forehead with his blue bandanna. Now that he'd already broken his promise to Catherine, he couldn't go back to the cool of the basement when the whole damn garden needed spraying.

It was nearly ten-thirty when he sprayed the last leaf. The heat had soared while he worked making him feel faint and a bit sick to his stomach. Gathering his garden tools, he shuffled back to the basement. George drew a cold drink of water from the basement faucet and plopped onto the old chrome and plastic chair to rest. What an idiot, he thought. Would he ever learn to be less compulsive about his garden? If he had another heart attack trudging up the stairs after steaming his body all morning, Catherine would never forgive him for spoiling the wedding.

"You were out in that heat a long time," Catherine said when he finally met her in the kitchen.

"I know. I don't feel too good, either."

"Why would you? You've just had heart surgery, and you're eighty-two."

"Eighty-one."

"Either way you're old."

She placed her cool hand on his forehead. "You're

burning up. Take a cool bath and a nap."

"What if I die in my sleep?"

"At least you'll look rested for the funeral."

George glared at her. "You're not very sympathetic."

"You're not very smart."

After downing a turkey sandwich to settle his queasiness, George shaved, took a long bath and a ninety-minute nap.

While struggling with the studs on his tux shirt, he said, "I guess we won't have to postpone the wedding. I feel fine."

Catherine was standing in her slip at the bathroom mirror curling her hair. "I'm glad you're feeling better, George, but I'd already decided we were going through with the ceremony even if we had to prop you up and hire a ventriloquist to move your mouth and say the vows."

George stared at himself in the full-length mirror on the closet door. "That won't be necessary. I feel as good as I look, and I look fantastic."

That afternoon at the chapel George and Catherine were married before their families and a smattering of neighbors.

Since the reception at the City Club more closely resembled a family gathering, Catherine eschewed a formal receiving line. Instead, while everyone ate appetizers and sipped drinks, the newly married couple made the rounds thanking each guest for sharing their day.

As the afternoon progressed, George approached Anne who had just finished nursing her son. "Can I introduce Gregory George to everyone?"

"Are you sure you want to walk around holding him?"

George hesitated. "I'm kinda out of practice. What if I sit down and hold him? Everyone could come to me?"

George pulled up a chair away from a table in the

front of the room. When he was seated, Anne carefully placed his grandson in his arms, and George cooed and made faces at the tiny infant.

Jill watched them for a moment and then scurried off. "We need a picture of this. I'll get my camera."

George gently raised his grandson into an erect position with his bent arm supporting his head. While the cameras clicked he announced, "Feast your eyes on Gregory George Jackson. Soon to be called George."

When the flashing stopped, George said, "Now I want pictures of me with all my grandchildren." He motioned to Lily. "Come over here, sweetheart."

She ran to his side and Anne and Jill took a few shots of George, Lily and the baby.

"I have four more grandchildren. I worked hard to get these kids, so I want them all in a picture."

Kyle and Peter laughed and arranged themselves behind his chair. Then little Rachel Alexander came over and sat at his feet. George patted her head. "I want you in a picture, too, honey. But for now I just want my grandchildren. Where are Nicole and Peter?"

Marianne rounded up her children and placed one on each side of George for more shots.

Finally Catherine pushed a chair next to her new husband. "Doesn't the grandmother belong in a picture?"

After pictures of Catherine holding the baby, and surrounded by all the grandchildren, Rachel, Kevin, Jimmy and Sean O'Hara joined them for a group portrait. When the children dispersed, the adults formed varying combinations for snapshots with the bride and groom.

Finally, George broke away, picked up a beer from the bar and slipped off to a spot at a table away from the hubbub. He took his tux jacket off, pulled off his cufflinks and rolled up his sleeves. While he sipped his brew, Mike O'Hara approached and sat next to him.

"You've gathered quite a family since Cheryl and I

moved next door."

"Having them all here today is humbling. I keep saying I'm the luckiest man alive."

"In my book, you're a most deserving man. Since we got reacquainted, I've tapped into your wisdom countless times."

George grinned at his neighbor. "Just because we've solved the world's problems over a few beers doesn't give you the right to BS me."

"I wouldn't BS you, George."

"I know you wouldn't. I just embarrass easily."

O'Hara lifted his glass and toasted George. "I wish you and Catherine a long and healthy marriage." They clinked glasses.

"That was very touching, Mike. Thank you."

"And I wish you many fine chubby little babies."

George laughed and shook his fist as O'Hara strutted from the table. "Get out of here, you shyster!"

After O'Hara cleared out, Gert joined George. She was wearing an attractive gray dress he hadn't seen before.

"You okay, Georgy Boy?"

"I'm having a great time. Just taking a break."

"Mind if I sit down?"

He motioned for her to sit in the chair next to him. "You look very nice."

"A little number I picked up at the Salvation Army Outlet just for the wedding."

Studying her face, he asked, "Still down in the dumps about Walt?"

"I've felt better. I've been worse. If I hadn't broken off the relationship, he would have dragged me down. I couldn't allow that to happen."

"But it still hurts."

"It sure does." She sighed. Suddenly her eyes sparkled, and she smiled at George. "But nothing hurts as much as losing my Georgy to the Old Lady."

George deadpanned. "I can understand that. Unfortunately, there's not enough of me anymore to go around."

"Well, there's plenty of me to go around, but no one's buying." Gert got up and walked behind George and wrapped her arms around him. She kissed him on the cheek. "I need a father, and I'm so grateful it's you, Daddy-O."

"Me too, Gert."

She took George's hand and pulled him to his feet. "I was sent by my sister, Marianne, and Jill to fetch you."

"Why?"

"How would I know? I'm just the cleaning lady." As they started toward the others, she asked, "By the way, what do you think of my sister?"

"She's very charming."

"More charming than me?"

"Something tells me she wouldn't take me to a biker bar for dinner like you did."

"She's the Ritz type."

"I liked the biker bar."

When he reached the others, George pulled a chair up next to Catherine and reached over to clutch her hand. She turned her head and smiled. It was at that moment with Rachel, Nicole and Lily tearing around the room, and Anne holding his grandson, his knee not hurting and his bypass surgery behind him that George realized he was the happiest he'd ever been in his entire life.

Jill and Marianne gathered everyone into a small semi-circle surrounding Catherine and George. When Jill had everyone's attention, she began, "We understand that Catherine and Daddy are waiting until winter to honeymoon on a Caribbean cruise. We adults have discussed this and found it totally unacceptable."

George looked around and saw Curtis and Bret nodding. When he caught Mary Alexander's eye, she grinned at him.

"What's happening here?" he whispered to Catherine.

"Darned if I know!"

"Soo . . ." Jill continued. "We all anted up and bought you two plane tickets and vouchers for an Alaskan cruise." She held up two envelopes and handed them to Catherine along with a hug. "They're for the twenty-fifth of June, Daddy," she said as she kissed him.

Marianne stepped forward. "And since you'll be flying to Seattle first you'll be staying with us for a few days so Bob and I can get to know George better and Nicole and Peter can spend some time with their grandparents."

Catherine squeezed his hand. It was time for him to say something. He glanced at her for inspiration. She was no help. She was crying. He rubbed his hand through his thinning hair. "This is a total surprise, at least for me." He eyed Catherine suspiciously.

She gave him a palms up shrug, "Then your gift is a wonderful surprise for both of us. Frankly, I never even considered an Alaskan cruise, because I associate cruising with winter. But, it's a whole lot better idea than the alternatives I came up with, and the more I think about it the better it sounds. Other than that, I don't know what to say except, thank you, thank you, thank you."

When Catherine rose to her feet, she said, "I'm not usually the crying type, but your wonderful gift has totally overwhelmed me. It's the perfect end to a perfect day. We're both very grateful, aren't we George?"

"I should say."

Mary Alexander spoke up. "I have something to add to the gift that should make the trip even more enjoyable for George. While you are gone, my husband, Dan, and Jimmy and Kevin have promised to weed, hoe and pick your garden. George, you won't have to worry about anything except pleasing Catherine."

"They'll even pick the worms off the cabbage?"

Everybody laughed.

"Of course. You'll have the best cabbage crop ever."

George dabbed at his eye with his knuckle. "Now that makes *me* cry."

R.L. Paul

About the Author

Raymond L. Paul was born in St. Louis, Missouri on February 25, 1936, and has been a resident of Rockford, Illinois since he was four. At West Rockford High School he was a top student, three-sport star and an All-State football player. He attended the University of Wisconsin on a football scholarship, majored in insurance and finance and graduated after four years with a Bachelor of Business Administration Degree.

Immediately following graduation in 1958, he passed up an opportunity to play minor league baseball in the Dodger farm system choosing instead to marry his college sweetheart and begin a career with Massachusetts Mutual Life Insurance Company. Forty-six years later, he is still smitten with Jo Marie and proud of his ongoing relationship with Mass Mutual.

Ray's writing career had its genesis in college, where he eschewed his business electives for creative writing classes. Though this period primed his heart for creative writing, fighting for a toehold in the financial services industry and being a good father to three daughters precluded any serious involvement. His hiatus from fiction writing lasted almost forty years.

Nine years ago Ray finally reached a comfortable stage where the demands on his time and energy were diminished. Their older daughters had moved away and started families of their own, and he and Jo Marie had weathered the crisis of losing their youngest daughter to meningitis. With his golf scores soaring and time on his hands, he needed a new challenge. Two college writing classes and a couple of workshops later, he had found a new avocation. With the first click of the keyboard, he began writing himself toward retirement.

In the past five years, Ray has written *Cabbage Requiem* and approximately forty short stories. Twenty-two of his short fiction pieces have been published in a variety of literary and commercial magazines, such as *Potpouuri, AIM Magazine,* and *The Acorn.* He has finished a second novel.

Printed in the United States
41103LVS00004B/70-90

9 780972 301190